THE PIANO CEMETERY

JOSÉ LUÍS PEIXOTO was born in 1974 in Galveias, Portalegre, in Portugal's Alentejo region. A journalist, novelist, poet, dramatist, literary critic and teacher of languages and contemporary literature, he is also a heavy-metal fan and produced a book and record called *The Antidote* with Gothic band Moonspell. His work is published and acclaimed in many languages and has won major prizes in Portugal and Brazil, including the José Saramago Prize in 2001 for *Blank Gaze*.

A NOTE ON THE TRANSLATOR

DANIEL HAHN is a translator of fiction and non-fiction, mainly from Portuguese. His translation of *The Book of Chameleons* by Angolan novelist José Eduardo Agualusa won the *Independent* Foreign Fiction Prize in 2007.

THE PIANO
CEMETERY

José Luís Peixoto

Translated from the Portuguese
by Daniel Hahn

B L O O M S B U R Y
LONDON · BERLIN · NEW YORK · SYDNEY

FT
Pbk

First published in Great Britain 2010
This paperback edition published 2011

Funded by Direcção-Geral do Livro e das Bibliotecas/Portugal

Bloomsbury Publishing Plc
36 Soho Square
London W1D 3QY

www.bloomsbury.com

Bloomsbury Publishing, London, New York, Berlin and Sydney

A CIP catalogue record for this book is available from the British Library

ISBN 978 1 4088 1009 5

10 9 8 7 6 5 4 3 2 1

Typeset by Hewer Text UK Ltd, Edinburgh
Printed in Great Britain by Clays Ltd, St Ives plc

www.bloomsbury.com

AUTHOR'S NOTE

Francisco Lázaro was a Portuguese athlete who died after completing thirty kilometres of the marathon at the Olympic Games in Stockholm, in 1912. The character in this novel who shares his name is based only circumstantially on his story, and all the episodes and characters depicted come from the realm of fiction.

RESURRECTURIS

But for those like us, our fate is to face the world as orphans, chasing through long years the shadows of vanished parents. There is nothing for it but to try and see through our missions to the end, as best we can, for until we do so, we will be permitted no calm.

Kazuo Ishiguro, *When We Were Orphans*

Neither pray I for these alone, but for them also which shall believe on me through their word; that they all may be one; as thou, Father, art in me, and I in thee, that they also may be one in us: that the world may believe that thou hast sent me. And the glory which thou gavest me I have given them; that they may be one, even as we are one: I in them, and thou in me, that they may be made perfect in one; and that the world may know that thou hast sent me, and hast loved them, as thou hast loved me. Father, I will that they also, whom thou hast given me, be with me where I am; that they may behold my glory, which thou hast given me: for thou lovedst me before the foundation of the world. O righteous Father, the world hath not known thee: but I have known thee, and these have known that thou hast sent me. And I have declared unto them thy name, and will declare it: that the love wherewith thou hast loved me may be in them, and I in them.

John 17, xx–xxvi

WHEN I FIRST BEGAN to be ill, I knew right away that I was going to die.

In the final months of my life, when I was still able to make it from our house to the workshop on foot, I would sit on a pile of planks and, unable to help with the simplest things – planing the frame of a door, hammering in a nail – I'd watch Francisco working, absorbed, in a mist of sawdust specks. I'd been like that when I was young, too. On those evenings – an impossibly long time after I was young – I made sure that he wasn't watching me and, when I could bear it no longer, I would rest my head in my hands. I held the immense weight of my head – the world – and covered my eyes with my hands so as to suffer in the darkness, in a silence I feigned. Later, in the final weeks of my life, I went into hospital.

Marta never went to see me in hospital. She was pregnant with Hermes. It was in the final months, and the way Marta is meant that she needed a lot of attention during the time of her pregnancy. I suddenly remember when she was small and so happy on that scooter I bought for her second-hand; I remember when she used to go to school, I remember so much. While I was in the hospital waiting to die, Marta was in another hospital, not too far away, waiting for Hermes to be born.

'How's my father?' Marta would ask, stretched out, hair unkempt, the hospital bed-sheets covering her belly.

'Just the same,' someone would reply, lying. Someone who was not my wife, nor Maria, nor Francisco, because none of them had the strength to lie to her.

The last evening I spent alive, my wife, Maria and Francisco went to see me. During the whole illness, Simão had never wanted to visit me. It was Sunday. I was separated from the other sick people, because I was going to die. I was trying to breathe and my breathing was a thick, hoarse buzzing that filled the room. At the foot of the bed my wife was crying, choked by her tears, by her contorted face and by the pain – the suffering. Without choosing her words, she spoke them in long, drawn-out, stretched-out howls, interrupted only by impatient drawings-in of breath. They were words that burned in her wasted body, her body dressed in a knitted jacket, a favourite skirt, polished shoes:

'Oh my precious man my friend who's my best friend and I'm left without you my precious man my companion my great great friend.'

Maria was crying and tried to hug her mother, to console her, because the two of them had the same feeling of a definitive and terrible emptiness in their breasts that I would have felt too if I had lost one of them. Francisco was looking out of the window. He was trying not to see. He was trying not to know what he knew. He was trying to be a man. Then he came closer to me, serious. In eternal time, in concrete time, he stroked my face, and rested his hand on my hand. On the bedside table, under the grey iron lid, he found a cup of water and a stick with a cotton tip. He wet the cotton in the water and placed it in my dry, open mouth. I bit on to it with all the strength I had, and Francisco was surprised to feel my strength for the last time. He removed the cotton.

He looked at me, and cried too, because he couldn't bear it any longer. Maria hugged him and treated him like she had when he was small:

'Don't be scared, my little boy, we won't leave you alone, we'll look after you.'

All my strength. I used all my strength and all I managed was a horrible, deathly sound. I wanted to say to Francisco and Maria that I wouldn't leave them alone either; I wanted to say to them that I was the best friend they would ever have in their lives, that I would never leave them alone, would never stop being their father, and looking after them, and protecting them. Instead of this I used all my strength and only managed a horrible, deathly sound. The sound of a voice that could no longer speak, the sound of a voice that, using all its strength, managed only to make a hoarse sound with its throat, a horrible sound, a deathly sound. They looked at me, and they cried more, and they felt a terrible, black emptiness all through their hearts – deep down, deep down – which I would have felt too if I had lost one of them.

They went to Maria's house, and each was left abandoned in a corner to their suffering. Far away, protected, Ana was two years old and was at the home of her paternal grandparents. Unprotected, my wife, Maria and Francisco waited for the telephone to ring. They waited for the call from the hospital with the news that I had died. This was what the nurse had said:

'In theory we should be calling you today. We'll phone as soon as your husband passes away.'

This was what the nurse had said. Without noticing, perhaps, that my wife was no longer anyone. Without noticing that the words she said to her disappeared without an echo inside her darkness.

The night, drifting. With the immoderate drift of worldly things, the night covered over all the places in the world that all existed only there: Maria's house – the imitation porcelain dolls on the cupboard shelves, the covers on the sofas, the folded-over corners of the rugs, the imitation crystal lamps, the prints on the walls – and the house of birthday parties in which we tunelessly sang happy birthday, clapped our hands out of time with each other and laughed – and the house of Christmas parties, where I would sit on the sofa, and the tablecloth with the pictures of pine trees and bells would be laid out, and we would use the long-stemmed glasses. In this house, each person was left abandoned in a corner to their suffering.

At nine o'clock at night, the telephone rang. The telephone rang for a long moment, because no one wanted to answer it, because they were all afraid to answer it, because they all knew with great certainty that when they answered it the hope that lasted to the final second would definitively end, the almost three years of my illness would end which we always knew would lead me to my death, would lead me to that telephone ringing that no one wanted to answer. The telephone rang. The sound passed through the house and through the breast of my wife, and Maria's, and Francisco's. It was Maria's husband who answered it. His words in a black suspension of time, as if in a shadow of time:

'Yes, yes. All right. I'll tell them.' He approached my two children and my wife and told them. An invisible wall between his face and the words he spoke. An invisible wall between the world and the words he spoke. A wall that didn't allow the immediate understanding of such simple words. Hermes had just been born.

Hermes had just been born.

The words were:

'He's been born, Marta's boy.'

Hermes had just been born.

In the hospital Marta was resting. And nobody knew how to be happy, but happiness was so strong, and it grew inside them. It was as though they had a spring of water in their breasts and happiness was that water. There was a miracle that turned tears into tears. They had their hands resting on their breasts. They had their eyelids closing very slowly over their eyes to feel the gentle rain of this happiness that covered them, flooded them.

An hour passed. The telephone rang again.

I had just died.

THE MORNING LIGHT DOESN'T feel the clean window-panes as it passes through them, coming to rest on the notes of the piano that emerge from the wireless and float in the kitchen air. The morning light, resting on the notes of the piano, pauses, speckled, in the reflections of the white wall tiles, on the corners of the formica-topped tables, on the drops of water that hang from the rims of the pans, washed and upturned over the draining board.

My wife goes past. She doesn't notice the invisible, luminous agitation of the piano notes that her passing leaves behind. Lightly, she goes by with her sleeves rolled up to her elbows. Without noticing, she bears the morning's lightness in her face. She goes into the corridor. Her skin shines under the shadows. Her muffled steps along the hall runner cannot be made out in the silence. She approaches the open living-room door and smiles, sees Íris's little body, sitting on the rug, surrounded by toys and broken pieces of plastic toys – dolls' legs.

My wife stays a moment like this. Íris is nearly three, and she doesn't feel the gaze covering and protecting her. During this moment my wife is ageless. She has no sense of the size of Maria's house, measured out by the creaking sounds of pieces of furniture in the distance: the wardrobe full of outmoded clothes in Maria and her husband's room, at the

6

far end of the corridor; the iron couch that my wife sets up every night before going to sleep and then disassembles when she wakes up, in the dining room halfway down the corridor; the refrigerator straining under the notes emerging from the wireless at the other end of the corridor.

Íris was born when there was nothing left of me but memories and photographs. Íris still doesn't understand all the conversations, and pays no attention to photographs of people she doesn't know. Her eyes are blue like a holiday-postcard sea; her hair is long and ends in ringlets that curl over her shoulders and her back. She is a lovely wild child. Some days she picks up speed; running on her little legs, she throws herself with abandon on to the sofa and laughs. Now she is peaceful, playing with her dolls. And like every morning, she woke up when her mother went to get her sister up for school. At the kitchen table, Ana, half-asleep, didn't reply to the questions Íris insisted on asking. Maria walked to and fro looking for little things – handkerchiefs, keys – and putting them in her bag. My wife was hurrying Ana, who wasn't finishing her food. In July there's no school any more, but Maria still takes her because there is a teacher who for a small amount of money continues to look after the children, to teach them sums and give them homework. Like every morning, my wife picked Íris up in her arms and went with her to the window to watch Ana, in her striped smock, heading away, down the road, running to keep up with her mother, then falling behind, and running again, and falling behind, running and disappearing with her mother at the bend in the pavement.

Now Íris is peaceful, playing with her dolls:

'You don't want your din-dins? Why don't you want your din-dins?' she asks the doll, bringing a little spoon to the rubber mouth. Then she combs her hair. Then she lays her down to sleep. She watches her sleep for a moment, then wakes her up. She changes her clothes and tries to feed her again.

My wife returns to the kitchen. In the cups hanging on hooks inside the cupboard, in the fruit bowl, in the washed cutlery, in the broom handle, in the cloths hanging by the side of the sink, in the box of matches spotted with fat, in the kettle resting on the unlit stove, her eyes recognise the peace of the morning. She opens the window and, after choosing a few pegs and an item of clothing from a full tub, she leans over the ledge to hang it out. And she repeats these movements. And each time she bends down to take hold of a pair of Maria's husband's trousers, or one of Maria's blouses, or one of her granddaughters' vests, she is submerged by a piece of piano music which fills the kitchen with the strength of a breeze. And each time she leans over the ledge and pulls on the line to fix a peg, she thinks about how Lisbon and the world are vast. Her torso, thrust through the third-floor window of a building in Benfica, has some sense of what it might feel like to fly. It is at that moment that she thinks of our son Francisco, who left early yesterday morning for the marathon, for the Olympic Games, as if he was heading off into a dream. This thought was always there under the others, like the glow of an ember that occasionally wakes into a flame. And, first, the pride – our son, our boy – the weight of all those tender memories – and that name printed in the newspapers, important. That name. We gave him my name, so that it should become his. That name which used to be mine now belongs to him entirely. That name and all those who utter it: Francisco Lázaro. And later, later, the pride.

As though she could speak silently to Francisco, she lowers her gaze to the streets, to the pavement with its missing stones – irregular earth figures in the shapes of the stones that are missing – then she raises her eyes. On the other side of the road, two buildings separated by plots where pieces of bricks, necks of broken bottles and rusty pram-wheels grow. A little further off, gardens of spring greens, surrounded by barriers made of rusty tins. Further still, the road where motorcars pass, in both directions, day and night. And after this road, the whole of Lisbon. And after Lisbon, the world and our son, our boy. And above all, in everything, the morning.

She lowers herself to the kitchen floor to pick up a blouse of Ana's – round, embroidered collars – and two pegs. The piano music continues, continuous, to come out of the wireless. She begins to lean over the ledge and, suddenly, a din is heard from the living room, a collapse, the explosion of some weight smashing to the ground – glass, wood, iron. Within that same moment, Íris's sudden cries. My wife drops Ana's blouse, not staying to watch it drift down on to the pavement because she is running towards the living room. My wife knows well the differences between Íris's different cries – when she's making a fuss, when she's just startled or when she really is upset – this is why she runs as fast as she can. Beneath Íris's piercing cries, the quick heartbeats of my wife coming to her. Her body goes down the corridor with the same movements as when she goes walking, but much faster, because that is the way she runs.

It was our house. My wife would sit on the yard steps, she'd spend pleasant early August evenings, and she'd stay there concentrating on her knitting. She would make woollen booties or little jackets for our son. There was a month to go before he was born and already she was imagining the size of his arms and the size of his little feet. Sometimes she would stretch the half-knitted pieces out in the palms of her hands, and at those moments it was as though she could see the arms or feet of our as yet unborn child.

I would hold the end of the hose, the water thick and fresh, hitting the feet of the trees and the plants. There was that fresh smell of earth drinking in water. There was a breeze that serenaded the skin on our faces.

At times, I would remember to tell her something. She would stop, and she would listen to me. She would rest her needles and knitting on her belly, and listen to me, and, sometimes, the knitting would begin to move all on its own.

It was our Francisco kicking inside her belly.

I would say:

'When he's big he'll have to be a footballer.'

Little did I know.

Years later, recollecting those kicks that at night would sketch angles in the skin of her round belly, my wife would often repeat:

'My Francisco started training to be a runner even before he was born.'

It was morning when I'd get to the workshop. I'd open the big door, and the echo of the key turning sounded natural from the sawdust-covered, dust-covered walls. With the sound of the first steps of my boots on the ground of the entrance hall, two or three sparrows would fly between the roof beams and hide in the shadows of the roof tiles. When the weather was fine, I would open the windows on to the patio. On the carpentry bench my tools would be where I had arranged them. Work was waiting for me just where, the previous day, I had decided to stop. It was morning, and as I held each tool for the first time – the hammer, the chisel, the handsaw – I'd feel the pleasant beginning of another day in the palm of my hand.

My uncle would arrive mid-morning. He wore the same clothes from the night before – his shirt half-untucked from his trousers, the buckle of his belt misaligned with the button. His left eye glittered in his unwashed face. When he was a child, during some game, my uncle had been blinded in his right eye. As he arrived in the workshop his right eye was the smoothest of eyelids, whiter than the rest of his skin, sitting over the empty socket. He had dry, cracked lips. His teeth bore a sticky film of red wine. He always wore a child-ish, genuine smile. He would say good morning to me. I would say nothing to him. Forgetting himself, he would say good morning to me again. Then he might perhaps take a crumpled handkerchief from his pocket and blow his nose. Then he would go out on to the patio. If I was measuring or marking something up I would hear the arc of his urine hitting the pine-shaving floor. After a time and the sound of his footfall approaching, he would come back in and perhaps wash his face in the cold water of the running tap. The water mixed with the sawdust of the floor. His eyebrows bristling, he would smile and, finally, approach the bench where his tools, heaped in disarray, awaited him.

Mornings passed with my uncle telling stories, stories which sometimes repeated themselves and sometimes never ended; they passed beneath the stories that my uncle would tell and that I sometimes did not listen to. As I worked

– hammer striking, saws crossing laths, files filing, sandpaper smoothing planks – I would stop listening to my uncle to concentrate on the sounds of the city that came in through the windows and the patio door as though from very far away – proclamations, lost voices, bicycle bells.

It was my father who left the workshop to me. Some days, when I was coming back from the market holding my mother's hand, I would ask her:

'Let's go to my workshop.'

If someone heard me and understood, they'd laugh, with me so small talking like that. My mother didn't laugh because she had been the one who had taught me to use those words.

My father died far away from my mother, exhausted, on the same day that I was born.

Throughout my childhood, on certain evenings, my mother would boil a pan of water and ask me to go out to the yard to fetch a leaf from the lemon tree. Our lemon tree had large, thick leaves, hard to detach and noisy as I tore them from the lower branches. My mother would wash the leaf and submerge it in the boiling water to make our tea. It was at that moment that she would bring to the middle of the table a parcel wrapped in brown paper which, very slowly, under my gaze, she would open. In it were two cakes she had bought from the bakery and which she would cut in half with the tip of her knife. I'd get up on to a stool and take two mugs out of the cupboard. We would sit at the table, mother and son, eating our halves of cake and drinking tea. Then my mother would tell stories that always ended with my father's laughter. My mother almost always laughed when she described my father's laughter. Then my mother would say that my father was priceless.

Then a pause. Silence. And my mother would tell me how, without any doubt, my father would have been proud to know that I was going to look after the workshop. That was the moment she would speak of my workshop:

'Your workshop,' she'd say, serious, looking me in the eye. My mother's voice was fragile and secure, it was gentle, it was firm.

The workshop remained out of action until the day my uncle offered to take care of it, paying the small rent with which my mother managed things. There were months in which my uncle, through confusion or through drink, was late paying. My mother counted on this, and for just such occasions she would save a little money at the bottom of her sewing box. It rarely happened that, after his deadlines had passed, she had to go, determined, up the two blocks separating our house from the workshop to claim the rent. When my uncle saw her arrive, he would be ashamed; he'd lower his face, beg a thousand heartfelt apologies and, almost always, weep.

I started working with my uncle a few days after turning twelve. During my apprenticeship I tried to make out what he was telling me to do from amid the torrent of incomprehensible stories he would tell me. What my uncle had to teach me was the little he had learned from watching his father working and what he had learned from his own mistakes and attempts. At fourteen, I was already more perfect in my work than he was, and I taught him things he had never known, or that he had forgotten.

I was fourteen when my mother fell ill. In a week every bone and every vein in her body became visible. Her skin yellowed. Her gaze remained fixed on a certain point. I begged her not to die. I asked her, begged her by everything. But a few weeks passed, and she died.

It was as though she had only been waiting to see me raised.

The following weeks my uncle remained in silence. One morning he began to tell a story which never came to an end, and time continued to pass.

Absorbed in the stories he himself was telling, my uncle would rarely hear people arriving with heavy tread on the earth floor of the entrance, people who would appear at any hour to commission work or see if the work they had commissioned was ready. So he would be surprised to see them appear at the shop door. He would circle them, thrilled, speaking to them loudly and smiling. These people, even if they didn't know him, ignored him and made straight for me. That was exactly what happened the morning the Italian arrived.

The fine moustache danced over his lips to the rhythm of the words he was saying. As he spoke, the fine moustache, waxed, assumed the most varied shapes: a tilde, a line, a right angle, a curve. At the same time he used his clean, smooth, white hands, his slender, well-tended fingers with their slightly long nails, to gesture and thus to sculpt the air before him into all manner of shapes: a noble horse with silver harnesses, halls with engravings on the ceiling, a piano. Then sometimes he would stop abruptly to check whether we had understood, and straighten his cuff buttons with the tips of his fingers or pluck at the bright collars of his morning-coat. Then he would decide that we had not understood him, and he would continue.

But we had understood everything. Everything, perhaps. From the moment the Italian started speaking, my uncle's voice faded away, weaker, weaker, as though going down a flight of stairs, until he fell completely silent, and with his left eye wide remained just listening with lively and genuine interest. When the Italian became tired, or when he simply no longer knew how to explain himself, my uncle and I looked at one another to confirm that we had understood. The Italian played and sang at dances. He had a broken piano and someone had told him that we would be able to repair it here.

With the Italian between us, we crossed the carpentry shop and the entrance hall, walked as far as the street, and there on a cart pulled by a pair of tired mules was a grand piano, reflecting the clouds in its black sheen, held down by the ropes. Before I could say anything, my uncle looked at the Italian and held out his hand, gravely saying:

'You can count on us to get your piano repaired in time to play at the dance.'

The Italian ignored my uncle's hand, smiled and, turning towards me, said that the dance would be on Saturday night. We had three days. I turned to my uncle to discuss the decision, but I was halted in the middle of my first word for he had already turned his back and, skirting round the puddles of oil from the moped mechanic who had a workshop a little further up the road, was walking hurriedly towards the *taberna*. Mutely I looked at the Italian and shrugged my shoulders in a moment of shared incomprehension, but with the same haste my uncle emerged from the *taberna*, leading a group of men – ragged men, unsteady men, old men, crooked men and cripples.

Under my uncle's orders, the men began to untie the piano. It was my uncle who opened the big workshop doors completely, and who got up on to the cart and began gently to push the piano, which slid on its little wheels into the arms of the men.

'Hang on there.' And he got down to help them.

My uncle counted to three and, with a sound from deep inside his chest, said, '*Hup* . . .' At that moment they lifted the piano higher and took shuffling steps that dragged the sound of the dust on the ground. They carried the piano as though they were carrying the whole world. The men's bodies, clutching the piano, and their legs, bent under the weight, were a black animal, like a spider. Their voices, stifled by the weight – don't let go now, push towards your left – surrounded the piano. They crossed the entrance hall to the workshop and headed towards the carpentry shop. There were men who went in backwards and others, going forwards, who raised their heads to direct them.

As they disappeared through the door to the carpentry shop, the Italian handed me a card – the Flor de Benfica boarding house. I was still looking at the card when the Italian held out his hand. I offered him mine and he, quickly, squeezed my wrist and shook my arm. He smiled broadly, wiped the polish of his shoes on the back of his trouser legs, climbed up on to the cart and, with a word of Italian to the mules, set off up the road.

When the men came out, as though they had seen the whole world between the walls of the carpentry shop, they disguised their efforts with a smile and clapped their hands together as though cleaning off the dust, wiped their hands on their stained trouser-legs as though cleaning them. My uncle came with them, leading the thread of their voices. He came out with them through the doorway, and they all skirted past me as though I was invisible, took some steps down the dirt road and went into the *taberna*. My uncle rested his elbows on the marble counter and bought each of the men a glass of wine.

It was still morning. I was alone, standing in the street, at the open door to the workshop. I held my arms straight down against my body and an abandoned card in one of my hands. Fragments of wind brought the ringing of bells chiming distant hours. I was twenty-two years old, my arms were straight down against my body, I had never repaired a piano and couldn't imagine myself capable of doing it.

At the living-room door it was as though my wife had stopped, though without actually stopping, because for a single moment an image – complete and clear – was suspended there in front of her: little Íris, sitting, her mouth open in a continuous scream, surrounded by pieces of broken glass, tumbled-over jugs, headless china dolls, sitting beside the corner cupboard, which was tumbled on the rug like an old corpse fallen face-down; and Íris holding up her hand, open, the palm of her hand covered in blood that ran between her fingers. In three steps, with pieces of glass crunching under the soles of her slippers, my wife picks her up under her arms and lifts her into the air. Our granddaughter's cries tear the landscapes printed in the pictures on the walls; they cut my wife's face and stop her from breathing.

'There now, there now,' she says, as she turns on the bathroom tap over Íris's hand, but the girl's cries are reflected in the rust-stained mirror and the white bathroom tiles.

The telephone starts to ring. Over the pine table – the drawer of scrawled papers and ballpoint pens that don't write – over the lace doily; my wife's godmother choosing

17

balls of thread at the silk merchant's – by the chrome-plated frame – the photograph we all took together in Rossio – the telephone screams. Strong as iron, it stretches out with a persistent urgency, which stops to catch its breath, then carries on again with the same panic and the same authority.

The telephone continues to ring. Íris cries and screams. Tears draw hot streaks on her red cheeks. My wife holds her hand under the open tap. The blood is diluted on the cracked washbasin porcelain and disappears. In the palm of Íris's hand a splinter of glass buried in a wound. In a single movement, my wife pulls it out with the tips of her fingers and feels the inside of her flesh.

'There now, there now,' she says, bringing her hand back under the cold water. Íris's cries make the white light of the bulb hanging from a cable turn strident, they make the little bottles of lotions arranged on a shelf tremble, and as they enter the bathtub they scratch the surface of the enamel with squeals.

The telephone continues to ring. Each ring is a hand that grabs my wife's body and squeezes it, that grabs her head and squeezes it, that grabs her heart and squeezes it. In her arms, Íris's voice begins to find some comfort, and, slowly, some peace. My wife turns off the tap, wraps Íris's hand in a white towel from the bidet and, holding her in her arms, runs out of the bathroom and down the corridor.

The telephone continues to ring. My wife's steps are quick on the carpet because usually nobody rings during the day. She fears, inside, that it is bad news, she fears it is news that will floor her, that will destroy her, that will condemn her again – death. She squeezes the girl to her breast and moves anxiously across the carpet – as fast as she is able. And the telephone stops ringing. My wife's steps lose their meaning, they diminish and stop.

In the kitchen, the piano music is still being born from the wireless and is pushed by the wind that comes in through the open window.

I didn't want to say anything to my uncle, because I wanted to see the result of his enthusiasm. He encircled the piano with words and steps that, all of a sudden, would change direction. At a distance, my arms crossed over my chest, I watched him and I didn't believe anything he said. In the sawdust that covered the floor an irregular shape had been sketched, which was the track my uncle was following. On impulse he broke off from this flow of marked steps and went to fetch a little stool – covered in splashes of paint and bent nails – which he brushed off and placed in front of the piano. He sat down, lifted the lid that covered the keyboard and ran his gaze over it. Almost moved, he said:

'Your father would have been so happy, if he was here.'

That was the moment everything made sense for me. My father. Like a finger on a key rousing a hammer from its slumber, I understood.

At the entrance to the workshop, to the right, there was a closed door, covered up by time and by chairs that were missing a leg, by tabletops and other remains that had been accumulating into a disordered heap. That afternoon my uncle and I moved everything away, and since we had no idea about where the key was it was left to me to break down the door with two kicks to the lock.

The piano cemetery. My mother avoided talking about this closed-off section of the workshop. Whenever she did, she said there wasn't anything there that would be of interest to me. When this explanation ceased to be sufficient, she spoke to me of frights. She said:

'There are some real frights in there.'

Aged ten, this explanation was enough for me. Then summers and winters passed. I stopped asking questions. There was a closed door at the entrance to the workshop, slowly covered over with boards, with bits of junk, and I didn't think about it. I thought about other things.

That afternoon we remained standing a moment at this suddenly open door. There, inside, absolute darkness covered all the shapes. It was as though we had opened a door into the night. In front of us, in the darkness of the piano cemetery, there could be fields covered by the night, or a river covered by the night, or a whole city – asleep or dead – covered by the night.

My uncle went in first. I could no longer see him among the shadows of the shadows – a shape among shapes. He knew the way, and it took only a few steps, a few mysterious sounds in the darkness, until with the sleeve of his sweater he had begun to clean the pane of the little dust-covered window. Through his movements, rays of light came in.

Slowly, brightness filled the whole piano cemetery. The light slipped across the surfaces of dust. You could barely see the grime on the walls, and the weight of the low ceiling was made much more real because there were pianos of all sorts rising up, in heavy tiers, almost touching the ceiling. Stored against the walls were upright pianos, one on top of another – in the arrangement in which my father, or his father before him, had stacked them. In the middle there were walls of stacked pianos. The light crossed the empty spaces between them, and even from the door it was possible to make out the labyrinth of passageways they were obscuring. And on one grand piano there was another grand piano, smaller and without legs; on this there was an upright piano, lying down; on top of this, a heap of keys. Near by, separated by a slit that the light came through, two upright pianos, the same height, leaning on each other, bore a more solid upright piano that at its top supported a smaller upright. Pianos were crammed in in every possible way. In the gaps where they didn't completely fit together, the brightness came through abandoned spiders' webs that held drops of water, points of sheen. The fresh air of the piano cemetery came into our lungs, bringing with it a damp touch of the gummy dust that was the only colour in the room – the smell of a time everyone wanted to forget, but which still existed. This light and ancient colour exuded silence. The light came through the silence. On the ground there were scratched piano lids, upended, leaning on other pianos. In some corners, there were metal rods, keys, pedals and piano-legs bound to one another with wires. Through the space between two pianos, from the little and now lit-up window, my uncle looked at me with a smile. When I looked right at his face, he smiled more, jumped to the ground with a thundering of boots and disappeared between the pianos.

I went in, choosing where I put each foot, as though afraid of something unknown. In the shadows I imagined secrets from a time before I was born, a time from which I would always be excluded – eternity – and which in the same instant became as concrete and simple as the objects I touched every day, like the way from the house to the workshop, like the memories I had and which guided me. Alone, feeling myself being watched by all the chaotically stacked pianos, I moved forwards. I skirted round an upright, and at the end of this new passageway saw my uncle with his arms inside a grand and rushed towards him. He took a step back, put a hand on my shoulder, gestured towards the piano's mechanism with his other hand and said that this was one of the pianos he would be returning to for parts. I looked at him, incredulous, but encountered such confidence that for that moment I stopped doubting that we would be able to fix the piano.

That afternoon, and the following day, and the next, and the Saturday morning, I learned the most important part of what, for my whole life, I was to learn about pianos. Solemnly, my uncle looked straight at me with his left eye when he wanted to explain the points that I should never forget. I nodded my head and paid attention to every one of his words. They remained engraved in me, as though inside me there was a place made of stone waiting to receive the shape of these words' meaning. In just the same way I paid attention to all the stories my uncle told. When he lost himself in details and began to forget to tell the ending of one of them, I would ask him what had happened after the point at which he had drifted off. He was not surprised at my sudden interest in his stories, and continued.

In the stories that my uncle told in those days, I understood a little more of my own story. My father, like his father before him, had spent years making doors and windows because he couldn't live on just repairing pianos. When my father wasn't making doors and windows, he made stools for people to sit on, he made tables hoping that people had soup dishes to place on them; but in all his fantasies, he could hear pianos, as though hearing impossible loves. When he finished repairing a piano, alone, without ever having learned a note, my father would close up the whole workshop in order to play – right in the middle of the carpentry shop – pieces of music he knew and pieces of music he made up. He would perhaps have liked to be a pianist, but even before he had given up on all his dreams he'd not allowed himself dreams of this size. My uncle fixed his left eye on me to be sure that I would never forget, and said:

'Your father, when he talked about or thought about pianos, he had whirligigs of music inside him.'

During those days my uncle sent me many times to the piano cemetery. At first he'd point out the piece he needed – a damper, a lever spring, a knob – and then would hide his face inside the piano again. The first few times my mother's voice, repeated by memory, would come back to say those words to me from when I was a child and I spoke to her of that closed door in my workshop. Later, bit by bit, I began to convince myself of my uncle's words:

'Your father would have been so happy, if he was here.'

And I began to believe that, whatever my mother's idea – to protect me, to protect my father's memory – I would be honouring her because I was giving new life to my father's dreams, just as I was giving new lives to the dead pieces of those pianos.

Sometimes I took a little longer than was necessary because I stopped to listen to the calm, or to look at the pianos that surrounded me and imagine the story that each one of them held – wooden stages, dances, instructors teaching, girls with lace cuffs learning. When I returned to the shop my uncle never noticed the delay and smiled at me as I held out the correct piece he had requested.

Early on Saturday afternoon we looked at one another with a shy satisfaction when we knew the piano was ready. Mid-morning my uncle had gone out to fetch the tuner. He arrived, leading him by the arm. The tuner was blind. He tilted his head upwards or to places where nothing was happening. His head turned independently on his neck. He was older than my uncle. He had smooth hands. He spoke little. We spent hours setting each note right. The tuner tightened the strings with a silver key that he held, tightly and carefully, between his fingers. And the pure sounds – distinct in the silence – drawn in the air, lingering briefly, echoing in the memory and leaving another silence – another silence – another, different silence.

When there was a word to be heard, at last, it was my uncle asking me to go and tell the Italian. I smiled at him, I nodded, but couldn't say anything because, inside me, there was an infinite whirligig of infinite music.

I could sense my wife awake. I might have remembered that there were only a few days left to the date the doctor had given, but I remembered only the nights when the heat had stopped her sleeping. It was the beginning of September. She turned impatiently in bed. Each time she turned the world would be suspended in her movements, because it was all very slow, because it was difficult and, at times, it seemed impossible. Her body was too big. Her arms tried to grasp the sheets. She couldn't settle into a position. The joints of the bed creaked. I was awake, asleep, awake, asleep. When I fell asleep, I remained half-awake. When I awoke, I was still half-asleep. In my vague thoughts I believed it was the heat that was stopping her from falling asleep completely.

Half-asleep, I opened my eyes when I felt my legs hot and wet, when she shook my shoulders, shouting and whispering:

'Wake up! My waters have broken.'

I had trouble getting my feet into my trousers. I tried to get one foot in and hopped around on the other. She locked herself in the bathroom. When I knocked on the door she asked me to go and tell Marta. I went into our daughters' bedroom in the dark. Marta awoke, startled. I waited for the silence, until all we could hear was the breathing tides of Maria sleeping. Then I said to her:

'Your mother is about to have the child. We're going to the maternity hospital now. Take care of your brother and sister when they wake up.'

In the gloom Marta's eyes listened to me, very serious.

I left our daughters' room. Marta was left sitting on the bed. Her eyes were worried and shining. I opened the door to Simão's room. He was still so small, and he was sleeping. I closed the door gently. I looked for my wife. I walked down the corridor. The truck was less than a year old, and in the final months of my wife's pregnancy we had kept it parked outside the front door. I helped my wife into the truck. I ran to the driver's door. I started up in second gear.

The first times we stopped in traffic I wiped the sleep from my eyes with my index finger. I hadn't paid much attention when that morning had started. Occasionally my wife's complaining would get louder. Then I would speed up, jolting on the tram rails, overtaking honking cars and running red lights. Then there were motorcars in front of me and I couldn't pass. I turned to my wife and asked her if she was all right. I looked at my watch – time was very fast. I asked her again if she was all right. I revved the engine and drew a roar without moving; I looked at my watch, time was very fast. I asked her again if she was all right and, when I was able to get going, accelerated again – jolting on the tram rails, overtaking motorcars, running red lights.

She said to me, in her suffering:

'Take it easy.'

I was getting irritated:

'How am I supposed to take it easy?'

She said to me:

'Easy . . .'

And we arrived at the maternity hospital. I ran to her and we went in with our arms linked together, me pulling her, her weighed down with her pains, and me pulling her. I made for a nurse and before I was able to say a word the nurse said to me:

'Take it easy.'

And she took her away. My wife turned around to see me on my own, my arms and my eyes abandoned. And I waited. I looked at my watch. The morning. The morning the size of a summer. The whole morning. I looked at my watch. Time was very slow. The nurse passed by me; I followed her and before I was able to say a word she was the one who spoke, saying:

'Take it easy. Go and eat something.'

And I gave up.

It was past lunchtime when the nurse came back into the waiting room and said to me:

'So, don't you want to go see your son?'

My feet slipped on the tiled floor, my body went through the grey-walled corridors with their lights nearly blown, blinking, flickering. My eyes couldn't see a thing. And I went into the room. All at once – my wife lying in the bed holding our Francisco in her arms. Smiling at life. I walked dumbly, slowly to the bed. I couldn't say anything. Later I would say that right then I had understood everything he would be capable of. Later I would say so many things. At that moment, I couldn't say anything. I touched the boy's cheek with the tips of my fingers. I touched my wife's forehead with my lips. Time did not exist.

Without a moment to waste on questions that have no answers, my wife goes back into the bathroom with Íris in her arms, and when she opens the medicine cabinet she doesn't want to think about who might be calling her.

Íris is already heavy. My wife sits on the end of the bidet and puts her down on the floor. In front of her, Íris is standing there, her hand open and stretched out towards her. A grandmother and a granddaughter. On her knees my wife balances cotton wool, tincture of iodine, sticky tape and a roll of bandage. Her voice is gentle because she doesn't want Íris to cry any more. She tries to smile, and she tries to distract her.

'So, now you've come to the hospital to be made all better. So tell me, madam, have you had an accident?'

Her lips pressed tight and her eyes wide, Íris murmurs injured moans, almost pretend, and holds her hand out further.

'Oh, we'll make that all better.' And she pours tincture of iodine on to a ball of cotton wool that she brings towards the wound.

Íris makes as if to start crying, but my wife manages to distract her. She says to her:

'There, there.' And she rolls up her little hand in a strip of bandage that she fixes with sticky tape.

Then she finds a moment to run her fingers through Íris's hair – tenderly – and slowly brings her lips to her forehead. She smiles at her:

'All gone.'

Íris is on her tiptoes, holding her chin over the sink while my wife washes her face that's still a mess from the crying. She feels her face. She feels her face through the towelling fabric, and it is only then, putting a hand on her shoulder, that she asks her how it was that the piece of furniture came to fall over.

'It was the dolly,' says Íris.

My wife understands that our granddaughter wanted to climb on to the cupboard to get the Nazarena doll that Maria kept to decorate one of the cupboard shelves. It's a plastic doll Maria bought on a trip. It has the seven skirts of the fisherwomen of Nazaré and a black hat over a flowery kerchief. It has painted lashes over its painted eyes. It is barefoot on a round base which says 'Souvenir of Nazaré'. No matter how many times her grandmother has scolded her, Íris still has an immoderate passion for that doll. As my wife is getting ready to scold her, the doorbell rings.

Her heart, again. It's already past the time the postman might ring the doorbell, it's early for our daughter's lunchtime and there are not usually other visitors during the day. My wife leaves Íris waiting for her in the bathroom.

'Don't touch anything,' she says to her, sharply.

And she makes her way along the hall runner. As though there were an idea also walking along the hallway, heading towards her, and passing her, she suddenly gets the thought that the person ringing the doorbell might be the same person who phoned minutes earlier. It might be someone who needs to tell her some dreadful piece of news that

28

has already happened, that will floor her – death – that will destroy her – death – that will condemn her once again. She tries to push this black thought away. She presses down on the button that opens the street door down below, and that moment hears the electronic echo of the door opening into the building's hallway. She waits. She tries to make out the steps that must now be coming into the building, or that must now be coming up the marble stairs, but instead, she hears three knocks on the upstairs door – close to her – three firm knocks on the wood. With a start, alarmed, she asks:

'Who is it?'

But no one replies.

She asks again:

'Who is it?'

But no one replies.

The Flor de Benfica boarding house wasn't very far. It was my eagerness to get there which meant that, that day, the way over seemed so long to me. The streets of Benfica, which I had known for ever, appeared new because I couldn't see them. As I walked, I didn't see the abandoned scabied dogs leaning up against the walls, fearful, heavy lids over their eyes; nor the ruined houses, windowpanes broken by thrown stones and walls painted grey by time; nor the dirty children, hair shaved because of the lice, who pulled at the sleeves of women's coats and thrust the palms of their hands out to them. It was Saturday and the early afternoon was bringing activity to the streets. More motorcars were passing than was usual – horns honked and startled the old women under their shawls who jumped and cursed. Groups of barefoot little kids ran after iron hoops, the sound of the wand sliding inside the hoop. Girls carried little errand baskets in the crooks of their arms and averted their blushing faces when they passed the café doors. Apart from all this, I continued on my way, attentive to the images that only existed within me, or which would be the whole world were I to happen to close my eyes – my uncle's face in the morning, my face when I arrived home in the early evening, and the Italian's face when I told him that the piano was ready. The two previous mornings, since the piano had arrived at the workshop, when I got to the top of the road, I could already see my uncle leaning on the big door, waiting for me. He had an alert look to him, and even from a distance I could already begin to make out his childish smile. When I approached with the key he'd pat me on the back, and as soon as I opened the door he'd pass in front of me and walk straight over to the piano. At the end of the day, he didn't stop at the *taberna* once. Before going up to the front step of my house, I saw him go down the road and away, shut off in his dreams, towards the room where he was living in those days. It was early evening when, in the house where I dined alone, I filled the basin and, having splashed water on to my face with both hands, stopped to look in the little bathroom mirror. In my eyes, I could make out a feeling that I was only then starting to recognise and that made me invent all manner of dreams. That Saturday, as I walked, I was sure I knew what enthusiasm I would find in the Italian's face when I told him the piano was ready. As soon as I saw the boarding house at the end of the road, I began to hurry. The distance of these final steps was greater.

I knocked on the door and no one opened. I knocked again and an uninterested lady in glasses appeared, who looked silently at me from head to toe, still holding the door, as if to ask what I wanted there. It was her gaze that undid my smile. I asked after the Italian, and she replied to me at once that the Italian gentleman did not want to be disturbed. I told her I had come with news about the piano he had left for repair; she continued to stare at me in silence; I insisted, and only then did she let me in. With a movement of her chin she gestured me towards a corridor that ended in a door to a room of armchairs and lace doilies. She followed me and waited for me to sit down.

When she left – her steps stabbing into the waxed wood – her absence remained, controlling every move I made. My hands resting on my knees, I could feel the fine sawdust that covered the fabric of my trousers, and as though the vases of ferns were watching me, as though the curtains were watching me, I remained still, trying not to breathe.

Her face – the same uninterest – came back in and went out in a moment. She said:

'The Italian gentleman will be down in a moment.'

The passing of time made me see how ridiculous my enthusiasm was when compared to reality. Reality was that tidy old room. My enthusiasm was an illusion I had constructed on my own from nothing. Sitting there, I watched the shadows growing from the armchair legs.

It was then that my life changed for ever.

Preceded by the quick taps that the floorboards made under the lightness of her step, she came into the room and was startled to see me. I would have been merely ashamed had it not been for the white softness of her face. She had her hair tied in a ribbon, she was a girl and, in her face, there was a kind of miracle – purity – that I couldn't describe. Big eyes – the sky. If I had been close enough, I believe I could have seen birds gliding within her eyes, it would be a month of spring within her eyes – endless. She was a delicate girl and my gaze rested carefully on the skin of her neck, on the shoulders under the flowery dress she wore. She was a delicate, barefoot girl – the start of her legs, the slender ankles, the bare feet that seemed not to touch the ground. Under her gaze I could feel an invisible force drawing my hand towards her hair, slipping it invisibly through my fingers, but I remained seated and still, eyes raised, imagining it all. It was only after the moment had passed and the Italian came in, perfumed and coiffed, that I realised that I was a carpenter with my body covered in sawdust, unshaved, my hands rough. The Italian smiled at her as though rescuing her. He put his hand on her waist and said some words to her in Italian that also made her smile. Then he turned to me, and as though not realising, left his hand resting on her waist. He left his hand resting on her waist. It was my voice telling him the piano was ready, but I didn't hear his response, I didn't see his face, because though I looked at him all I could see was the hand he had left resting on her waist. Then he said we should go and fetch the piano, and at the same moment he took his hand from her waist and in came the woman, eyes wide, telling her to go and do something unimportant. She disappeared. Then an empty moment. As I made my way along the corridor runner towards the door I breathed in all the air I could because that air still carried the perfume of her passing by. In silence, sitting on the cart, next to the Italian, I travelled quickly along the streets towards the workshop.

My wife decides not to be afraid, and suddenly, in an impulse, wraps the strength of her fingers around the knob and opens the door.

32

In front of my wife, an arm's length away, is a gypsy dressed in black. In his burned skin, between the wrinkles that open pathways in his face and transform it into something arable like earth, the serious age of his brown eyes is looking at her. The white beard, knotted up like a cloud of spider's webs, ends at the collar of his faded black shirt. He has a hat, also black, shapeless, wedged on to his head. And an old belt, of worn cobbler's leather, holds his faded trousers to his thin body, the trousers grey and black, black with grey stains. On the carpet of the entrance hall, his boots covered in dry mud.

My wife doesn't speak, watching him. There isn't any word she could say. Behind him the plants, supported by long sticks, become suddenly distinct in their pots. In just the same way the fresh emptiness of the staircase in the middle of a Friday morning becomes distinct. The clarity awaiting an echo becomes distinct.

A movement of the gypsy's arm shows Ana's little blouse that my wife had dropped while she was hanging out the clothes. Then, that way gypsies speak, a hoarse voice. And the words:

'Did you drop this?'

Between his fingers – thick gold rings, earth-scratched nails, index finger cigarette-stained – is Ana's blouse. My wife, her face lowered, but her eyes raised, receives the blouse, and her voice, very faint, says thank you. The gypsy lowers his eyelids as though replying and turns his back, takes two steps and begins to go down the stairs. Leaning on the doorpost, my wife sees the gypsy go down, focused, half his body obscured by the cement handrail. When the image of him disappears, leaving only the dragging sound of his boots on the lower floor, my wife slowly closes the door.

Behind the door, she holds Ana's blouse with both hands and thinks of a whole world behind her open eyes. She focuses on listening to the sounds downstairs, but hears a tap running in the bathroom. She leaves the blouse on the little telephone table, next to the chrome-plated frame with the photograph we took together in Rossio, and hurries up the corridor. In the bathroom, Íris has the bidet tap turned on, running on to a mixture of soap and torn-up toilet paper. Suddenly she stops to watch her grandmother coming in.

'You're really just ruining everything,' says my wife, as she turns off the tap.

She rolls up Íris's wet sleeves and, holding her hand that is wrapped in a bandage, pulls her down the corridor to the bedroom. She changes her blouse and vest. Then she leaves her sitting on the bed and lowers the blinds. Íris already knows. My wife looks for the white blanket and the two of them lie down. My wife murmurs, to herself:

'Now we're going to have a little sleep because you woke up very early.'

Íris doesn't reply, but after a moment she says:

'Granny, tell a story.'

Dragging her voice over some whispered words, my wife begins to make up the story of a girl called Íris who ran a race against other girls and won.

'She was like Uncle Francisco, wasn't she?'

'She was.'

'He also ran a marathon, right?'

'Right.'

'Hey, Granny – tell it again.'

'No. Now we're going to sleep.'

And there they stayed, the two of them. The sounds from the street – the motorcars, the buses – are distant beyond the window. Íris:

'Hey, Granny, don't steal my blanket.'

And there they stayed, the two of them. The air in the room is the colour of shadows. Through the gaps in the blinds come lines of light, in parallel, gently slanted, crossing the gloom and settling on the two bodies lying on the little bed. In the wardrobe mirror there is an identical room, with a grandmother and a granddaughter lying under a shadowy gloom, crossed by parallel lines of light.

In Íris's skinny little chest, her breathing softens. Her little lips lose the shape of being able to say a word. They surrender to their loss of strength. She sleeps. My wife, when she feels her sleeping, gets up with great care. She tucks the blanket round Íris's body which, feeling it, breathes more deeply, as though sighing.

It was Sunday because it was sunny, because I had decided I wasn't going to work, because not many cars could be heard in the city, because the world seemed infinite, because my daughters had dressed with ribbons they tied round their waists and because I had slept until I was woken by the church bells calling the people to mass. My wife was smiling and the morning bore the lightness of her smile. My wife was younger on Sunday mornings when she smiled. Our children were still small. Francisco was not yet born. Marta was already helping her mother.

The previous night, when my wife had told me about the octopus she had bought at the market, I could imagine her coming back home laden with baskets hanging from her arms the whole way, the handles of the baskets marked in red furrows in the palms of her hands.

That morning, when she drew back the strips of ribbon from the door to the yard and called me, I was looking for a bill in my document drawer. I crossed the little kitchen tiles and took the basin as she handed it to me and said:

'I've already cleaned it. Now it's got to be beaten.'

I chose a plank from the pile of firewood, and on the laundry tank started to beat it. On the ground, the drain was covered with the bloody mess that my wife had taken from inside the octopus.

Simão and Maria were little. They were sitting on the ground, playing, and they were watching me. Marta and her mother were waiting, and they watched me very seriously.

It didn't take much to realise that the octopus was too tough. I approached the steps at the entrance to the house and began to beat it with all my strength against the cement.

My children were shocked. They only realised they could laugh when their mother started to laugh. To make them laugh more, I exaggerated my actions as I beat the octopus against the steps.

I wanted my wife and my children to laugh and to be happy.

The bitch we had at the time was old, and pregnant, and she took fright. She came running into the kitchen, tail between her legs. After handing the basin with the octopus to my wife, for her to run it under the water, I washed my hands with a worn bar of blue soap that was in the sink, passed a wet cloth over the steps and went back to the kitchen. The bitch was lying on a heap of two or three old sweaters my wife had put in a corner, next to the unlit fire, where she knew she liked to lie. She looked at me hurt and I bent down to stroke her, as though asking her pardon.

I was still looking for the bill in my document drawer when Marta came in to start laying the table. I didn't stop looking when my wife, coming from the oven we had in the yard, entered holding the clay dish and saying not to come too close, even though there wasn't anybody near her. I didn't give up looking when my wife went to the yard door to call Simão and Maria. I gave up when my wife told me, in a sweet voice that told me all was well:

'Go and sit down or it'll get cold.'

I don't know what we talked about. The sun was coming through the window and pouring a constant torrent of light that crossed the air, that illuminated the agitated dust and set itself against the tiles. My wife, seasoning the salad, looking for napkins, running with Simão's plastic plate, was crossing this torrent of light, disordering the movement of the dust and smiling.

Simão was eating all by himself. Sometimes he would raise his fork into the air. Marta and Maria were looking vaguely at their plates. I was watching my wife serving herself. It was at that moment of silence that Simão pointed at the bitch's place and said:

'Hey, Ma . . . The dog's dying bleeding.'

At the same time we all looked over to the bitch. One of her puppies was being born. Our daughters began to scream, spitting the half-chewed octopus into their plates, got up thunderously and went out into the corridor. Simão's body was turned in his chair. He still had his beautiful child's eyes. It was out of the corner of his right eye that, without understanding what he was seeing, he was looking at the bitch. My wife got up, took him up in her arms, and took him out to the corridor. I got up too and followed.

In the corridor Marta and Maria were recovering their breath and mixing laughs with little screams. Simão started to cry. My wife was trying to comfort him, and at the same time she was laughing at our daughters. It was Marta who said to me:

'Go and see if all the puppies are born, go and see if the dog's all right.'

I opened the door slightly and put my head through into the kitchen. Around the bitch there was a puddle of water with traces of blood. Little puppies were still being born, with sticky fur, their eyes closed. I brought my head back into the corridor, muttered some sound, mouth full, and nodded yes with my head. I had my mouth full of octopus I couldn't swallow.

After loading up the piano – using our whole strength, the whole limit of our strength – after we lifted it till we were able to arrange it on the cart, I closed the workshop door. While the Italian looped and knotted the rope, he'd turn now towards me, now towards my uncle, telling us how well the piano was, better than new; he had seen so many pianos, his fingers had been over the keys of so many pianos, but not one – well, perhaps one – but almost none was as smooth and as well set-up and tuned as that one. And he told us, in Italian words, to come to the dance that night. We didn't take much convincing, but he insisted. I didn't take much convincing myself, but he took me aside and whispered that he would pay for the repairs once he had received his payment for the dance, and then speaking to everyone again he raised his voice to insist that we go to the dance. The men my uncle had called from the *taberna* looked at him with mouths agape, with almost toothless smiles.

I accompanied my uncle and the men to the *taberna*, and that afternoon it was me buying everyone a glass of wine. The glasses were filled until a red shining surface was about to spill over. The men stopped what they were saying, raised their glasses, and as though suffocating downed them in a single draught. Then they stuck the thick base of the glass on to the marble countertop and continued talking. We were happy. My uncle paid for another round. Again the conversations stopped for a moment. The *taberna* owner had spots of red wine on his shirt, and with his arms resting on the bar he watched us with an expression of amazement. All the men spoke to my uncle, who replied at random. Occasionally he would tug at someone's arm, point at me and say:

'That's my nephew.'

The men already knew, but it didn't matter because none of them was really listening to him. I paid for another round and we left. It was May. There was a kind light over the streets. The brightness was approaching the end of the afternoon and gradually took on its warmer colour. My uncle and I walked together and we were happy. When I arrived at the door to my house, before we parted, we smiled and we didn't say see you tomorrow as we did every day, because not long afterwards we would be seeing each other again at the dance.

I picked two or three pieces from the pile of firewood to light the stove, filled a pan with water and left it to heat up, and sat on a stool to think about her – to remember her face. In that rapturous moment I wanted to believe in everything. I was twenty-two years old, and I was capable of believing in everything. In that way, time passed. Night had fallen when I got up from my stool and went to pour the pan of water into the basin where I washed. In the dark the water slipped down my body, giving it glistening shapes – over my chest, over my legs, I raised my hands filled with water, poured them over my head, or my shoulders, or my stomach, and they were still wet when I ran the palms of my hands over my body as though moulding it. I cleaned myself – the towel soft from years of use – and struck a match with which I lit the lamp. I put on my best shirt, my best trousers, my best jacket, put my best boots on my feet. Then after combing my hair I took some time in front of the bathroom mirror pretending I was still combing. I opened my shirt buttons to spread a drop of eau de cologne, buttoned them up again and left.

Night over the houses. The door to the hall where the dance was going to begin was surrounded by a crowd of men and children. They were all there together, surrounding the light. You still couldn't hear any music, you could hear many voices on top of one another. I approached and began to find a bit of space to get past the shoulders and elbows. By the door sitting at a little table was a man with an open cardboard suitcase. When I made to go in he put his arm in front of me:

'It's one *tostão*.'

I told him I knew the pianist, but he kept looking at me with his eyebrows knotted. I looked inside and saw the Italian talking to her. I felt the skin of my face warming up, I felt my blood beat fast in the veins of my temples. I raised my arm and gestured to him, called him, shouted to him, but I was invisible. The people's voices filled the room. The people's voices were a compact bulk, like a rock, in the whole room. He was talking to her. She was laughing. I continued to gesture to him, put my fingers to my lips and whistled at him. But I was invisible. I lost all movement, I forgot my own arms, when the Italian moved away from her and began, determinedly, to walk in the direction of the piano – on a platform, at the back of the hall – the piano my uncle and I had repaired. Without taking her eyes off him she took two steps backwards and sat in an empty chair, next to the woman who had opened the boarding-house door for me that afternoon. All the voices were transformed into silence when the Italian sat down, pushing away the tails of his morning suit, and raised his two hands in a suspended moment over the keyboard.

When the first notes sounded, even amid the crowd of people at the door – the children crawling under legs – no other noise could be heard. Normally dances were accompanied by an accordion. Most of the people there had never seen a piano before. The Italian's melodramatic movements on the stool, now approaching the keyboard, now moving away from it, accompanied the torrent of music that was launched over the room like a tide. Some of the women, submerged, raised embroidered handkerchiefs to their faces to contain their tears. Bringing his hands, fingers open, suddenly down twice on to the keyboard, the Italian finished this first piece. Applause broke out all across the room and the Italian, on his feet, bent over the hand he had placed across his waist. After some time, when the applause was beginning to fade, he sat down again and from his hands came some looser notes; then, lifting his face towards all the people who were watching him, he began to sing in Italian. The women smiled, then immediately concealed their smiles when several men crossed the room and offered them their arm. Two couples, then three, then four began to dance. It was at that moment that I felt a hand take hold of my arm.

I turned to see my uncle, newly shaved, smiling at me under a side parting, the skin of his forehead pale without his beret, his clothes washed and ironed, his shoes polished. I paid two *tostões* to the man at the table who in exchange gave me two stamped squares of paper, and with my uncle following me I went down the stairs on to the tiles of the hall.

She saw me. I was sure that she saw me come in. I saw her face seeing me, then obscured by a couple who set themselves swaying, dancing in front of her. I stopped behind the wall of men who stood watching the couples dancing, who smoked cigarettes and waited for the right song before they would go up to the one they had chosen and with luck they would dance, too. Surrounding the dancers, in chairs pushed up against the walls of the hall, were the single girls, and beside them, their mothers. In the middle were the circles made up of the dancing couples – spinning together, a few inches between their bodies; the lads held the girls' waists, the girls would put a hand on their backs and with the other hand they held the hand the boy held up in the air. At the back, on a wooden platform, the Italian played piano and sang, looking frequently at her as she sat there beside the woman I took to be her mother. At the other end of the hall, behind the wall of waiting men, behind me, there were words and there were the faces of the men who spoke them, and who sometimes would go in through a door to where there was a bar. Behind me, tired of looking at nothing that caught his eye, my uncle was one of the men who went into the smoking room. He asked for a glass of wine.

With his hands rummaging in his pockets, he opened his left eye wide, smiled and asked for a glass of wine. When I turned back to face forwards, she was watching me. Her fixed stare was crossed by couples dancing past, but it continued fixed and immobile. I could see her now. She wore a velvet choker – her smooth neck, white and pure. Her eyes were asking something of me. I was sure that her eyes were asking something of me. In the corners of her lips arose a very subtle smile. Anyone else wouldn't have been able to make it out. The song ended, a few women clapped, the couples parted and she continued to look at me. The shape of her eyebrows spoke to me with a word – a request – but I didn't know how to dance, and that was why I remained with my hands in my pockets, sad, looking at her watching me and understanding that I had disappointed her. When the music returned and the couples resumed their dancing, she turned her face towards the Italian and, her hands empty and resting on her legs, she stopped watching me. I went into the room where the men were leaning on the bar and approached my uncle. He was with a group of men, talking loudly and laughing a lot. In the quick movements he made with his arms my uncle carried a half-full glass. When I rested my elbows on the counter and asked for a glass of wine, I listened to my uncle a moment and could not understand anything that made any sense. When my uncle saw me, he pointed at me, proud, and said:

'That's my nephew.'

And he stood me another glass of wine. And one of the men paid for another. I returned to the hall to see her. She looked at me again, and then immediately turned her face away. I went back in to ask for another glass of wine and my uncle stood me another glass of wine, and one of the men, another one, paid for one more glass of wine. I went back into the hall to see her.

In an instant I decided that the next dance I was going to hold my hand out to her and she would accept. She would accept. In my thoughts I tried to convince myself that when I had her in my arms, like a miracle I would be able to dance, but there was always something that prevented me from believing it completely. As I thought, I didn't want the song to come to an end, because at that moment I would have to go through with my decision.

And the song ended. A few women clapped, the couples parted and I crossed the wall of men standing there and began to walk towards her. As I walked she turned her face towards me and beneath her gaze my steps were very slow and difficult. And then, face to face, I looked her in the eye and felt her breathing being breathed in my own chest. The woman who was sitting beside her, who had opened the boarding-house door to me, who I took to be her mother, looked at me, too. Then, in a movement I imagined being drawn in the air which I foresaw before each of its moments, I held my hand out to her. And I waited.

Suddenly her face and the face of the woman beside her and the faces of all the people in the room turned towards the room in the corner, where there was a bar. From inside came shouts muddled together with voices. At the door there was a crowd of men trying to see, who stood on their tiptoes and held the shoulders of those in front of them to see better.

I started to run, my arms pushing away anyone who stood in front of me. I opened up a path between the ones who were standing at the door, and when I managed to get in saw my uncle lying face-down on the ground. He had the knee of one of the men he had been talking to earlier stuck in the middle of his back. He had one side of his face right against the floor and he was shouting groans under the shouts of the man who was repeating to him:

'You just say that again.'

Nobody could anticipate what I did. I threw myself at the man and pushed him. When the others made for me they did so without much conviction and I pushed them off, too. I lifted my uncle and a path opened up in front of us to let us out. As we left – my uncle with buttons torn from his shirt, his hair falling all over his forehead – I looked at her and, in the distance, I saw her face watching me.

My wife is sitting in the chair that stands between the rack of coats forgotten since winter and the telephone table. She had come to fetch the blouse of Ana's that the gypsy had picked up on the street. She had not yet taken two steps towards the kitchen when the telephone began to ring behind her. Before a moment had passed she answered it.

It was Francisco's wife. It was her shy voice. She was phoning with few words, merely to say that he had arrived well. Francisco had phoned her to say he had arrived well. My wife tried to find out what the city was like where he was. She wanted to know if it was as she imagined it. She tried to learn the exact words he'd said, but when she realised she was not going to be told any more she asked her how she was. Francisco's wife is pregnant. As soon as her belly began to show she stopped working at the hospital. She was sent home. Her voice is very low – as though dissolving into dust. It was with this voice that she said that she was well. After the silence, they said their goodbyes.

Having hung up the telephone, my wife sat down on the chair. First, she stared into emptiness. Then she held the chrome-plated frame and looked at Francisco's face in our family photograph. He was six years old. To anyone looking at us there, we will always be the same age. We will always be in that moment. We are always in that moment. Francisco is very serious. I have my hand on his shoulder. Beside me is my wife between our daughters. Next to Francisco is Simão, apart, almost out of shot. It's Maria who is smiling the most. Marta is still elegant. Simão is in a bad mood. Behind us, the Rossio Fountain. In the photograph there are still many years to go before our first granddaughter — Elisa — will be born, even more till Ana is born, even more till Hermes is born, even more till Íris is born. Marta is not yet thinking about getting married. Maria has not yet met her boyfriend. In that moment, we were happy. Before that there had been gestures that brought us to that moment; afterwards there were gestures that took us away from that moment; but, in that moment, we were happy.

The punishment I chose for myself was to know what happened next.

We went round and round Rossio waiting for the photograph to be developed. Maria and Marta walked together. Francisco walked beside me. My wife and Simão walked on their own, two steps ahead of me, each to their own side. Sometimes I would look to the middle of the square and see the photographer get himself under the cloth, lift an arm and take photographs of couples with babies in their arms. Tired of having passed repeatedly by the same chestnut-sellers and the same flower-sellers, tired of dodging people walking towards us, when the time had elapsed and we received the photograph in an envelope, we all agreed that we hadn't come out well.

In those days the truck wasn't all that old, and that was how we got back home. Francisco and Simão travelled on the back. When they lowered down I could see their faces in the rear-view mirror. The wind disfigured their expressions. They clung on more tightly and tumbled when the truck tyres went through some pothole in the road. My wife was next to me, talking to our daughters. I was silent.

The punishment I chose for myself was to know what happened next.

After we'd had dinner, under the kitchen lamp, the curtains moving slightly in the windows, the embers fading in the grate, it was winter, my arm, my thick hand in a single movement, like an impulse, but not even an impulse, like a desire you have for a moment and which becomes concrete in that same moment, another person's desire within me, a desire which is not thought, but which rises up like a flame, and my arm, my thick hand crossing a straight and invisible distance, me looking at her face and lessening this strength a little, and my hand meets her face and her mouth, the tips of my thick fingers touching her hair and her ear, the coarse sound of flesh against flesh, the expression on her face changing, tense under my hand, and my hand ceasing to exist when she falls flailing, the disordered sound of her body falling to the floor, her back knocking over a wooden stool, me now wanting to pick her up, now wanting to hold her, now wanting to undo what had just happened, but just standing waiting for it to happen, I can't do anything, I can't go back, it's impossible, and her body stopped, I began to feel the burning memory of her face, mouth, hair and ear still on my hand, and all the objects in the kitchen seeming to burn, the scales for weighing grams of flour, the tile with a Lisbon landscape hanging on the wall, the ashtray of shining porcelain, and the children crying, the children crying, but the smallest came running and clung on to my legs, I felt his thin body clinging on to my legs as though he wanted to stop me, as though he was holding on to a mountain that was much stronger than him, and I held him by his arm, opened the door and sent them to their room, my arm pointing to the open door, and them afraid to pass between me and the open door, I shouted words, the eldest was crying, she couldn't hold back her tears, her face flushed, red, her sister was crying all the tears she had, her nose curving down, the brothers were crying like little men who already didn't want to cry, who had already begun to want to unlearn how to cry, and they passed me and I closed the door. She got up and sat on a stool, in the light, crying. I rested my closed fists on the table, my breath racing, close to tears.

It was Sunday. I awoke mid-morning with a bitter, gummy taste enveloping the whole of the inside of my mouth. I put on some trousers, and bare-chested opened the yard door and took two steps – the earth under my feet. Slowly I got used to the light that dazzled me, but I couldn't bear the sun on my head, which was why I stopped beneath the lemon tree.

On Sundays, the birds are freer. They show themselves off looping round in the air because they know people will notice them more. On Sundays, the noise of the streets is different – the voices, unconcerned, settle over the empty space left by the harsh voices of the weekdays. That was one of those Sundays, it was a Sunday Sunday, but I was waking from a world in which there were no Sundays and that day seemed strange to me, just as any other day would have seemed strange to me.

I rinsed my mouth with water. I washed myself under the yard tap. I breathed. Drops of water, settled on my eyelashes, gave a glisten to the corners of the outdoor sink where my mother no longer washed the clothes. I went into the house, wiped myself down, and as I got dressed my bones clicked dryly like vine branches splitting.

I tried to think as I walked down the street. It was Sunday. I passed gentlemen with their watch chains coming out of their pockets, and ladies on their way back from mass. Bit by bit I was getting back to being something closer to myself. Bit by bit it was as though I was regaining the gestures in my hands, regaining the movements in the movements of my legs. It was as though I was returning to my own body.

Knocking on the door with my knuckles, that moment seemed to me the distinct and definitive entry into reality – all the outlines returned to their objects, the colours stopped drifting into stains. As I waited, I focused on the door, immobile, in front of me. Behind it, I could hear a current of steps approaching. And the sound of a lock opening. And the door moving away, opening.

It was her. It was her face, there in front of me, looking at me. It was her lips, suspended, the infinite depth of her eyes, her skin. If I stretched out an arm I could touch her. A blanket of heat enveloped me. The sun stuck to my whole body and transformed itself into hot skin. She wasn't expecting to see me there either. Her face took on new shapes as she looked at me. Anyone else wouldn't have been able to make it out. In the corner of her lips arose a very subtle smile.

In that glowing silence, I don't know how I was able to say the words of the banal phrase that simply asked for the Italian. I don't know how I was able to understand, in her fragile, incandescent voice, that the Italian had left early that morning. I don't know how I was able to float in the vastness of her eyes – the horizon – and ask her if the Italian hadn't left anything for me. I don't know how I didn't die – my heart bursting in the middle of my chest – when she, never stopping watching me – purity and beauty – shook her head, so very slowly, to one side and the other – the smooth skin of her neck – the way my fingers could have slipped, slowly, across the smooth skin of her neck. The Italian had left without paying me and all I could do was look at her and smile.

When we said goodbye, each trapped in the other's eyes, we kept smiling because there were many things we wanted to say. When she shut the door, I remained where I was. For an immeasurable length of time I kept looking at the closed door, smiling and feeling everything that still remained of her presence.

I arrived at the workshop. I went into the piano cemetery. I leaned on a piano – my body leaving a mark in the dust – and I remembered the image of her face. I talked to the image of her face. I listened to the image of her face. And hours went past. It was only much later that I remembered the Italian. He left early in the morning and didn't pay me for the work with money, he paid me with something that was worth much more – the pianos and the indelible image of her face.

For a moment, my wife leans over the ledge and casts her gaze over the empty street, as though looking for the figure of the gypsy. In the kitchen, looking at nothing, she freezes – only she knows what she's thinking – and then, after a shudder, she starts to move again. She is holding Ana's damp blouse. She cleans off the pavement dirt with her hand and decides to hang it out because she can't put it in the laundry basket wet.

This blouse used to belong to Elisa when she was smaller. All our grandchildren inherited clothes from one another. Even Hermes, when he was a baby, wore clothes from his sister and from Ana. The few times Marta went out with him, people would be misled by the colours and said:

'What a delightful little girl.'

When Hermes started to walk, Marta stopped dressing him in his sister's and cousin's clothes.

It was a cardboard suitcase, marked by scratches, worn at the corners, old. On the side where the fastener was, under the clasp, it had the tin figure of a running man, his arms and legs stopped mid-movement. All our grandchildren tried to tear the tin man off. None of them could. He was stuck there for ever. It was Marta who packed Elisa's clothes away in the case and took it over to Maria's house a few months before Ana was born. Maria packed these clothes back in the case, added to it a few she had bought, and took it fuller than it had been to Marta's house a few months before Hermes was born. Marta packed these clothes back in the case, added to it a few she had bought, and took it fuller than it had been to Maria's house a few months before Íris was born.

My wife hangs out the blouse and thinks vaguely about eternity. One day, this blouse that had been bought for Elisa, and which is worn by Ana, will also be worn by Íris. Even after that day, the future will go on.

'Ah, my little monster!' I'd say, and Ana would come running to me in the kitchen. It was a weekend, because Maria had come to visit us. Ana was not much more than a year old, but already she would run to me saying:

'Grampa, Grampa, Grampa.' And she was almost breathless. I was very ill. I had pains, and I knew I was close to dying. Ana was very like Maria when she was small – the dark hair and very blue shining eyes. When I saw her eyes with the child's smile I felt sorry, because I thought that when she was big, she wouldn't remember me. I didn't remember my grandparents who died when I was her age.

'Ah, my little monster!' I'd say. She would come running and jump into my lap. I was sitting on a sofa that had come from Maria's house when she had bought better sofas. I'd hold her in my lap and we played a game. Maria was making the dinner with her mother. For a moment I forgot all about them. I was playing a game with Ana. Her little hands slapped at my face. I smiled at her, very thin.

After a few weeks, even my uncle noticed.

During the daytimes, without there being any pianos to repair, I would spend hours lost in the piano cemetery. I was always late in, in the mornings, and many times I found my uncle waiting for me by the big door, as yet unshaved, hair uncombed, holding his beret in his hand and looking at me in wonder, his left eye open very wide. At the end of the day I didn't want to be alone at home and stayed with my uncle in the *taberna*. But I didn't want to be in the *taberna* either.

I drank glasses of wine and stayed at one end of the bar, not allowing anyone to talk to me.

All my thoughts were her face repeated.

At lunchtime I'd leave my uncle sitting at a table to eat and I'd go out into the streets. It was the start of summer, and I walked on, over the top of the light. The people who came into the workshop would say:

'I saw you, yesterday, out in the street, I tried to call you, I waved to you, but you didn't see me.'

I didn't see anything. When I got to the corner before the boarding house I would stop with my body obscured by the wall, I would lean my head out and wait. Sometimes she would come to the door – her profile. At other times she would come out – her body drawn on the pavement. On more than one occasion – her voice greeting someone – her voice saying a phrase – her voice brought by a breeze – her voice floating – her voice fragile.

In the piano cemetery, all afternoon for a week, I wrote and tore up, and wrote again, and tore up again, and wrote again the letter where I said a part of what I felt about her. Hours could pass in the time I spent choosing a word. When I wrote it, moments would pass before I tore up the piece of paper where I'd written it. I knew by heart all the words I'd decided to write, and all the alternatives to each of them. That was what I was thinking about when at the end of the afternoon, at the start of the night, I leaned on the *taberna* counter, not allowing anyone to talk to me.

It was perhaps the hottest day of the whole summer. The sun burned in the streets. I made my way over the sun. In my pocket I had the piece of paper. On the paper I had the words I had managed to assemble, written in my hand, written with a carpenter's pencil. The paper, like a piece of sun folded in my pocket, also burned me. I had finished writing it three days earlier. The two previous days I'd waited for her at the corner before the boarding house. The previous day, she had appeared at the door for a moment, and then immediately went back inside. That day I waited for her at the corner before the boarding house. When I already believed I was going to be returning to the workshop without being able to see her, she came out of the door and walked away, down the pavement. I stopped thinking. I crossed the road and, taking steps much larger than hers, I walked, looking only at her back getting ever closer, ever closer, till it was just two steps away, till it was just my arm's length away, till it was beside me. As I passed her I put the piece of paper in the soft, soft and fresh palm of her hand. She shuddered and I felt her fingers closing at the tips of my fingers. I pulled my hand away as though I had never touched her and looked her in the eye. I didn't stop walking. She looked at me, softened, closed the piece of paper in her hand and didn't stop walking.

When Maria arrived my wife had already hung out the clothes, had already switched off the wireless and already had a pan on the stove, wreathed in steam. My wife wasn't startled as she heard the key entering the lock and turning, but she was set in a thought and as she abandoned it she began to move about more quickly, only stopping when Maria came into the kitchen.

Without asking, but understanding the house's deserted calm, knowing, Maria came in angry with my wife.

'It's always the same. How many times have I told you that if she goes down in the morning she doesn't want to sleep at night?'

My wife didn't reply. She waited. Maria continued to be angry. She said two or three things that all meant the same. Her voice was all the more severe for existing alone amid the silence of her movements. The other sounds – the whistle of the flame on the stove, the water boiling – were like shadows that surrounded the words she spoke. The moment ended when Maria pulled back a chair and sat down. My wife, feeling herself a girl and a mother and a grandmother, took a breath, approached her and told her what had happened.

Maria listened to her, her eyes wide, resisting in those moments when she almost couldn't resist interrupting her. And as soon as she stopped being able just to listen, she leaped up and went along the corridor. Her mother followed her, trying to keep up with her speed. And suddenly there they were, both standing in the door to the living room. A brief moment had passed since our daughter had heard the whole explanation, since she had understood every word, but there, looking into the living room, she seemed not to understand the cupboard fallen on the carpet.

Ignoring her mother – her gaze frozen – she took slow steps towards the cupboard. Following her gaze, her mother followed her. The gloom of the living room was fresh like the silence, like a journey to a time past. Rays of light, straight, symmetrical, came through the gaps in the blinds and stretched into the living room air. Mother and daughter walked towards the rays of light, drawn by the rays of light. Although neither knew what the other was thinking, it was as though they thought the same thing because they bent down at the same time on either side of the cupboard, and slowly, lifting the weight of their own bodies, began to lift it up. Their movements crossed and interrupted and freed the rays of light. Their movements sketched themselves in the straight and parallel distance of the rays of light.

The touch of my hands had no weight and no texture, the people who spoke to me were always very far away, all colours were pale in my eyes, the glasses of wine I drank tasted of nothing and intoxicated some other person, my body walking along the pavement was so light that it didn't belong to me, because I only thought of her. I could only think thoughts that imagined her. I only existed deep down inside myself thinking of her. A tiny movement inside me – believing for a moment that she might never want to see me again, believing for a moment that she might have laughed at the letter I gave her – any movement inside me was felt with my whole life; but the touch of my own hands was inexact. In the world, I was not I. I was a reflection that someone vaguely remembered. I was a reflection that someone was dreaming without believing.

The last days of May were dull sun – on the streets of Benfica, lost from myself at lunchtime; in the piano cemetery, my gaze locked on the little window that tried to illuminate the impossible and was giving up, resigned. Each moment felt like the tiring repetition of identical successive moments from previous days. In the morning, arriving at the workshop, I would think it was again morning and I was again arriving at the workshop. I recognised the temperature and the sounds and the smells of the day being born. I knew every detail before it happened – the people who arrived at the workshop, my uncle telling stories attached to stories attached to stories – currents of words snaked in the air of the shop. I watched each gesture unfold without interest. And at lunchtime I felt myself

suffocating. I walked the streets towards the boarding house –
I again walked the streets again towards the boarding house.
Every day, at the corner before the boarding house, with my
body hidden by the wall, I stuck my head out and waited
again, again, again. She didn't appear, and I always made the
same plans – to jump over the walls of the neighbouring yards;
to look through the windows and see her through the curtains;
to knock at the door, wish that she should be the one to open
it or ask some question of the woman I took to be her mother,
some question I didn't yet know but which was reasonable
and allowed me to see her. I believed that if I saw her I would
instantly know what she was thinking. But the time came
when I had to return to the workshop, and I never, not on
any of those successive days, I never dared to get any closer
than the edge of the corner where I waited. Returning to the
workshop, without any news, floating without any strength
over the pavements, I always thought I was again returning to
the workshop, without news again, floating again without any
strength over the pavements.

The piano cemetery was enormous. The afternoons were
as vast as linked generations. I would choose a piano, open
it and stay there, looking at its suspended mechanism. Every
time I could not help thinking that my life, diminished by
those afternoons, was exactly like the suspended mechanism
of a piano – the fragile silence of the aligned strings, the
perfect geometry of its almost death, able to be resuscitated at
any moment that never came, a simple moment like so many
others would be enough, a moment which could arrive, but
which never arrived.

And it was in a moment that my uncle came into the piano
cemetery. I raised my eyes towards him. He approached me.

He stopped and stood a pace away from me. In that concrete distance which separated us, in silence, it was as though I was passing on to him a part of all the hurt that I was capable of imagining. Then I lowered my face, as though I really was able to cry. I'd already stopped trying to hide what I could not hide. My uncle looked at me, with his left eye saddened, with the blind space of his right eye, ever sad, and in the concrete distance which separated us, in silence, it was as though he almost nearly hugged me and was able to speak to me with words of courage. We returned together to the carpentry shop, and as soon as we resumed our work my uncle resumed the telling of the stories I didn't hear.

As night fell, the *taberna*. Then home, alone.

It was the morning when more than two weeks had passed since the moment when I'd handed her the piece of paper, the letter in which I had written the word you and that word was her, the letter in which I had written the word me and that word was me. I reached the big workshop door and my uncle wasn't waiting for me. I didn't pay too much notice to this absence as I believed I'd known it even before it had happened. And I spent the morning in the solitary hours of my thoughts, between the hours in the carpentry shop and the hours in the piano cemetery. It was June, and for me, there were no birds singing, there was no freedom of the people on the streets. At lunchtime I walked slowly along the pavements that each day took me to the boarding house. I stopped on the corner where I stopped every day. I waited. I waited. And when I thought that this was a moment just like any other, her body appeared at the door. She looked towards me and went back inside.

Returning to the workshop, my feet walked along the pavements, my movements avoided people who stopped in front of me or came towards me, but inside me there was a shadow that avoided even more obstacles, that walked even faster. I didn't understand whether she had come out to see me, or whether she had gone back inside because she had seen me. From a distance there were no answers to be found in her face. And my feet walked along the pavement. And by avoiding fear, I was avoiding hope.

I crossed the entrance hall of the workshop. The high walls were the limits of the world. My steps on the earth, against the silence, were the only sign of life. I went into the shop. I crossed it. I opened the window and, arms open, holding the shutters, it was as though I was trying to grasp the whole afternoon and pull it into my chest. In the immense time that began in that early afternoon, not much time passed. I heard steps in the entrance hall and I didn't turn to see who it was, because I believed I knew in advance what was going to happen, nothing could surprise me; I believed it was my uncle. Sensing that, strangely, the steps had stopped at the door to the shop; sensing someone's breathing beginning to calm, sensing the silence, I turned. It was a boy, in shorts, arms folded across his waist, dirty cheeks, looking at me fearfully. Without my saying a word to him, he reached out his arm, holding a folded piece of paper. I took it from his hand, gave him a coin, and in the time it took me to lift my gaze I saw him running out. I opened the piece of paper before I was able to breathe. It just said – I like you a lot, too.

Light, light – the sun can cover every object with its brightness after all. The sun slipped across the surface of pine shavings on the patio floor, came into the carpentry shop, wrapped up my skin and came inside, too. Within me, I was infinite. June was born within me again. The sun expelled all the shadows and brought only brightness. Smiling, a child in this world, I ran round the workshop, looking for my uncle. I wanted to tell him of my happiness and I wanted to see him smile with me. I went into the piano cemetery, I looked out on the patio, I almost called out his name, but I couldn't find him anywhere.

I stopped looking for my uncle when I anchored myself to the carpenter's bench. Resting my gaze on a point where I could see her – she was clear, she was beautiful – I kept smiling and, like a child, so I remained. It was only after the night had passed without seeing my uncle at the *taberna*, after he didn't show up for work the next day, after asking the men at the *taberna* if they knew anything of him and them saying no, after I had been to the house where he rented a room and asked if they knew anything of him and them saying no, it was only after spending another night without seeing him at the *taberna*, it was only after he didn't show up for work again, that I understood that my uncle had disappeared.

My wife says she wants to telephone Marta. Maria doesn't reply. Maria is still cross. If my wife just stopped to think, just to look for an answer, she would end up concluding that Maria is cross over some problem at the factory.

Maria spends her day at the factory sewing items of women's underwear – bras, knickers. Around her are six or seven women who do the same job. They have already become used to talking above the noise of the sewing machines. The factory is a warehouse filled with women sitting at sewing machines. The factory is always lit by the same light – white lamps sticking out from the ceiling when it's daytime, when it's night-time, when's it's raining, when it's the height of summer. Normally my wife knows the stories, the conflicts and friendships of the six or seven women who surround our daughter at the factory. Normally, at lunchtime, sitting on a kitchen chair, my wife hears Maria talk to her about these women – their ambitions, their sacrifices, their scares, their fears, their secrets.

My wife doesn't stop to look for an answer, and so she, too, becomes angry. Being angry is being haughty, speaking with superiority. It is a statement that expects no reply, when she says:

'I'm going to phone Marta.'

Maria, angry, doesn't reply. My wife lifts the receiver.

On the day Marta's husband came back from his mother's funeral, he chose a hurt expression and announced that he no longer wanted to live at the house by the workshop. On that same day, respecting a son's mourning, Marta started to pack things away in cardboard boxes and packing cases she asked for at the grocer's.

Hermes hadn't yet been born and Elisa wandered round the house, contented, dodging table lamps spread around the floor.

Marta's husband borrowed a truck. For several days he did one trip after another between the two houses, between Benfica and the plantation land where he was born. Each time he arrived, Marta had everything organised in piles and told him what to take.

On the final trip – the house completely empty, the walls, the house suddenly bigger – the final thing to be taken was the living-room armchair. Marta's husband asked two friends to help, who also used all their strength to get Marta up and on to the back of the truck – her husband pushed her rump, one man held her under the arms and another by the waist.

When Marta managed to install herself on the truck, when the men had recovered their breath and her husband had thanked them, Marta stood herself up, took a few embarrassed steps and sat down in the armchair. As the truck made its way along the streets, each time it stopped at the traffic lights people would stop on the pavements and look at her, pointing in her direction because they had never seen anyone like her before – squeezing her legs together, setting her elbows on the arms of the armchair, her head held up on her neck, Marta's body spilled over in waves of flesh and skin that covered the armchair; the existence of the armchair could be inferred simply because Marta's body was in the position of sitting on something.

With the speed of the truck a breeze passed Marta's face which ruffled her hair, but her cheeks were coloured a vivid red. Her lips were pressed together in a line.

When my wife comes back into the kitchen, the muscles of her face tense. She says:

'Marta has asked me to go and spend the weekend at her place.'

Maria keeps eating, leaning over her plate, in silence. A spinach leaf slips from her spoon but she moves her head, swallows the spinach leaf and then the spoon of broth and continues eating, leaning over her plate, in silence.

I wasn't surprised when I went into the piano cemetery to look for some part and, lifting the lid of one of the pianos, found piles of Maria's romance novels. I knew very well that Maria would escape from her mother and spend hours sitting in a corner of the piano cemetery, leaning over a book which rested on her knees. When this habit began, my wife worried a great deal and said to me:

'I don't know what Maria was up to all this afternoon. I asked her and she didn't want to tell me.'

As soon as I realised what was going on I calmed her down. She only spoke of it again when she was angry:

'So you have no trouble hiding yourself away to read your romance novels, but when it comes to helping out . . . Or did you think I didn't know?'

My wife would say this because she knew it hurt her. The romance novels were the secret everyone knew but which everyone respected as a secret.

If any of my children had continued with their studies, Maria would have been the one who would have got furthest. She was always the most dedicated.

Those were evenings when I would be doing something silent behind my bits of wood. I would hear her steps on the pine shavings that covered the patio floor, raise my head slightly and see her with her books hidden under the dress altering the shape of her body, squaring her belly or her rump or her shoulders.

Later, when I lifted the lid of one of the pianos, I would find piles of romance novels. The books were written in Brazilian Portuguese. They made up collections with women's names – Sabrina, Bianca, Júlia. Reading the authors' names my daughter would imagine women in love, who knew life – Rosemary Carter, Violet Winspear, Anne Mather, Vanessa James, Lynsey Stevens, Elizabeth Pretty, Ann Cooper, Penny Jordan, Casey Douglas, Rebecca Stratton, Flora Kidd, Jane

Donnelly, Linda Harrel, Rachel Lindsay, Essie Summers, Katrina Britt, Amanda Carpenter, Anne Hampson, Janet Dailey, Marjorie Lewty, Carole Mortimer. Before she started reading my daughter would select a solemn voice and in the silence of the piano cemetery would whisper the title of the book she was holding: *Lost in Love*, *A Time for Love*, *Only a Woman*, *The Perilous Rival*, *No Way Back*, *The Seduction Game*, *It All Happened in Paris*, *Love without Marriage*, *The Man of Steel*, *Afraid to Love*, *The Stranger from Next Door*, *Slave to Pride*, *Sublime Obsession*, *Stolen Heart*. And she would enter a world of envy and love, of pride and love, of fear and love, of jealousy and love, of betrayal and love, with strong, sensitive women she would never forget, and who were called Cherry, Vic, Laura, Helen, Jane, Polly, Kate, Casey, Sarah, Raine, Luenda, Rose, Sally, Lee, Sophy, Jensa, Brooke, Viviane, Magda, Robyne, Madeline; with handsome coiffed men who smiled in the enamoured photos on the jackets and who were called Max, Gwill, Mark, Rick, Brandon, Flint, Marcus, Adam, Jeremy, Leon, Karl, Magnus, Ric, Nick, Cole, Dean, Kley, Robert. And hours would go by like that, afternoons would go by like that. In the final pages, after all the frights, bad omens, obstacles, when it seemed impossible, Maria would give a long sigh because she once again believed what she had never stopped believing – that pure, true love always triumphs.

Through all the nights of that summer, the stars were liquid in the sky. When I looked at them, they were shining liquid points in the sky.

The first time, we met during the day – I smiled at her, she smiled at me. We said two or three words and held ourselves back within our bodies. Her eyes, for a moment, were an abyss where I was surrounded by a luminous lightness, where I fell as though floating – falling through the sky within a dream.

That night I waited for her, leaning against the wall, a few metres before the entrance to the boarding house. The people passing were happy. I was thinking about something that made me feel bigger inside, like the night. The ivy leaves that covered the top of the wall, and which hung over the pavement, were a single nocturnal shape, made only of shadows. First I felt the ivy leaves being moved; then, I saw her arms grasp the wall; then, her face still against the bright night-time sky. And my heart missed a beat. The world stopped. Shadows rested, transparent, on the skin of her face. The fresh air, cooled, moulded the skin of her face, and the world continued. I helped her down. We ran along the pavement hand in hand. My hand enveloping her slender hand, the strength of her fingers in mine. At night, our bodies running side by side. When we stopped – our breathing, our faces wondering at one another – we looked at one another as though seeing one another for ever. When my lips slowly approached her lips and we kissed, there were shining reflections, like dust thrown into the air, falling through the night that covered us.

Later, there were interminable days which I spent alone at the workshop. In July, for the first time, I repaired a piano without any help – the upright piano of a lady with children and grandchildren.

'It's not for me any more. It'll be for my grandchildren,' she said.

Later, there were the men from the *taberna* never asking me about my uncle, and me remembering less and less to ask them about him. There were whole days, and whole nights.

As soon as I awoke, I pushed away the sheet and remained sitting on the bed, watching the first light coming through a slit in the window, and I knew that during that summer the days had neither a beginning nor an end. Time was a permanent succession which didn't stop with the night. I would get up slowly, drawing shapes with my movements and beaming at the clothes I put on. When I went out into the street the city was misty shapes that were reborn and perhaps, perhaps, happiness was within its reach. I would arrive at the big workshop door, and as I went in, even before going in, I would begin to count the time that separated me from her. However, I was comfortable in the workshop. In front of me I had wood, and I had the peace of knowing the shape I wanted to give it, and of knowing just how to give it that shape. In front of me I had the piano of a lady with children and grandchildren, there was a keyboard and my finger resting on a key, and inside a note I would never know – a single note – the whole space of everything I wanted to imagine – her face – her face – her face. It was morning, and for some moments I saw only the image of her face, I could hear her voice, and it was still morning, I saw her again with the same face, and it was still morning, I saw her again, and heard her, and it was lunchtime. In the afternoons, too, I lived between dreams. With just a few differences it was like when I was five or six and my mother sweetly let me sleep on Saturday mornings – there was sun beyond the window and I would go on waking and sleeping, thinking dreams and dreaming ideas.

I would go into the *taberna* when, after the afternoon, before the night, the dark blue colour would fall over everything – the workshop's earthen path. The sounds of the city, distant, came through the dark blue. I would drink three or four, or five, glasses of wine because it was still too early to arrive home to get myself ready. That was the time each day that I just allowed to pass. I didn't worry about existing. The marble countertop wasn't important, nor the men's toothless smiles, nor the men's limping conversations. I witnessed everything, unconcerned, light, I smiled easily. I existed during that time that I allowed to pass, that I barely felt, but I existed far away. I returned to my body when I left the *taberna*; it was too early when I arrived home and, without eating, began to get myself ready. Hours passed, dimly lit. In the bathroom mirror, my face.

Then there was a moment when I would put my right foot down by the front step of the house, on the pavement stones. And I would walk against the streets. I would get closer. And the streets would walk against me. When I reached the boarding house I knew for sure that inside was her. Her her her. This simple certainty was filled with miracles and I was almost surprised not to find the walls of the boarding house engulfed in flames, or filled with what seemed like a flood of magnificent voices. My waiting then was serene. I knew there was nothing that time could do against our inevitable, insatiable, indomitable will. There were breezes that came from black corners of the night and that touched my face. There was that nocturnal summer. I waited, and in a single moment: her steps on the other side of the wall, my heart lost inside me, her movements drawn in the silence, and me lost inside myself. And, in a single moment: her, at last, the weight of her body being much more than just weight, her, the shape of her body being much more than just a shape, at last, me feeling almost ready to cry, and her, at last, her body being much more than just her body, at last, in my arms. Her head resting on my shoulder. Her hair touching my cheek.

On those nights, I already knew that the woman who lived in the boarding house wasn't her mother. The woman who ordered her about, whose face was stone, was her godmother. She had raised her from very young, as though she were her mother, as though she were her daughter. Her real, distant mother was the dull image of a poor woman, with a sad expression, locks of hair falling down her face. The first nights we walked, we ran far, before we embraced. Later we stopped being able to wait. We embraced as though exploding when we met, and only then we walked, we ran. For a week we had a park bench and we had all the shadows that shrouded it. Then, we had my key opening the big workshop door, the darkness and the piano cemetery. Our bodies.

'Marta has asked me to go and spend the weekend at her place,' my wife says. She repeats.

Maria remains silent.

Íris has woken up and got out of bed on her own. She is coming along the hall runner, her face cross with sleep. Her eyes almost closed. Her eyebrows as though she is angry. Her skin warm from the flannel sheets. She comes whimpering a lament which is her way of complaining at having woken up.

'Oh! Come here to Mummy!' says Maria, reaching her arms out to her.

Íris rubs her little eyes with her small hands, her fingers closed in her small hands. She whimpers, as though everyone believes and understands that waking up is a bad thing that has happened to her.

Maria takes her on her lap. She sits her on her knees. She examines her bandaged hand. She tells her she has to behave herself well. She talks to her about the little hurt. And she falls quiet. There is silence.

Her voice faint, but looking directly at her mother, Maria says: 'Don't go . . .'

My wife remains silent.

Íris, sitting on her mother's lap, has her gaze directed at the window and she continues to wake up, slowly. My wife is turned towards the sink. Her movements are too small to fill the kitchen.

'Don't go . . .' Maria says. She repeats.

Maria puts Íris down on the floor. She approaches my wife's back and touches her arm. My wife pretends not to feel it. Maria says:

'Please.'

My wife has already decided that she's going to spend the weekend at Marta's house, but she remains silent. Without knowing what she wants, Íris pushes a chair across the tiles. Maria shouts:

'Stop that!'

With that shout, Íris begins to cry. Maria continues talking to her mother:

'Please, I'm afraid that the worst is going to happen today.'

My wife remains silent.

The kitchen clock – in a few minutes Maria will have to go out, back to the factory. When she crosses the threshold

69

my wife, ever silent, will have begun to give Íris spoonfuls of soup. Maria will go down the stairs, she will find the street, the light, the size of the buildings, the motorcars, July, the abandoned mangy dogs, and, the whole way, she will feel regret, pity and fear.

Our bodies. In the piano cemetery the night was black, it was absolute. In this opaque time, our bodies existed. My arms saved themselves, surrounding her. My hands sought peace in the sure surface of her back. Our lips knew how to meet. Our mouths constructed shapes – so many details – shapes that no one in the history of the world could imagine, they were impossible to imagine for living people with the common thoughts of people, unrepeatably concrete shapes. Our lips. Our tongues sensing the taste of our mouths – the warm saliva, the warm blood. And my lips extended. And my lips reached out to the skin of her face. I held her head – my fingers in her hair – and my lips mixed in the skin of her face. The palm of my right hand went down her body, down the line of her body, passed her waist and went down, trying to find the end of the dress, found her legs and moved up. It went up, on the inside of her thighs. And my lips were still there and on her lips too because we breathed the same breath. The tips of my fingers slipped up the warm, smooth inside of her thighs. This way was a long one. She put a hand around my arm. The tips of my fingers slipped and, the moment I touched the cotton of her panties, I felt her hand tighten around my arm and, still, we breathed the same breath. My fingers, squeezed by her legs, felt, slowly, the middle of the cotton panties, soft beyond the cotton, hot beyond the cotton. The palm of my hand, on the panties, felt the hairs under the panties. My fingers – my whole body – my fingers felt, slowly, the cotton, hot, damp. Our bodies drawn black on black. A piece of the dark night sky came in through the window of the piano cemetery. It was this almost no light that showed the shadows and the outlines of her body at the moment when I lifted her dress above her waist and slipped her panties down her legs. And I lay her on a piano – her body – my body – our bodies.

At the end of the summer, we learned that it was that night that we had made Marta.

September. As though preparing to cross autumn together, we were less and less able to bear the pain of parting. More and more people came to the workshop asking for jobs that were not ready. Every time I excused myself with my uncle's disappearance – most expressions changed to understanding – but I knew the real reason was the vital urgency of always meeting her.

I had closed the workshop door and I had run through the invisible streets of Benfica. When I reached the market, I knew where to find her. I began to walk beside her, or behind her, or in front, far enough that, occasionally, our elbows would touch, that I would feel the smell of her skin, far enough that no one would understand that we were together. She would look one way, and I would feign no interest in looking that way. She asked the cost of the apples, I asked the cost of the pears. Trying not to move our lips, barely looking at one another, we exchanged whispered phrases – simple phrases that tried to say love – like questions, like answers. That morning I spoke furtive phrases to her, and she remained silent and serious. I would say something else to her – a smile expecting a smile – and she remained silent. In an instant she turned towards me, stopped, looked me in the eye – serious – and said that she was pregnant.

I don't know where the whole world went.

After we said goodbye I walked, lost, wordless, in the hubbub of the market, until in silence we met at the corner before the boarding house, at lunchtime. She said:

'I have to tell my godmother.'

I said nothing. She said:

'I'd rather tell her before she notices.'

In the street, in front of anyone who might pass by, I hugged her. Inside our closed eyes we hugged. Time passed, I opened my eyes and saw her move away. And her body, alone, ever further from my arms, crossing the street and walking up the pavement, along the wall where I waited every night of this summer. And her body, alone, disappearing through the open boarding-house door.

As I waited, I didn't know what to be afraid of. I concentrated on the entrance to the boarding house and tried to believe in the images I imagined for my eyes – her coming out, coming towards me – her smile – her returning to my arms. For a time I waited, a time in which only I got old. The ivy leaves on the wall lifted when a breeze pushed them further over the pavements. And it was sudden – the thunder of the door closing, the shutters of all the boarding-house windows closing. I witnessed this moment without knowing how to exist.

I felt a hand touch my shoulder.

I turned.

The blind, dirty face of my uncle.

The start

I don't want just to have this name, I want to own it.

at last. I imagined this day every time I had hope – when I was lying beside my wife, my hand resting on her round belly, pregnant with our son; or when I was a lad, I'd come back from the workshop with my father and see him going into the *taberna*, hear him sending me home and I'd continue alone along the dirt road, my clothes, face and hair covered in sawdust; or when I was small and I would sit in the piano cemetery, side by side with time. I had hope, I imagined this day and believed that I wouldn't be afraid; I repeated it a thousand times within myself – I won't be afraid, I won't be afraid – and I could see distinctly, clearly, this moment, these faces. And I believe that all the moments when I imagined this day, together, added up, are longer than this day, but I also believe that this moment, now, is deeper, is an infinite well, and if I were to dive into this now, it would take my whole life to fall into its size and I would die before I touched the end. At this time in the afternoon

within the marble. I rest my hand on the white surface of this wall – and it's as though I were touching the frozen inside of the limestone. I have arrived here. I put my cardboard suitcase down on a worn out bench. It is a new suitcase which my wife bought, with money she'd saved and which she hid from me – the change from the grocer's. I was angry, happy, angry, happy, just happy, the moment she handed it to me – the case sitting on the kitchen table. Beside the fastener, under the clasp, it has the tin figure of a man running – my wife's expression smiling when I notice the little man running and lift my head to see her. It was my wife – her hands, her voice, her face that smiles before being kissed – it was my wife – my wife – who bought a tin man and kept it wrapped in paper hidden at the bottom of a box, until the moment when she stuck it on the new suitcase, beside the fastener, under the clasp, where I could always see it. I open the case – the vest ironed and folded, the shorts, the running shoes, my father's pocket watch and the tin of special grease. I had the idea when

everything again – we still believe. Time hasn't passed. The days are once again the surface on which we dream. The afternoons

also during the thing I want. Time is dislocated within itself, moved by anxiety and by desire. Time has no will, it has instinct. Time is less than a running animal. It doesn't think where it's going. When it stops, it is anxiety or desire that obliges it to stop.

went back to being the size we were when we walked across the gardens, hand in hand. The sun that illuminates us, that illuminated us, must always exist. Forgive me. The same lightness that filled us continues, like light, like light. I'm asking you: forgive me. We are everything again – we still believe. Time hasn't passed. The days are once again the surface on which we dream. The afternoons

was laid out there: special grease. It's a mixture of oil and tallow and grease. Almost asleep, but unable to sleep, I could feel the warmth of my wife beside me. A body breathing. I had my right arm over her and my chest stuck to her back, the bend in my knees fitting in behind the bend in her legs and the inside of my arm going under her arm, following the shape of her ribs, surrounding her, enveloping her, protecting her, and the palm of my hand rested on her belly – our son. My hand on her belly, on our son, was my way of falling asleep telling them my thoughts and my dreams. I thought about our son as though I was speaking to him and I thought about the races and I thought about what it is to go to Sweden, representing your country in the marathon for the best runners in the world: the Olympic Games. I was imagining our son's face when he's born. And I thought about the races again. Stockholm, I thought. And it was a word which had no connection to anything I knew. I was almost falling asleep when I was awoken by that idea. If it had been up to me I'd have got up and begun to prepare the grease there and then; but it wasn't until the next day that I went to buy one part oil, another part tallow, and another part grease. I allowed the mixture to sit for a night. As evening fell on the following day, after work, it was the coolness of June, and I spread this special grease over my whole body. I didn't have a watch on, but I was sure I ran much faster. I became lighter. My legs slipped more quickly

75

through the air. I didn't need to drink so much water because I didn't perspire. I became stronger. This grease I've got here was made

silence made up of the runners dressing themselves, some of them crossing themselves, and by the voices of the stadium, invisible, beyond the walls, as though they didn't exist and as though they existed more than anything, like fear. Then the silence of the nervous little steps the runners pretend to take, as though doing their exercises. I begin to spread the grease over my body. I immerse my fingers in the tin full of grease, and when I slip them across my legs, arms, shoulders, cheeks, I begin to shine. My body is transformed into muscles that shine. The sleeves of my T-shirt mark the line where the skin turns from brown to white. My hands spread grease over this line, and give it a shine. This is the science that is going to make me win. I feel my own hands touch my body as though they were someone else's hands. In these seconds, seconds that are marked by running shoes being tied with a bow and a knot, I feel the looks and the hidden astonishment of the other runners. They turn their heads away, but they look at me because they've never seen anything like it. I clean the walls of the tin and spread the final remnants of the grease

a man in a tie gesturing to call us. In a disordered queue, not speaking, the runners all come out. I come out, too. Under the brightness, voices crack. The expectation of a thousand mixed voices is a skin resting over the light. The size of the stadium opens itself up to the sky. The sky could pour down over this stadium now. You'd need the whole sky to fill it up. If I come to a bit of shade, I feel the cool on my oiled skin. Before the trip, a man who met me at the entrance to the workshop explained to me that Sweden is cooler than Lisbon. Either he was trying to fool me or he didn't know. It's the same heat we usually get in Lisbon at the height of August. It's a living light that makes the faces of the people in the stands incandescent – the women with parasols, hats and dresses are shining; the black of the men's top hats is bright and shining; the children shine who watch us and imagine in us lives we will never know. The runners' steps bring up the smell of the dry, burned earth. I put the palm of a hand against a barrier and move my feet just to get used to the new running shoes. The others run slowly back and forth. Some do exercises. I don't want to tire myself out yet. I look at them. I stop looking at them. In the crowd of mixed voices that fill the stadium stands and that surround me I can make out bits of my father's voice when he called me over to learn something – come have a look – or my mother's voice saying my name in the middle of a conversation – Francisco – or my brother's asking me for something, or my sister Marta and my sister Maria, still small, taking care of me and always wanting to play with me. No time has passed. All these moments

as though a sudden new day were being born inside me, inside my flaming eyes. It feels like it's not the world that exists burning before my eyes, but that it's my eyes that create and burn this world before them. A whole world created by the flames that flow from my eyes. Now

from my heart. Again we are

———

because they're calling all the runners to the starting line. I'm in the front row. Runners behind me come closer. I have my right shoe stuck to the line. There are runners, men of every race. Those next to me touch my arms with their elbows and I feel them slipping on my shining skin. We're looking ahead, because we can see the future. Each of us has a heart beating in his chest. There's a man in white trousers, a dark jacket, tie and straw hat who fires a shot into the air. The explosion spreads across the field and disappears, like a release of pigeons, like a useless memory, and it's the voices of the people in the stands that really explode and fill the air, the sky and everything we can see and think. I take my first quick steps, trying to get away from the arms that are pushing to open a path. I stick out my arms to push open a path, too. Now, each step

a ray of sun, like a hand that grabs me and squeezes me against its skin, red-hot. It's fire that each movement of my body passes through. They are flames in my eyes that open a path into which I go and through which I make my way. I am a unique force, incandescent and true. I get further and further away, and I know that forty kilometres from here I will be back. I'm getting further away and closer. There are forty kilometres between me and being here being someone else. And forty kilometres may be my whole life. All time from the moment I was born until the moment I die within a single moment that might be forty kilometres. Time won't know me. I will be someone else. I won't know the distance of time. And I will return to the stadium. I will return here. Myself alone, over metres and time a shower of stones on to the track of the stadium. When I realise that one of my legs is going to take a step, it's already the other leg that's taking a step that's even bigger and even faster. My legs – I marvel at their strength. The people who are filling up the stands are like a choir of shots, voices firing from every direction. Sometimes we notice a voice that's left behind; then we notice another also left behind. We pass by as though we haven't seen their faces, but we see them without looking at them. We sense them. Breathing doesn't yet weigh on us. We have our heads to look around us. We don't look. We complete a lap of the track and the confusion of the opening metres has been left behind us. We run spaced out enough to be strings of men

you are lovely in my heart.

in my skin, the voices of the stadium fade. Bit by bit, the sounds of the city begin – a team of horses held by the bridle, which almost take fright as we pass, which take a couple of nervous steps; the engine and the horn of an enthusiastic motorcar; dogs barking angrily; children

after work, I'd already gone out to train, I'd already come back home after my training, I'd already run water under my arms and down my neck, I'd already been sitting by the fire for quite some time, when my mother asked me to go and call my father from the *taberna*. I looked at my mother lit up by the oil lamp. I said nothing. I put on my jacket and left. It was night-time, it was cold, it was February. I walked in a lot of nights like this. I knew what would be waiting for me – I'd go into the *taberna*, the gaze of all the men, and one of them saying: look, he's come for you already. And my father unable to let them be right. When I was smaller I'd pull at his arm saying: mother sent for you. And the other men would laugh and he would laugh, too. Later I stopped doing that. I didn't want the word mother spoken there. I didn't want my mother, lit up by the oil lamp, to be named there. That's why I would just go in. My father and all the men knew why I had come in, without saying good evening, without looking anyone in the eye, walking towards my father. I didn't have to say anything. They laughed, they offered me wine and I didn't accept. Once one of the men, as a joke, held a glass of wine to my lips. My father pushed his arm and the glass broke on the floor. My father was looking at him, very serious. He looked away, fearful. There was silence until one of the men said: 'Oh, what a waste of wine!' And everyone laughed. After a beat my father laughed, too. Sometimes my presence would hurry him up. At other times it seemed he'd only leave when he wanted to leave. At other times we'd be the last to leave and I'd have to carry one of his arms over my shoulders, or had to grip him by the elbow, or had to walk behind him to stop him falling. And I had to listen to him. I had to reply to him. I had to wait for him if he wanted to throw up. That night, even before I reached the *taberna*, I stopped to listen. It was my father talking. With his voice moulded by the wine, he said: 'As soon as he was born, I knew right away what my Francisco was capable of.' He said, 'Listen carefully to what I'm telling you, that boy will be capable of great things.' Then someone started talking about something else. I hoped they'd forget the moment when those words were spoken. I went in. The gaze of all the men – look, he's come for you already – and I don't remember if we went home early or late that night, what I could never forget were the words my father said, that he never would have said to me directly, but which are repeated again and again in my memory. Whenever

to another street, to other houses. I run faster so that time will pass faster. The colour of the tall houses. The roofs of the houses. My breathing. I don't want to focus on my breathing. The colour of the houses – toasted yellow, orange nearly brown, clay-coloured

this permanent sun, this heat, I feel a fresh breeze coming from the water which appears with the sudden recollection of a winter's day, with the memory of the day my father died.

of my father lying under the light of the candles. Me looking at his dead face and remembering only his living face.

that the rhythm of the running shoes on the road becomes faster. I overtake a runner who, feeling me getting closer, turns his head to watch me pass

father's face covered by a transparent tulle cloth. I looked at him, white, still, and the natural thing would have been for him to open his eyes and say my name, for him to look at me and say, 'What are you waiting for, lad?' The cold black echo of the chapel. I looked at him and found it hard to believe his voice would never be heard again.

even faster and I know that that's why people age more quickly, they die, children are born. There is only one runner ahead of me. Each pace of mine is bigger or faster than two paces from this frightened runner, who still

my father dead, white, still, and I tried to retain the image of this sadness that destroyed me because I knew it wouldn't be long before I didn't even have this, didn't have anything. They would take my father away and I would have to live my whole life without ever seeing him again.

going forwards, and the runner is getting closer and closer. The nearer I get the faster I want to run to overtake him. I keep on

for my sister Maria and my mother. They were together, sitting in chairs. The happy absence of my sister Marta was there, too, still recovering from the birth of Hermes. My brother Simão's absence was there, too. Ever since the night when it happened, that thing we will never forget, Simão and my father never saw one another again. My father, his arm shaking, pointing at the door shouting: 'Out!' Shouting, 'Out!' Simão shouting, 'You'll never see me again!' Shouting, 'I'm never setting foot in this wretched house again!' Then, years of silence. We didn't talk about it, but we wanted to believe that on that day Simão would still appear. He was our father. Our only father, who had died. We wanted to believe that he might still appear. He didn't. And we had no words, only hurt. My mother was next to Maria and had her head in her hands. My sister looked at me with dark eyes. There at the back I saw the face of the piano-tuner. I went towards him. His head tilted towards shadowy corners, towards the surface of the roof or towards empty chairs. He recognised me by the sound of my footsteps. In silence, in my hands, I took the hand he held out to me. The tuner had known my father for many years. His blind face was old and hurt. We looked at one another, as though we were exchanging secrets. And again, the echo of my footsteps – and I approached my father again – my father

I see the runner's body ahead of me

the tips of my fingers lifting the cloth that covered my father's face

I launch myself forwards and begin to overtake the runner

I leaned over my father

I overtake the runner now

my lips touched the icy skin of my father's cheek

time stops. Time has stopped. What exists are our two breathings and a group of people suspended on the side of the road. A cool breeze. Colours smudged. A cool breeze as much for my mother, as for Maria, as for me. We'd already left the hospital, we were walking towards the exit – we knew the streets were enormous – when she came running. My sister and my mother didn't see her. They were walking ahead of me, two frail shapes continuing on their slow way. She took my arm and held my father's watch out to me. Her face wasn't a smile, nor was it just serious, it was precisely the face required at that moment – her gaze under a fringe combed to one side, wavy hair. She placed the watch in the palm of my hand, then let the chain slip and fold and settle – a nest – in the palm of my hand. Then it was her voice, going through me, suddenly made of velvet, kindly. As though whispering, she said it would be better for me to take the watch with me, she said that someone might take advantage of my father's condition to steal it. I thanked her, and I noticed her, but I barely noticed her. It wasn't till I came back

by time. My mother couldn't come into our house, the empty corridors weighed down on her. In Maria's house, Ana was two years old and my mother looked after her with slow steps and few words. Ana was asleep, Maria and her husband were working and my mother was sitting in an armchair. The afternoon was reflected in the window-panes – my mother's eyes reflected the relief image of the windowpanes. Nobody could know what she was thinking, but there were whole years inside her, unrepeatable laughs and unrepeatable silences. On those afternoons my mother

believed that, in a single instant, everything could be transformed into nothing. She believed in silence

with the gentleman from the undertaker's, when we arrived
at the morgue, that I really noticed her. The whole sky was
falling in grey rain on to the city. On the pavements people
ran from door to door. Then we were at the morgue – the
thick walls. Water streamed from my hair, on to my coat,
down my skin. She approached me, and as though we knew
one another well she gave me her condolences. It seemed to
me then that her voice carried images of some other time. I
looked at the walls of the morgue, at my hands, and it was
only on the surface of her voice – as on a river – that I was
able to relax. Her choosing words and silences to console
me. And me managing even to find comfort in that voice,
closing my eyes to listen. And me, faced with my dead
father, feeling guilty for being able to find comfort in the
sweet memory of that voice – fragile grace. In the weeks that
followed I would come back just to hear it. She later told
me what time she left, and on other days I would return at
that time and accompany her to her front door. On the way
I heard tales from the hospital. They were told unhurriedly,
as though they had no end. Her voice was serene. The nights
– the moon, the city, the stars – imitated her. Weeks passed.
She began to smile at me. I began to smile at her. And before
falling asleep I began to hear her voice inside my head. I fell
asleep listening to her. The house was immense. Night filled
the house. The walls were undone by this absolute night,
and yet the darkness was all made up of many walls, one
over another. I tried to live. As I lay down, as I waited to
fall asleep, her voice was the calm world in which I forgot

everything else. In the mornings and the afternoons, I tried to see only the planks of wood I carried on my shoulders and which I laid out in front of me, on the carpenter's bench, I tried to see only the tools, only the lines where I imagined cuts, only the points where I imagined nails stuck in, but in spite of myself I still expected, always expected my father's voice to sound at some indistinguishable moment. Which was why in the morning or the afternoon I'd go into the piano cemetery when I wanted to hear only her voice in my memory, when I wanted to rest. Before going off to train I'd stop by Maria's house. I told myself that I was going to check that everything was all right, but even before knocking at the door I knew that I'd find my mother with her voice dismayed, Ana running around me holding out her arms for me to pick her up, Maria tired and her husband, on his tiptoes, his face raised towards me, trying to interest me in some subject which didn't interest me even remotely. And I'd run round the streets at maddening speed – the air leaving me heavily. I'd come back home to wash, and in the mid-evening I'd get to the hospital entrance, combed, when she would smile at me and I'd smile at her. She was the best moments

utterly. My mother's sadness also got into Maria, but never to the point where it was shared completely, because only my mother knew the time and the secrets of that sadness. Perhaps that was why there were moments when Maria couldn't understand her or what troubled her. More than a week after the burial of my father, Maria managed to convince my mother that they should go and visit Marta and meet Hermes. On the days that followed the burial of my father Maria wandered round the house and said nothing to her. She'd say to her: 'Come and eat something.' She'd say to her: 'Then why don't you go and lie down?' But she said nothing to her because these were the tiniest of words, they were silence. After a few days Maria began to sit down in chairs to talk to her. She said, 'We've got to go and see Marta's boy.' She said, 'Tomorrow we'll go and see Marta's boy.' My mother responded with a nodded yes, but on two occasions as the time to set off approached she was taken ill. It was more than a week after the burial of my father. Maria's husband didn't want to go, and at one end of the corridor he held Maria by the arm and, shouting whispers at her, shook her. At the other end of the corridor my mother and Ana waited by the door – hand in hand. They went by train. On her mother's lap, Ana leaned her whole body up against the glass of the window. Only her gaze – all of it – managed to get through it. On the front seat, my mother's silence was more invisible beneath the sound of the train on the tracks. It was still morning when they arrived at the land where Marta had gone to live. The sky

Kilometre three

was shining. It had a grey shine that filled the puddles of water with light. On the streets people stood watching my mother, Maria and Ana pass. My mother walked as though she was moving forwards on her own and no world existed. Maria and Ana went hand in hand. Maria pulled her arm and hurried her. Ana raised her head, and with her neck she turned it from side to side. It was still morning. They arrived at the little iron gate a cool breeze. This breeze is coming from within the stones of the houses. It comes from within memory. It comes from the depths of the waters. When we were at the party on the boat, my fencing teammate told me that in winter these waters freeze over completely. He told me that if you want to you can walk on them. I found it hard to believe. My companions had come to take part in the track races, the Greco-Roman wrestling and the fencing. Their hands are clean and soft. They have white shirts. They have property and education. I call them 'sir', they call me 'Lázaro'. Sometimes, before they laugh at something, they say, 'Good old Lázaro.' Next to them I'm a brute. I don't know things. That's why my companions like to joke around with me, and that's why I found it hard to believe. But it might even be true. At least it's true that at that point we were on a sailing boat I've not seen many like in Lisbon, lovely, there was still the lightness of daytime, and we'd already had dinner and it was already nearly eleven o'clock on that night that was still day. I'm sure of that because I saw the time on the watch that was my father's and which, ever since I've had it in my pocket, like for all the years it was in my father's pockets, never ran a single minute fast. I was sure that time respected the numbers on the watch. I was sure that the numbers on the watch were the secret and the lie that we all use in order to believe in simple things. But this teammate told me that Sweden is a very big country, and that in the north the sun shines at midnight as though it were midday. At first, I thought he was teasing me. I said to him, 'Hey, come on . . .' He looked at me, his face still, but we had already had dinner and it was almost eleven o'clock on my watch and I ended up believing him. And it was only then that I understood that not even numbers could bring certainty. Time exists between the numbers, it crosses through them, and confuses them. Many numbers can exist between each number. More numbers might exist between one number and another than between that one and the next. It is time that determines the numbers, that stretches them out or shrinks them down, that kills them or allows them to exist. There is nothing numbers can do when faced with time. Here, this breeze on my face makes me think he was being serious. These waters really do freeze over in the winter. At least, this breeze is all of a piece with those January mornings that chill your ears and make the frost grow

of my days. She was a single world. At that time, when we were together – it was night-time and we walked the streets – I knew that my mother's black sadness was very far away, as though it didn't exist, the cold of the lone house was very far away, almost as though it didn't exist. As we took these steps her voice would tell me I had the right to some peace. And we walked the streets, passing through shadows. Sometimes our elbows touched. I focused all the strength of my senses on that point where my elbow, for a moment, touched her. And in her voice, telling stories from the hospital – lads coming in the door to the emergency room, disoriented old women in the wards, broken men lying on stretchers – I could make out a slight change in tone when our elbows touched. Like me, she also felt these wordless moments that illuminated, blossomed, caught fire. At that time neither of us would have been capable of using words to speak of those moments or of the waves that washed over us. At that time we reached the door to her house and stopped, not knowing what to say or how to move. We lowered our gaze, our faces filled with shadows, and from the invisible insides of those shadows we laughed, pretending to laugh, because we didn't know what to say or how to move. Then, to say goodbye, we would reach out a few fingers to one another. It wasn't a handshake, it wasn't anything, it was us reaching our arms out to one another, it was our open hands and the tips of our fingers touching in the air, as our hands began already to lower and part. Then there was a night when we kissed cheeks. I closed my eyes when my lips felt the skin of her face, the smell of inside her wavy hair. Then there were other nights. The moment wasn't planned, the moment when I didn't make that move I knew just how to make – that I merely had to let my neck make it – and in which our lips met. Our lips burning. My hand holding the nape of her neck – the weight and shape of her head. When our lips parted, her eyes didn't leave mine. My eyes fleeing, and hers, serious, seeking them out. My eyes no longer able to flee – a smile. Her eyes seeing me and smiling, too. After that night, we started always walking hand in hand.

Kilometre four

from Marta's house. No sooner had Maria opened the gate than Ana let go of her hand and went in on her own. The dogs ran round her, giving little leaps, wagging their tails and licking her. Happy, Ana shouted or laughed. Maria scolded the dogs – settle down. My mother, forgotten for a few moments, continued in her silence. Elisa came out of the front door at full tilt and ran over. She approached

Ana and waited to be hugged. The dogs circled round them, high-stepping, impatient. Elisa, well-behaved, gave two little kisses to her aunt and grandmother. Ana was already heading for the door and Elisa followed her. In a straggling line, the four of them walked down the corridor. At the entrance to Marta's room, Maria was frozen mid-word by the silence and by the sight of Marta lying in bed, in a white nightshirt, her hair falling over her face. And Ana, and Elisa behind her, ran to the crib. Ana still didn't reach the top of the crib, so she rested her forehead against the wooden bars. When Hermes woke up my mother started walking. Maria went between the bodies of Ana and Elisa to lift him out of the crib. Moved, she said something – oh, so very tiny – and showed him to my mother. In that silence my mother felt a shapeless emptiness that was like flames tearing through her and she only cried when she took him in her arms. Innocent. Hermes looked out at the whole world and no one could imagine what his eyes saw. Marta took him from my mother's arms. The light weakened as it came through the curtains and mingled with the shadows. All-knowing, Marta took a breast from inside her nightshirt and brought the nipple to Hermes's little lips. And Ana remained in silence, in wonder. Elisa had already seen her mother breastfeeding her brother many times, but she too was still, she too was silent, wearing the same expression as her cousin. Maria continued to be moved. My mother remained in a silence so absolute that her body almost disappeared. That morning, Marta was already very fat. Her shoulders were thick in her nightshirt, her arms were thick, her belly was a high, round bulk under the bedclothes, her legs were thick. On that morning, and in everything that was known at the time, it was impossible to imagine that Marta would continue to get fatter to the size she is today, to the size she was the night before I left when I went over to say goodbye. Be careful out there with abroad, she said. Hermes wanted to play. Leave your uncle be, she said. When it was time to go back to the station and wait for the train, I opened my arms out wide to try and encircle her and the most I could do was rest my wrists on each shoulder. But that morning no one thought of this and everyone – even my mother – paid attention to the suckling boy. It was a gentle time. The morning

and I love you almost too much

at the foot of the walls. This perpetual sun comes in, lighting up every corner, this breeze reminds me of when I was small and my father took me to the fishmarket and showed me the blocks of ice which the men arranged on the crates of fish. It is as if, in this perpetual sun that's burning skin and walls, there exist veins that are made of this ice. It was almost eleven o'clock at night and it was still day. These waters freeze over in the winter. It's Sweden. My teammate wasn't kidding me, in spite of having laughed when I looked at the dinner cutlery not knowing what to do, and in spite of having laughed as I practised holding tight on to the cutlery, and having laughed again when he said, 'Good old Lázaro.'

the morning. I was looking at a wooden lath, my hands feeling its shape – the angles, the lines – but I didn't see it, and I didn't feel it, really. Time dissolved into the light, but I ignored time and the only true light was that which lit up her face within my memory – her walking beside me, her voice, her standing at the door to her house, her silences – her thin arms reaching out, her hands, her belly under a cardigan, her breasts, her legs below the end of her skirt – the serene certainties of her face – her before a kiss – her lips – voice and silence. I might have been looking at a piece of wood when the lady came in. Her little thin body, dressed in black, appeared at the door to the carpentry shop unannounced. That was the moment I lifted my head to see her approaching me – her face contented and casual, her steps on the sawdust that covered the floor. I walked over to her and before saying anything else apologised for the sawdust, for the dust and for something else I didn't know what. It was a lady with a gold pin, with polished shoes and who looked at me, contented, almost as though she was smiling. A lady who was

Kilometre five

distinguished. Never, not even when my father was alive, had I seen such a distinguished lady come into the workshop. Without having heard her voice I already thought her face friendly – the wrinkled skin, white hair, hat with a black tulle brim behind it. Her voice was friendly. As though pleasantly making a statement, she asked me if I repaired pianos. I could only reply yes. Then I was already taking the pencil from behind my ear and making a note of her address on a small bit of board I picked up off the floor. I'd go by the following day. The lady's smile made me smile, too. I stayed there, watching her move away towards the exit. The sounds of the city returned to the open windows. The morning returned. The image of the lady – her friendliness

– remained, slowly dissolving and I only thought about her again when, the next day, I went along

am trying to remember the happiest moments, I always end up seeing the vague image in my memory of a Sunday lunch. The diffuse clarity of the light. My mother possibly plucking a chicken. The smell of boiling water poured over the chicken's body. My mother, in the yard, sitting at a basin, in a shadow. The noise of the feathers being yanked out in fistfuls by my mother. It was always spring. It was always May. Maria might be hiding in her room, inventing fantasies, reading romance novels under the shade of the shutters; or she might be helping my mother; or she might be standing in the yard, absorbed, listening to the long tale my mother was telling in every detail as she plucked a chicken. There were birds that suddenly rose up in flight from the orange trees in the yard and which awoke a rustling of leaves. Simão came up the streets with an empty bottle in his hand, he went into the *taberna* and didn't need to say anything. The man reached out his arm over the marble countertop. My brother held the bottle out to him. The marble was colder than the shade. And my brother waited as the man fitted the funnel into the neck of the bottle and as the noise of the wine that flowed from the barrel sounded alone in the empty *taberna*. He opened the palm of his hand where he held the sweaty coin and walked the path back home. Alongside the wall, his face was serious as he walked. His left eye fixed on a point that didn't exist, and which was ahead of him. He made his way forwards, drawn by this. On the right side of his face, his eyelid rested over the empty socket. The lid sunk into the smooth hole that linked his cheek to his eyebrow. A black hand squeezes my heart. My breast

because time hurts as it passes. If I could only tell you what you were – what you are still – your face looking at me, not understanding. If only I could tell you everything I was hiding. Me not allowing my fingers to be delicate and pass through the air to touch the lines of your face – the skin of the face that encloses you. I, a criminal. You, kindly, looking at me not understanding. I – you. If only I could tell you all the sorrow I was hiding, and the tenderness, the hurt. If only I could tell you that in everything – in us – time

on Sundays, my father smiled. We were having lunch. My mother had bought fish at the market. My father was complaining about the bones. My mother was turned towards Maria or towards my brother, and she was saying, 'Don't eat so quickly.' I was seven or eight years old and my mother had chosen a piece of fish for me, and with the point of her knife had removed all the bones. Marta was still going out with the guy who is now her husband. It was the third or fourth time he'd had lunch with us. Probably someone was telling a joke, probably someone was telling the story of something that had happened, when Marta choked and started coughing. Her boyfriend got up and began patting her on the back. Marta kept coughing. My mother said to her, 'Eat a little bit of bread.' A thread of drool slipped from Marta's mouth on to her plate. Marta coughed and her face got redder and redder. She stopped coughing, and she remained for a moment with her head lowered. My father asked her if she was better, but she didn't reply. The boyfriend held her by one arm, his other hand on her shoulder, and he didn't know what to say. My father said, 'This fish is useless, it's nothing but bones.' My sister started coughing again, and when she managed to spit out the bone her plate was full of spit mixed with blood floating in the oil. As Marta recovered her breathing, my father raised his voice, saying: 'I did say that this fish was rubbish, it's money wasted on this complete swindle.' And he threw the cutlery on to the plate. Shouting, he asked my mother, 'What went through your head, spending money on this rubbish?' My mother didn't reply. My father said, 'What a swindle, what rubbish.' My mother continued not to reply. My father grabbed her by the arm, shook her and shouted: 'Aren't you listening?' My mother looked at him, her eyes serious. In a single movement my father took the plate and smashed it on the floor. Shouting, he said, 'Don't you look at me like that, you hear me?' It was that Sunday that my father stopped being ashamed of Marta's boyfriend. When Marta took him to the door

Kilometre six

to say goodbye, my father's shouting could be heard from the kitchen and Marta was crying with shame.

the streets I'd written on a bit of board and arrived at her door. I knocked, I waited, I didn't think of anything. The weight of the toolbox bent my body. The lady's steps approaching beyond the door – her smile. Going into the corridor I left behind the sun that filled the whole morning, that flooded the streets, that the men and women carried in their faces as they made their way along the pavements, the sun that lit up their certainties and heightened their hope. I slowed down to follow the lady's slow steps along the hall runner, passing the doorways to rooms full of old pieces of furniture, where whole lives had taken place, and where at that moment there was a tidy silence of coppers, silvers and crystals. We arrived

through Stockholm. Ahead there I can see the beginning of a bridge. The air – this hot air – it's now completely still. The sun fills up the air. As I approach the bridge, I want to run faster. Behind me, I hear the steps of a runner and I begin to run faster. I look at the bridge down there, I run faster, and when I slow down I can no longer hear anyone pursuing me. The bridge is closer and closer. I manage to make out the people who are at the start of the bridge. I want to get closer to the water because I believe that when I get there the air will be cooler. I put a foot on the bridge – this bridge. I pass by people cheering me on. Voices within cries. Here – the first bridge in this city that's broken into pieces and linked together by bridges. Here the air isn't any cooler than it is in Lisbon. The sun burns my skin, the special grease that covers my skin. Behind me I hear the quick steps of another runner. I hear the same voices of the same people cheering him on. And I run

into a huge hall – tall windows behind curtains that reach down to the floor, rugs spread over the waxed wooden floor, armchairs covered with cloths of cornucopias, a chandelier hanging from the ceiling over a thick mahogany table. The lady pointed me towards a piano in one of the corners of the room. There was no need. It was a grand piano.

Imposing and antique. I approached, assessing it, admiring it. It was certainly a piano the lady had first known right there, in just this same spot, when she was born – just like her parents, grandparents, great-grandparents – and which would remain there till the end of her days, and beyond and beyond. The gaze of all the generations it had survived would have been enough to wear it down; it was a solid enough piano, however, solemn, eternal, like an old oak. I put down the toolbox, sat on the stool and with a movement of my fingers lifted the lid from the keyboard, removed the cloth that protected the keys, and then after looking at them, after feeling the perfection of their surface, I touched each one. I didn't need to look behind me to know that the lady had left me alone. I knew solitude too well. It was a problem with the soft pedal. And I was leaning into the inside of the piano when I felt her approach. Her steps were silent on the rug. Her presence was like a clarity that, delicately, expanded and from afar touched my skin with marks which were at once fragile and certain. I said good morning to her. Her startled look replied to me in a whisper almost impossible to hear. In her body a shiver which if you weren't looking closely could pass unremarked. Her fingers flexed in and out. Her face, maybe curious, maybe concerned, seemed to want to approach – she tried to look inside the piano, and when I caught her she looked at me shyly. At just that moment I knew the piano was an extension of her body. As if to free herself from suffocation she needed to play. There – shy – she could feel any contact, however small, that I had with the piano. That was why I explained to her what the prob- lem was and what I had to do. Smiling, the lady came in. She got between me and her. Without losing her smile, she said, 'So I see you've met my granddaughter.' Behind her, her face, serene, shy, continued

as fast as I can, as though I was fleeing from the thing that most scared me, as though it was possible to flee from that thing I have inside my skin and which goes with me every-where, I run

to see me. Her hair, long and smooth, arranged just so. The lips without a speck to spoil the perfection of their lines. The lady asked me what was wrong with the piano. I stopped listening to myself as I explained all the unnecessary words I was saying, and just watched her over the lady's shoulder, just imagined the world of peace that existed

as fast as I can, as though I could leave myself behind, as though I could run so fast that in an instant I could come free from myself and leave myself behind me, as though I were moving ahead out of my body, and through my speed was purifying myself, I run

Kilometre seven

as fast as I can, I run

in her eyes. When I leaned back over the piano and pulled the pedal rod, there was a moment of silence during which they both went out. The lady's voice: 'We'll leave him to work.' For the rest of the morning I couldn't erase her face from my memory, I didn't want to understand the reason for her face, single and clear, in my memory. I came to believe that it was out of pity for her wanting so badly to play, needing to play and not being able to. It was getting to lunchtime, and when the lady came into the hall I was already putting away my tools. I explained to her that I had things to do in the workshop that afternoon and said I'd be back the following morning with a few parts I needed. The lady smiled at me. I told her that the piano should be ready the next morning. She continued to smile at me. On the street I looked at all the windows searching for her face behind one of the curtains. I even stopped on the pavement, pretending to look at my watch, but I didn't see her. I spent the whole afternoon thinking about her. I went into the piano cemetery to look for the parts and I thought about her. After work, when I went out for training, I thought only about her.

during or after dinner. Simão lived on odd jobs, and when he got home he'd go straight to his room. My father followed him with his gaze, as though he was angry with him and waiting for some gesture to fight with him, or at the same time as though he wanted to see if he really could cross the kitchen in silence without looking at anyone. Simão crossed the kitchen in silence, without looking at anyone. When he had gone through and closed the door, my father said, 'There's something wrong with that boy.' I slept in the same room as Simão, and when I went in his eyes were the only points that shone in the darkness. His voice was calm and soft. It was my brother's voice. He asked me, 'Is there anything left to eat in the kitchen?' I didn't have to answer. I would go back, and if my father had gone to sleep I'd ask my mother for food for Simão. The oil lamp transformed my mother's movements into shadows. I waited a moment and she put a tray into my hands with a full meal, covered with napkins. If my father was still awake it would just be me discreetly palming a hunk of bread and something to go with it.

not even impossible. Truth – like silence – exists only where I am not. Silence exists behind the words that awake inside me, which fight and destroy themselves and in that struggle gashes of blood open within me. When I think, silence exists outside what I'm thinking. When I stop thinking and focus, for example, on the ruins of a house, there is a wind that unsettles the abandoned stones there, there's a wind bringing distant sounds and then the silence exists in my thoughts. Untouched and untouchable. When I return to my thoughts, silence returns to that dead house. It is also there – in that absence of me – that truth exists.

hand in hand. For the first time, we walked in silence the whole way. She didn't tell me tales from the hospital. It was as if that day no one had broken a leg, or died, or gone mad. I didn't ask her any questions, but I missed her voice on every street. It was as though the streets themselves – the houses, the people passing us – were different without her voice. Only our steps, steps, steps. When we reached the door to her house she looked at me with her eyes covered in shadow. She asked me, 'Do you still like me?' I made as if to reply with a kiss, but she moved away and asked me again: 'Do you still like me?' I waited, as though I didn't know what to say because I had nothing to say, and when I brought my lips towards hers she didn't move away. That was the night we walked across the city hand in hand, arrived at the workshop, went into the piano cemetery and made love for the first time. We didn't go into her house because of her godmother. We didn't go into mine, because in spite of the solitude it was still too much my father's house, my mother's, my brother's and sisters'. It always will be. We went into the piano cemetery. Then, wordless, we crossed the city again, the day being born slowly behind us. Lisbon – the streets

was enormous beyond the curtains – the size of the world. When Hermes finished breast-feeding, Marta leaned him over her shoulder and began to pat him gently on the back with the tips of her fingers. Neither my mother, nor Maria, nor Elisa, nor Ana said a word. In this silence of gentle taps on Hermes's back, it was Marta who asked after Simão.

is six years older than me, but sometimes it's as though we were the same age. Other times it's as though I were his older brother. It was two days before I was going to make the trip that would bring me here. I wanted to say goodbye to him. After leaving the workshop I ran to Rossio, and then hung off an electric tram as far as the house where Simão rented a room. I went up the wooden stairs – the sound of my weight on each step. I knocked on the door – broad, uncertain rumblings approaching. The door was opened by a woman with grease stains around her mouth, with dark eyes. I asked her for my brother. She said she didn't know him. I explained to her that my brother rented a room there. She said again that she didn't know him. Suddenly, without anyone having called her, just her head appearing at the top of the spiral staircase, the upstairs neighbour said that Simão had gone away and no longer lived in that house. Then she answered no to all the questions I asked her. Thinking about my brother, imagining him, fearful, I ran back home. It was night-time when I went up my sister Maria's street. I looked in the windows – shadows pointing fingers, shapes that were perhaps too close, and perhaps too abrupt. I don't know if I could make out my sister's voice or her husband's voice shouting

Kilometre eight

were longer when I returned home after meeting her. If I had thought about it occasionally, I might have understood right then that it wasn't just my will that led me to go and meet her, to desire her; it was also my lack of will, my indecision. Even when she was silent, I looked at her face and I could hear her voice. The velvet, appeasing, comfortable, sincere, living sound of her voice found ways of getting into the inside of my time, into my own inside. As it did, the body of that voice found the huge space of a person who was completely empty – a past covered in doubts, a vague present, a future that did not yet exist. And what little there was seemed like nothing to me – kilometres and minutes – legs trying to destroy the world in a way my arms couldn't. That was why her voice grew within

the house of the piano-tuner. I was carrying the parts I needed in the toolbox. Each of my steps made the noise of those parts and the tools rattling within the wooden box – a muffled sound which I sometimes imagined being the sound of my heart beating. The morning cleaned the city – even the rubbish abandoned in the crevices of the streets, even the weeds growing at the foot of the walls, even the stones scattered in the earth. When I knocked it was the lady who opened the door for me. Her smile didn't hide any bad thoughts. I smiled at her, and followed her along the corridor. I looked at each of the rooms as they passed us, because I was looking for her. I would have been satisfied with a piece of her clothing spread out on the back of a chair, the leaf of a plant still moving after her passing, but I found only the empty spaces where at certain moments she might have been, where her face – brought by a miracle – might materialise. We reached the hall. I went to the piano. Alone, I placed my hand on the varnish of the piano and it was as though we were speaking, as though we were the same age and looking at the world from afar. I opened the piano up, and the tools in my hands were as though turning over the mechanism of the morning, as though they understood it and were capable of repairing it. The morning, indifferent, continued to pass, and when the lady came in, leading the tuner by the arm, I almost believed that I wouldn't ever see her again. I had seen her face the previous day, and I wouldn't ever see it again. And at the same time as I felt something icy and burning, like hurt, I felt ridiculous because she wouldn't even be aware of my insignificance, because she existed in a place to which I would never have access, unaware of me, just unaware of me. I said something, because I knew in that way the tuner would be able to follow the sound of my words, would be able to take hold of the thread of my words and come to me. The lady replied, and went out. When we were alone, the tuner, blind since birth – a blind baby – asked me, 'What's up with you?' I replied, 'Nothing.' I was only able to deceive him because at that moment she came into the hall. I was the one who said to the tuner: 'It's the lady's granddaughter.' Turning his head in any old direction, the tuner smiled and was polite. Then he began to touch each of the keys and press on the piano strings. Her chin was right down on her neck, but she raised her eyes to see me. My gaze was fixed inside her eyes. There weren't three steps separating our bodies. She and I didn't breathe. At each note the tuner felt the strings vibrate with the tips of his fingers. The whole mechanism – springs, straps, levers – not existing between one extremity and the other – the key and the string – the sound. The notes rose up like pillars across the whole hall. And the fragile moments when the tuner fixed his little silver key and tightened or loosened the strings – the tip of the silver key – broken glass played on by the wind – and the strings stretching – silent groans passing through the air like a thread of breeze. In our linked gaze, another time was passing, another time through which those notes and that silence also passed. The tuner put his silver key away in his jacket pocket, moved away and

don't leave me

said: 'There it is.' Independent of her body, her feet made her light and without touching the floor brought her to the piano. At that moment she could see nothing else. She sat on the stool. She pushed her hair off her shoulders so it tumbled down her back. It was a moment of utter silence. She lifted her pale face towards me and her fingers touched the keys. She was smiling. Under her music, the air in the hall was crossed by invisible lines – a construction of light. These notes were her body, too. They were points of her skin that existed just for a moment, that remained in memory, until they came apart and transformed themselves into air, into life lived. Not even when my father closed all the workshop windows and sat down to play the pianos he had just fixed up, not even in my dreams, had I heard music like this. It was as though the invisible shapes of those sounds went into the joints of all the furniture, objects, bodies, it was as though they went into the joints of the whole house and divided each object clearly into each of its elements. It was as though all the air in the world was filled with specks blinking and, for a few moments, showing the air's secret shapes. She didn't take her eyes off me. Her thin body swayed on the stool, approaching the keyboard and moving away. The movements of her arms

Kilometre nine

were sure and elegant, like birds coming to rest on the lake in the park – her thin, smooth, white, porcelain wrists. And her face – in her eyes – was a sky where new meanings existed – a new life, created by her hand, more than eternal – and it was possible to believe in everything because there were nothing but certainties in the intensity of her eyes and in the music that came through me. In one corner, trying not to touch anything, the tuner had no face. The music from the piano had transformed his wrinkled skin, his worn lips, his blind eyes into a single smudge. The tuner didn't exist. She and I looked at one another and what we felt filled the hall and could have filled the world. When she turned her face away I felt lost, until the moment I looked over my shoulder and found the smile of the lady who had just come in.

against the doors. After Hermes was born, after the death of my father, my mother only stayed in Maria's house a few months. When Hermes began to be more work, at the start of summer, my mother moved to Marta's house, and it was around this time that she began, slowly, to wake up. At times the pitch of her voice rose. There were times when she laughed tenderly at something Hermes had done. Marta wandered through the house – she occupied the whole corridor with her body – and my mother became gradually interested in details – the cutlery arranged in the drawer, the pins stuck in the calendar, the different ways of the land where Marta had gone to live. There were late after-noons when Marta's husband would arrive home suddenly, demanding dinner. The three of them would sit and talk, in the evenings, perhaps about something that had happened – Marta, sitting on a stool, breathing heavily, anxious from the stifling heat of the August nights; my mother, sitting dressed in black, a black stain that spoke calmly; and Elisa, sitting on a patchwork rug, lit up by the whims of an oil lamp, playing with a rag doll. Over those evenings – like a breeze – was the calm of knowing that Hermes, submerged in the shadows of his room, was asleep, serene, safe, and he was a growing child. On those same nights, in Maria's house, time

a few days. I stopped outside her house and I didn't know what to do. When I was in luck, I'd lean against the wall and like a memory I could hear a little of the music she played. I knew that in the hall that music was like a whirlwind. There, it was like a breeze, like a veil carried by a breeze, something that floated and mingled with the voices of the people who passed, with the bells of the horses pulling carts or with the engine of the occasional motorcar. On one of those evenings I decided to knock at the door. I didn't know what I'd say – I forgot one of my tools, how are you? I forgot to fix a problem with the piano. I thought of nothing as I walked down the pavement, climbed the steps and

was much slower. All the streets of Benfica had fallen still. It was on one of those nights – August – after a dinner of soup – that Maria's husband broke all the dinner plates for the first time, kicked a chair and pushed Maria against a wall. Maria spent the night in the kitchen, sitting in a chair, falling asleep occasionally, spending the rest of the time awake, crying loudly enough that he could hear her and quietly enough that Ana shouldn't wake. The next morning he got up and finding her still in the kitchen he embraced her, crying too, asked her forgiveness, asked her forgiveness, grovelled, told her he'd never do it again, told her he loved her, told her he loved her more than life itself. She embraced him back, and believed him.

knocked. It was the lady who opened it. She smiled at me, and as I readied myself to say one of the phrases I'd made up, the lady began to walk ahead of me and I again followed her along the distant corridor. When we reached the hall, she was sitting at the piano, insubstantial. When the lady left I marvelled for a moment, but this moment passed very quickly because I threw myself towards her – her serious, white face, her smooth, long hair – and I embraced her. She embraced me, too. I was certain that she embraced me too. She stood up and I felt her whole body fitting within my arms. Then she walked silently towards the doors and closed them. We made love on the floor, on rugs, lit up by the brightness that hurled itself from the windows as if trying to kill us.

Kilometre ten

in my legs, like flames enveloping my skin. My arms, too. That's how come there's a star in the sky shining during the day – a distant, solitary, single star – a world covered in fire. I exist here. And the star, she exists up there, watching me. And accompanying me, wrapping me in fire. I make my way through the streets of Stockholm just as though I were making my way along a tunnel towards the sun.

a ball made of rags. My mother says to him: 'You're too old to be out playing in the street.' Simão was twelve years old. When the stonemason didn't have any work for him, he'd send him home. It wasn't common, but it wasn't unusual. There were times when the stonemason would notify him the night before. On those mornings I'd try not to wake him when I got up to go to school. There were times when the stonemason only told him he didn't need him when Simão arrived, his boots covered in dried cement, with his work clothes and the pot of lunch our mother had prepared for him. On those mornings he'd come back home and he couldn't get back to sleep. He'd walk round the kitchen and was always in our sisters' or our mother's way. He'd sit in a chair, and when he was told to move he'd discover he was in the way of one of them; then he'd lean on a cupboard which he later discovered was in the way of another, who told him to move; then he'd go somewhere else, in the way of another, who also told him to move. It was then that he'd head down three or four streets to the patch of waste-ground, between two vegetable gardens, where the lads got together to play ball. No weeds grew on that wasteground because every day dozens of lads would get together to chase a rag ball across the pitch. They were free lads, who didn't go to school, or who didn't have a father or mother. On this ground, of dirt in the summer and of mud in the winter, stones grew. The posts were measured out in bare-foot steps and made of little heaps of stones. Almost in the middle of the pitch was an olive tree that survived year after year, mistreated by the lads who tore limbs from it, and who dodged around it as they chased the ball, and occasionally bumped into its trunk and were knocked back. When Simão arrived he took off his work boots because he didn't want to ruin them with kicking stones. He left them carefully behind one of the posts and went on to the pitch to kick off one of the younger kids and start playing. Turning his head in every direction, always following the ball with his left eye, Simão ran surrounded by a knot of lads who came up to his chest and kicked every which way. It was on one of those days that Simão, coming out of the yard, let the bitch get out between his legs. Usually she was allowed out, she could go wherever she wanted and then, tired, she'd wait; she'd lie on the pavement and wait for someone to go back in. That day was different. In the late afternoon Simão wasn't surprised to get home, sweating, and not see the bitch. He didn't give it a thought. No one would have given it a thought if Maria hadn't soon afterwards come through the gate crying and disappeared through the kitchen door. I was sitting on the edge of the outdoor sink telling Simão stories from school, and when Maria ran past crying the two of us didn't notice. Maria came back to the yard with our mother. They walked towards us. Maria tried to recover her composure. Our mother approached, angry. Her eyes were angry. Her voice was only angry when it asked Simão, 'Was it you who let the bitch out?' She didn't wait for a reply, and asked again, 'Was it you who let the bitch out?' Maria had gone with an errand to the grocer's and found the bitch on the edge of the pavement, run over by a motorcar – her fur bloody, her tongue dry, her eyes closed and sad. Simão had no time, no words to say. Before taking Maria by the hand and going back into the kitchen, our mother said to him, 'When your father arrives, then you'll see.' Next to me, Simão went pale. Our mother came back through the kitchen door, handed him a burlap sack and told him to go and fetch the bitch. After putting the sack with the bitch's bulk down on the ground of the yard – the spots of thick blood, the arch of the spine recognisable in the shape of the sack – Simão wandered through the house alone, as though he was inventing solutions, all of them impossible. As night fell, our father came into the kitchen, and as soon as our mother told him he went out into the yard to look for Simão. He didn't look far. He found him scrunched into a corner of the chicken coop, covering his face but not hiding the terror in his eyes. Our father took off his belt, and against the dirty chicken-coop wall he beat him, letting the blows fall wherever they might.

against the wind. I was running down the streets, and for this time it was the whole city, it was the houses, the faces, the voices beginning to turn into night. During the days, fooled by the sawdust or by what I had to do, it was easy to lead my thoughts anywhere I wanted. If I started to think and to hurt myself, I'd stop at the part in front of me – perhaps an unfinished window, perhaps the beginning of a table leg – and I knew that at some point, with no effort, another thought would come, a more agreeable thought, which would either entertain me or soothe me. But when I went out to train, I ran along the streets and no one could imagine the world of words I carried with me. To run is to be absolutely alone. I've known it since the beginning – in solitude it's impossible to escape from myself. After the very first few steps black walls rise up around me. The world, harmless, moves away. As I run, I remain still within myself, and I wait. At last I am at my own mercy. At first, I was thirteen years old and I ran in order to find the silence of a peace I thought didn't belong to me. I didn't yet know that it was just the reflection of my own peace. Later, as life became more complicated, it was too late to be able to stop. Running was a part of me like my name. It was then I learned how to run against the words that were inside me, just as I learned to run against

when we're together

the wind. I ran along the streets, and as I got further from the workshop I might complete the remainder of some thought that had been broken by a word that developed into others – a first step, another, another and all the ones that followed it, indistinguishable from each other. It was a word too quick to understand where it had come from, but it was a vital word because it was through that word that I began to remember the nights – her voice and, in the background, the huge façade of the hospital. On a day that was getting ever further away, my father had died in that hospital. And as she spoke, we made our way hand in hand through the inside of her voice. And another sudden word reminding me of the evenings when I'd arrive at her house. The lady opening the door – me following her down, along the hallway – the piano music in everything – her face – her skin. And there was a moment when her voice and her face mingled together – her, and her. Her voice in the darkness of the piano cemetery, and her face, serious, on the hall rugs. My fingers in her wavy hair, or running through her long, straight hair. My hand squeezing hers. My hands holding her waist. I couldn't resist the thoughts that hurt me most. I never thought of the two of them at the same time, but they mingled together within me. I ran along the streets and no one could have known that there were plates shifting within me.

couldn't stay still. My mother had gone off to sort something out, she crossed paths with her and said nothing. Maria said nothing to her either, she said nothing to anyone. She went around concerned with strands of hair and specks of dust. Maria wanted everything to be perfect. It was Sunday, and it was the end of winter. Marta was helping her mother. Simão was far away. I was sitting on a bench by the fireside. Maria had on her best dress and a cardigan and a costume necklace.

Our father was sitting at the table – his arms resting on the tabletop. He waited in silence – a glass and a bottle. There was a knock at the door. Maria turned suddenly in every direction. It was my mother who said to her, indifferently, 'Go and open the door, what are you waiting for?' After a moment of muted sounds – the lock, uncertain steps – and silence – silence – Maria came into the room with her boyfriend. My father had already seen him on the morning he'd turned up at the workshop to ask if he could go out with Maria. He greeted him normally. Maria's boyfriend, nervous, greeted everyone and leaned against the cupboard. Maria stood beside him. There was a moment of uncomfortable silence. Maria was much taller than her boyfriend, but beside him she shrunk down, bent her back so as to be his height. He pulled himself up to his full height, stuck his chest out and lifted his chin. Maria's boyfriend, dressed in his best suit, began to talk about the weather and addressed my father by his full name: Senhor Francisco Lázaro. My father replied to him, and added something. Maria's boyfriend agreed, and added something. My father replied. And on they went. There was a smile on Maria's face, mixed with serious attentiveness, as though the conversation between her father and her boyfriend was interesting, important, as though everything they said was right.

our bodies. In the gloom of the piano cemetery, in the almost complete darkness, I could make out her body – shape, shadow – lying on a grand piano – legs bare, dress pulled up to where her waist began, hands abandoned to either side of her head, her face – her hair stretched out on the black varnish of the piano and her eyes, open and lit up, watching me. As I undid my belt, as I unbuttoned my trousers, I focused on her face, and in the silence of my movements, in the night, I could recall her voice. Very slowly I lay my body down on top of hers. I rested all my weight on my knees, digging into the surface of the piano, and felt the inside of her legs on my legs. I knew how to find her lips

Kilometre twelve

and how to kiss them. Our heads fled from one another – sought one another. Our mouths tore against one another. My hands closed with all their strength against the palms of her hands. My lips slipped slowly down her neck, when what I wanted was to sink my teeth into her skin. Perhaps that was the moment my hands slid down her shoulders, and over her dress felt again, ever again, the shape of her breasts. I felt her hands on the back of my shirt, pulling me – the strength of her fingers sticking in – talons driven into the earth. I lifted her dress higher and my hands held her waist, as though her skin was fire, as though her skin was fire, as though her skin was fire. Burning. We stopped breathing at the same moment, when in an instant that might have lasted forever, that lasted forever, I entered her. Then the weight of my body itself pressed against her body. I held her within my arms, under me, and I inside her, and her, inside of her, being fire, being fire, being fire. Burning.

might think that it's for a long time. I let myself go on like this. Unspeaking, without losing sight of them. When I get home I'm going to kiss my wife's belly, I'm going to embrace her gently, and then, I'm going to tell her – I was all on my own, out in the lead, then on a bridge I let two get past me, just so they'd think they could win, I let them go ahead for half a dozen kilometres, I waited for them to get tired then I pulled back into first place. I'm going to tell everyone. My sisters, my brothers-in-law, my nieces and nephew will all assemble around me and in the silence I'm going to tell them all the same story. Then I'm going to meet up with my brother, he'll come with me to the workshop and we'll go to the *taberna*. When we go in the men will stand up from their chairs or straighten up from leaning against the bar to greet me. Hey, the hero! There will be one or two men who'll offer us drinks, and then, when everyone has fallen silent, when the men's gaze follows each of my words, I'm going to tell them how I was on my own, how I let two runners get past me, and then, when no one expected it, how I got past them again. The grimy toothless faces

clocks had changed, it was getting dark earlier. Maria wandered the kitchen, flying. In the shadows of the oil lamp, when Maria moved from something she was doing neither space nor time existed between one point and the other. She was too quick. Maria was at the sink. Maria was at the table. Maria was holding Ana under the arms. When her husband came in, Maria's movements slowed and it was as though a blanket was drawn over the house. When her husband came into the kitchen Maria was waiting with her hands clasped over her belly and smiling. Ana threw herself at her father's legs. He lifted her in the air, laughed at her and put her back down on the floor. The table was set and he sat at his place. Maria put the tureen in the middle of the table. And she ate, waiting for her husband to eat. After the fruit, at length – an apple peel stretching out and rolling up, thinning to a point – Maria cleared away the dishes and found the moment she'd been waiting for all day. She approached her husband from behind, holding a piece of paper yellowed by the light. Ever smiling, Maria said that at the market she'd bought a leaflet with a poem. Her husband scolded, said she shouldn't waste money on rubbish, said that she was only interested in rubbish, said it was always the same, and fell silent. And then, still smiling, she sat down, moved closer to the oil lamp, and read:

> *when it was time to lay the table, we were five:*
> *my father, my mother, my sisters*

he took the piece of paper from the hand, and still looking her in the eyes crumpled it up

> *and I. then, my older sister*
> *married. then, my younger sister*

he opened up the piece of paper, looked disdainfully at it and raised his eyes to look even more disdainfully at her

> *married. then, my father died. today,*
> *when it is time to lay the table, we are five,*

rage, he tore the piece of paper into irregular pieces. He tore the pieces into even smaller pieces until he couldn't tear any more

> *except for my older sister who is*
> *at her house, except for my younger*

looking at Maria as though he could kill her

> *sister who is at her house, except for my*
> *father, except for my widowed mother. each*

threw the pieces into the air, bumped into a chair, threw the chair against the table and fell silent, breathing through his nose and looking at Maria as though he could kill her

> *of them is an empty place at this table where*
> *I eat alone. but they will be here always.*

as though he could kill her

> *when it is time to lay the table, we will always be five.*
> *as long as one of us is alive, we will be*
> *always five.*

when Maria got up, took Ana in her arms, and went out to put her to bed.

Kilometre thirteen

the sound of the wind across my ears, like the roaring of the universe. Maybe like the sound of moving through the inside of time, passing through it with your whole body – arms and legs passing through time, chest passing through time, face carrying all of eternity within it.

nor out into the street. Marta didn't like going to the grocer's because people would stop and look at her. They'd say hello but then they'd stop and look at her. Marta didn't want to think, but she knew. My mother said nothing. It was evening, as they sat chatting, when my mother looked at her face – excited, discouraged, devoted, nostalgic, irritated, amused in turns – and saw her face when she was little. My mother looked at her face and saw all her ages. It was like that when she saw her in the morning, too, when Marta handed her the basket, the purse, and told her what they needed. My mother always met the same women at the grocer's. They always had the same conversations. My mother greeted them and replied to them, but understood little of what they said because they were always talking about people she didn't know. That morning, while she waited, while the lady from the grocer's did sums on a sheet of brown paper, one of the women started talking to my mother. My mother didn't understand, didn't know the person she was talking about. The lady from the grocer's was doing sums on a sheet of brown paper – the nib of the pen wearing itself down against the paper, the marble counter underneath the paper, the grains of rock salt scattered over the counter. When my mother said she didn't know who she was talking about, the woman, as though it was quite natural, pronouncing every syllable, said to her, 'She's that friend of your son-in-law's.' As if it were nothing: 'She's that friend of your son-in-law's.' That evening as they sat chatting, my mother looked at Marta's face and saw all her ages. Inside

through the brighter light. I don't know what picture the lady can have seen in my face, but whenever she opened the door to me, whether it was still morning or almost the end of the afternoon, she always smiled at me. Then the distant walk down the corridor, and, in the hall, her, seated at the piano. For some time, after we had made love, we would just lie there on the rug. We'd be side by side, further apart for the silence, closer together for knowing the same things. I lowered my eyelids over my eyes, and when I raised them again she was sitting at the piano and she had started to play again. Her hands were just like butterflies dying on the keys. Each note she played was fragile when it alighted on a point on my skin. In this weightless, cloudy time, months passed, and years passed. Nearly two years passed. At night, in another existence, I would arrive at the hospital. I waited for her, and we took each other's hand. Sometimes we'd cross the city to the piano cemetery. On other days, in the morning, or in the afternoon, when it took my fancy, I would go to the lady's house and go into the hall. Some weeks I thought that it was the best of lives, I thought I was lucky, and I didn't think about what I didn't want to think about. Other weeks I didn't feel able to continue like this. I had to decide, I had to decide, but I couldn't. I hid even from myself the certainty that time would decide. Which was why when it was daytime and I was lying on the hall rug, I didn't remember the piano cemetery. In just the same way, when I was going in, out of the piano cemetery, I didn't remember the time I spent lying on the hall rug.

today and for ever. There's no difference between what actually happened and what I kept distorting in my imagination, over and over again, across the years. There's no difference between the dull pictures I remember, and the raw, cruel words I think I remember but which are merely reflections constructed out of guilt. Time – like a wall, a tower, any construction – makes there stop being differences between truth and lie. Time mixes truth and lie together. What happened mixes together with what I want to have happened and with what they told me happened. My memory isn't my own. My memory is me distorted by time and mixed up with myself – with my fear, with my guilt, with my repentance. When I remember being four years old and playing in the yard, I don't know where the images end that my four-year-old eyes saw and which remain with me to this day, and where the images begin that I invented whenever I tried to remember that afternoon. It was an afternoon that I was spending among the branches of the peach trees. The light, laid out on the earth, was like shapes in lace, like a lace bedspread with the pattern of peach tree branches and leaves that shivered. Beyond the tangled treetops, there must have been the sky and the birds, because it was a peaceful May afternoon. My mother was in the kitchen. Occasionally I saw her face looking at me through the glass of the window. My sisters were perhaps in their room, or somewhere else I didn't know. I was four years old and there were many things I didn't know. I was sitting

Kilometre fourteen

on the earth of the yard. I was stacking planks that were leftover wood my father had brought back from the workshop and which I was making into little huts. The bitch went slowly by, her brown eyes lost on the ground. Under an orange tree, half-buried, was a long piece of rusty wire. I think I can remember the moment when my four-year-old body got up to pull the piece of wire two-handed from out of the earth. I can see this moment with the same lack of clarity with which I now look to one side and can make out treetops, leaves mixed together, one after another as I pass. Like an image of liquid colours dissolving into one another. That day I sat back down beside my piled-up planks, which were the little huts I had made. I held the wire and began to find clumsy shapes with it. On my hands I had scratches of earth and rust. I heard the movement of the gate to the street opening. It was my brother, smiling. His clothes were dirty with sawdust because he was our father's apprentice and he was coming home from work. He said something to me in greeting before noticing that I had the wire in my hand. The flowerbeds my mother had been over with a hoe were blossoming behind him. Simão was a lad of ten years old. Sometimes he'd put his hands in his pocket and laugh. When I remember him in the days that came before that day, the first image that comes to me is him with his hands in his pockets, laughing. That afternoon he had his shirt untucked from his trousers. When he saw me with the wire in my hand, he took three quick steps towards me. From then it was all very fast, but now, as I recall it, it's all very slow. Simão's hands were bigger than mine and tried to get the wire off me. I don't know what words he chose to tell me I shouldn't play with bits of wire, because before I was able to understand them, perhaps as a reflex, perhaps because at that moment it seemed that that was how it had to be, perhaps because I also knew what ought to be done, perhaps for no reason, for no reason, I didn't let go of the wire right away. I held on to it with both hands. I felt my brother's strength on the rusty wire pulling with all his strength against the palms of my hands. And it was very fast, I know it was just a moment, but now it seems like it was every minute of an hour. Every movement split. Everything very slow. The tip of the wire moved towards my brother's face. As though there was a straight line there to show it the way. The rusty tip of the wire moved forwards. His face. In a single movement the tip of the wire touched the damp white part of his right eye, pressed it lightly and sank, irreversible, into a rip. My brother let go of the wire, stepped back and brought both his hands to his right eye. It was a moment of absolute silence. I was four years old and I knew that something terrible had happened. My brother was gripping his face and making sounds of pain like I'd never heard before. They weren't cries. They were the sounds of a pain that was destroying him slowly. I was four years old and I was still holding on to the wire. That was the moment our mother saw us through the glass of the kitchen window. The moment ended when our mother came running out through the door, asking, 'What happened? What happened?' I couldn't say anything. My brother was holding his face, and from behind his hands threads of blood were appearing that slipped down his arm and down his cheek and down his neck. They were threads of very living blood that ran down his wrists, over the light, smooth skin of his inner arms, and dripped off the tip of his elbow. Our mother, who had no idea what was going on, approached him, saying, 'Calm down, calm down.' With no idea what was going on, trying for a serene, motherly voice, she said to him, 'Let's see what's happened.' Simão, still wanting to believe there might be a possibility that what had happened hadn't happened, drew his hands away slowly. Through the blood my mother and I saw how the right side of his face was a bloody hole where there was the empty white skin of the eye, the flattened circular design of the iris, and that slipping down his face mixed with the blood was a thick, viscous substance, like the white of an egg, that had previously been inside his eye. On the left side of Simão's face, the other eye, hurt and innocent, waited to see my mother's reaction. I was four years old and I was still holding on to the wire. I let go of it when my mother couldn't stop the bitter cry that tore through her. My brother went back to covering his face. My sisters came running into the yard from the kitchen door. Neighbours came in from the door to the street. My mother shouted with all the strength she had in her throat. Someone went to fetch my father from the workshop. Someone grabbed me by the waist, picked me up off the earth of the yard and took me in to the kitchen. Between the bodies of the people who were supporting my mother, between my sisters clinging to one another crying, between the people who surrounded my brother with clean towels, soon drenched in blood, I was four years old and I was consumed by a fear like blades. I was silent, still, my eyes open, wide, being consumed by a fear like blades. At a certain moment my father came into the kitchen. No one could stop him. Only his breathing could be heard. He went through between the people, took my brother by the arm, and with the men who were in the kitchen following him they went to the hospital. When they left it was night-time. As the door slammed shut, all that remained was my mother's and sisters' anxiety, followed by the drawling voices of the neighbour women trying to console them. It was one of these neighbour women who, amid the shadows of the others, struck a match and lit the oil lamp on the table. From then, as my mother's and sisters' crying started to weaken, the neighbour women began to say goodbye and leave. We were left alone in the kitchen – the stones of the kitchen floor, the wooden table and benches. Through the light and the shadows of the oil lamp, my mother and sisters had their eyes open to a picture only they could see. Cold time passed, with shrieks and blades. Late in the evening, my father and Simão arrived in silence. My brother had the right side of his head wrapped in bandages that covered his eye. No one said a thing. We went to sleep. That night was like the nights of many months that followed. There was a heavy weight within us, pulling us towards our blackest insides. Months passed. My brother

Kilometre fifteen

never went back to working with my father at the workshop. After removing the bandages, for some weeks he wore the leather patch they gave him at the hospital. One day he appeared with his eye clean and uncovered, the lid stretched and white over the empty eye. In the hospital, the doctor told him he could go back to doing everything he did before; but when Simão talked about going back to the workshop as an apprentice, my father talked about a lot of things and, always in other words, showed him that it couldn't be. He asked him to wait a little longer and he changed the subject. One night, at dinner – he hadn't yet turned twelve – my brother decided to tell us that he'd fixed up some work as a stonemason's assistant. That was the first time my father hit him after the day he lost his sight. After that he got angry with him many times, and hit him many times. Over all those years he never got angry with me, and never hit me.

It was always clear to me that my father got angry with my brother and hit him because this was his way of dealing with the sadness, with the hurt he felt since that afternoon when my brother had become blind in one eye. This was his way of punishing him. It was always equally clear to me that my father didn't get angry with me and didn't hit me for the same reason. That was his way of punishing me.

because I don't want to look at the runners around me. I know that in their homes there are people who speak other languages and who are waiting for them in the same way that in my home they wait for me. They have names and they have childhoods. Without turning to face them directly, I see their dull figures on the fringes of my gaze. In this mixture of smudges of colour, I can tell they aren't looking at anyone either. Just as we're running here in the Stockholm streets, we're running within ourselves, too. At the finishing line, the distance and the weight of this inner marathon will be as important as the kilometres of these streets and the heat of this sun. As I raise a foot to take a step, the other foot grips the ground. If the world were to stop at the moment when I have one foot raised, moving forwards, and the other foot set on the ground, roots could grow out of this fixed foot that holds me. These roots could penetrate the gaps of earth between the stones of the street. But I don't let the world stop. After a step, another, another

second time. When she arrived, she gave me a quick kiss on the cheek and said nothing to me. She gave me her hand. We walked in silence the whole way from the hospital to her house. It was a night in mid-December. There was cold, and there was the cold wind that cut through us and awoke the sparkle in the puddles of water. The night was black. My hand wrapped itself around the fingers of her hand, and at certain moments squeezed them. I didn't find her silence strange, as I carried many words with me. I had words, whole sentences, sliding through me. I turned my face to kiss her and she moved away. I smiled because I thought she was just playing. I turned my face again to kiss her and again she moved away. She kept her eyes down. I held her hands and waited. The night existed. There were no people on the streets. There were no motorcars or carts. There were frozen stars in the sky. She began to lift her face, slowly – her wavy hair, her forehead, her eyes fixing on me from the depth of the night, and her whole face. Her lips – it was then that her lips said, 'We're going to have a child.' And her hands, parting from mine. And she opened the door and went into the house. And she closed the door. Suddenly it was no longer the same night. The world was clearer, and at the same time more imprecise. I felt a hand on my shoulder. I turned – the blind, dirty face of my brother.

WE GOT MARRIED ON our own.

Two Saturdays earlier, we walked downtown together. We didn't hold hands, but our smiles were only for each other. We went into a warehouse of displays with models dressed in the latest fashion. She didn't take long to point to a roll of fabric – end of season, a leftover bit. While we exchanged smiles, while we believed more, the metres were measured out on the counter.

That was the material, not too sober, not too extravagant, that the seamstress marked with chalk, cut, sewed, and through this skill made a dress that was just as my wife had imagined it. This was the dress she premiered on the Monday morning when we got married.

Everything was taken care of, we had the papers, but we went into the civil registry without realising we were doing it. I was the one who went up to the counter, and when a man walked past carrying a pile of papers to his chest I said good morning to him. He didn't reply. He remained indifferent, angry at the world and at all the archives. We followed him with our gaze for a few minutes that passed on the hands of the clock hanging from the wall. At some moment of his own choosing, the gentleman from the registry walked towards me, combed his moustache, stopped on the other side of the counter and – bored – as though asking a question, said

'Now then, if you please . . .'

I held out the papers to him, and explained that we'd come to get married.

He took the papers, put on his glasses and took his time reading the form that the other gentleman at that same counter had given me more than a month earlier. Without saying anything, he raised his face slightly and looked at us over the top of his glasses. He opened and closed, opened and closed the other documents. Without saying anything, he raised the board that allowed us through to the other side of the counter. We followed him between empty desks, piles of papers, cupboards full of files, until we reached a white room. He sat at a table, coughed twice, and opened a book that covered the whole surface of the table. We sat in two thick wooden chairs.

Never turning to look at us, the gentleman from the registry read a few lines quickly, not pronouncing the words completely – mixing up words – a buzzing of words. In the brief gaps where he paused, I said yes when I'd heard my name, and soon afterwards she said yes. The man from the registry breathed in deeply and blew out during the time it took me to get the wedding ring out of my pocket and put it on her finger. We were looking at one another, and smiling, as he finished up his lines. He turned the book towards us:

'Sign here.'

I signed and she signed. It wasn't until that moment that the gentleman from the registry noticed we didn't have witnesses.

'You don't have witnesses?'

Without waiting for an answer, he got up and crossed the room in short, quick steps. He returned with a thick book with the letter B on the spine. He opened it at a page and chose two witnesses for me, a man and a woman. He opened it at another page and chose two witnesses for her, a man and a woman. He copied the names on to the page of the other book: Bartolomeu, Belarmina, Baltazar, Belmira. With different scripts, he signed under each one.

We left, light-spirited.

That day I didn't go to work. The next morning, when my uncle arrived at the workshop, he said nothing to me.

The beginning of night-fall. July. The sounds of the town where Marta went to live. Carts passing on the beaten earth road. Men and women, greeting one another. The old olive trees bending under the fresh air. The iron gate to Marta's yard. Clothes hanging out on a line. Pigeons making their final circuits in the sky. My wife going into Marta's house through the kitchen door. The beginning of night-fall. Dogs barking in the yard.

'Look, it's Gran,' says Hermes in the sewing room. And he freezes — his mouth stays open for a moment while he waits for confirmation from his sister. His eyes remain alight. Without saying a word, but as though breaking the silences, his sister looks at him — she smiles — as if to say yes.

Hermes starts running through all the open doors to get to the kitchen. Elisa, who is older, and knows more, walks behind him. Elisa has time. It takes her just a moment — time for almost nothing — but when she reaches the kitchen Hermes is already in his gran's arms.

'Calm down, you'll knock your granny over,' says Marta, mouth full of bread, talking as though she can't understand Hermes's enthusiasm, as though she can't hear her mother describing the train journey, as though she can't see the dogs who've come into the kitchen and, tails wagging, surround my wife.

Elisa greets her grandmother with the manners of a girl who's grown up. My wife puts Hermes down on the floor, leaves him playing with the dogs. Elisa, calm, puts her hands on her hips and leans against the cutlery drawer.

At another time Marta would have scolded Elisa for not helping, for leaning against the cutlery drawer with her hands on her hips, but night has already fallen, it's Friday – July – and my wife has just arrived. Marta's body is enormous. It's in the small smile she keeps on her face when she isn't looking at anyone, in the almost agile movements with which she puts the dogs in the yard, in the sweet way she pronounces certain words, that it's possible to tell how glad Marta is that her mother has arrived.

She spreads the cloth over the table. My mother makes to help but our daughter doesn't let her, and when my wife tries to go to the plate cupboard Marta's body blocks her way. Without anyone having to say anything, Elisa begins to arrange the cutlery beside the invisible plates.

My wife hadn't seen Marta, or Elisa, or Hermes, for more than a month.

Soon after the day Hermes was born, the day I died, my wife went to Marta's house, went to help her look after her son. Hermes, hugged to his mother's breast, was a very wide-eyed baby, wrapped in flesh – skin – he was a little baby wrapped in Marta's huge arms, his head out, eyes wide. In that time my mother had watched Hermes learn to run across the kitchen, and learn to have tantrums when faced with closed doors. Sometimes Marta lost patience. Being heavy, she couldn't keep up with her son and she lost patience. Then my wife was a real grandmother – a mother in secret – and she felt alive.

Soon after the day Íris was born, my wife returned to Maria's house. She only went to Marta's house intermittently, but Hermes wouldn't forget his grandmother. When Marta allowed Hermes to speak on the telephone, he'd ask:

'Come over here, Granny!'

My wife, at Maria's house, was moved. She'd put down the receiver, and felt sorry that Marta no longer lived in Benfica.

There were months that passed too quickly. There were months that were lost, like lids on ballpoint pens. On the few occasions that Marta came to Lisbon, she'd go up the stairs of her sister's house very slowly, with her mother's help, stopping every half-dozen steps to rest. When she finally arrived she would sit in a chair and smile broadly.

My wife would take the train to Marta's town two or three days before these trips. She'd take advantage of the lift back. In the blue truck that Marta's husband had bought not long after the move, she'd sit at the window. Hermes and Elisa would sit between her and their father, who drove, bad-tempered. And it was always summer, or it was always spring, or it was always a day when you knew for certain that it wouldn't rain, because Marta would be sitting in an armchair on the back of the truck. Only once it started raining on the way. They stopped at the side of the road and took her all their jackets. Marta put Hermes's jacket on her head, tied the sleeves under the skin that hung from her chin, and covered herself as best she could with the other jackets, but when they arrived she was sad and soaked through.

Marta's husband promised to take her to Lisbon on Sunday. They'll collect leftover bits of wood from the workshop to burn in the winter, they'll go and visit Maria. Marta will take her bunches of spring greens from her yard, sprigs of parsley that she planted in a tub and sausages she bought at the grocer's. Her sister will say she needn't have troubled herself, and Marta, sitting in a chair, will smile broadly.

When they finish their dinner, my wife is quicker. She gets up and starts piling the dirty plates. Marta complains, but my wife is quicker. Marta's husband's plate is still clean, his chair is still empty and pushed up against the table. When my wife makes to take his plate away, Marta says to her:

'Leave it, he's probably just arriving.'

And they talk like they did when Hermes was a baby and the evenings were longer. They talk about Francisco. They talk about Francisco's wife and the child who is going to be born. Marta is sure it's going to be a girl. They don't feel the time pass. When Elisa's eyes start to close and her head drops, my wife looks at the clock on the wall and it's already late. Hermes is still playing, but my wife gets up and holds her hand out to him.

'Come, let's go to sleep.'

Marta says she'll stay up a little and wait for her husband.

'He's probably just arriving.'

My wife leaves with Hermes and Elisa. Marta's thoughts remain. Her steps remain – swinging from side to side, as though reeling. All over the house – in the walls – there is silence. For a moment Marta fixes a fist on the tabletop, leans part of her weight on to that arm, and looks into the air, remembering Francisco – she smiles. Slowly night comes into the house – fields spotted with crickets, dogs barking in the distance, a moped passing occasionally. Marta's body, solid, dressed in a blue smock, is a bulk of sheer flesh that crosses the kitchen, that lowers itself to open the cupboard door and take out a biscuit tin.

She is sitting, the tin resting at the end of her belly, on the tips of her knees. Her right arm repeats the movement that takes the biscuits from the tin and brings them to her mouth. Biscuits disappear between her lips. Sometimes she remembers and forgets her husband who has not yet arrived. She thinks of Francisco, she thinks of the child who's going to be born, she thinks of Francisco when he was little, she thinks of Francisco filled with dreams, she thinks and imagines him in Stockholm, wondering at the world and believing. Her thoughts are surrounded in light. There is a lamp hanging from the ceiling. There is the noise of the biscuits being chewed.

There is the noise, ever slower, of the biscuits being chewed. There are Marta's eyes, closing. Her head falls slowly back. She opens her eyes, straightens up her head, swallows the remains of the biscuit she has in her mouth, runs her tongue across her teeth and loses her energy again. Her eyes close. Her head falls slowly back.

My daughter's body, illuminated, stretched out over the corners of the chair, is shapeless. Her torso, covered in crumbs, breathing, is a mass in which it's impossible to make out where the breasts end and the stomach starts. She has one arm alongside her body – her hand resting on her lap, next to the biscuit tin – and her other arm is stretched out – hand open, frozen in a gesture of giving – the palm of her hand, the thick back of her hand, the thin fingers, thin fingertips. In her head tilting back, as though her neck was broken – her face – her skin, mouth open, and the face that used to be a little

135

girl's who came running to me, who had a little girl's voice and who laughed because the world was so simple, so simple. The world was so simple.

Hours pass, over the illuminated body of my daughter, over the plate on the table, over the unmoving cutlery. It's the heart of night. Far away there are dark, deserted streets, black, empty houses. My daughter's husband opens the door and his skin carries the smell and the heat of another skin. He is a man suddenly alone. He looks towards my daughter and he is not happy. He feels sorry for her, feels sorry for himself, he feels sorry for everything he knows how to name. He closes the door carefully, turns out the light, walks carefully across the kitchen. The hours remain, stretching out, filled up by the night. Time remains – time which passes without existing.

Day breaks. An almost clear light reaches Marta's body, covers her breathing. Little sounds settle over the silence. All of a sudden the dogs begin to bark in the yard. Marta opens her eyes. She realises that she's woken up. She straightens her body in the chair. She moves her shoulders to rearrange the bones in her aching flesh. She turns towards the window and, not understanding, sees the faces of Maria, Íris and Ana on the other side of the glass. She doesn't understand that they could be there. Not trusting her eyes, she closes the lids forcefully, wakes up a bit more, opens them again, and again sees the faces of her sister and nieces on the other side of the window. It is only then, not knowing what to think, that she gets up quickly and hurries to open the door for them.

Our daughters had gone out and I'd made them take Francisco with them. They'd gone out to see the streets, the parks. They'd gone out to wander about, to be girls. The clarity of Saturday came through the windowpanes and filled the kitchen with cloudy air, that mingled with the words, that you breathed in, and that maddened you. There was a reason, there was a reason, but now, try as I might, I can't remember.

I grabbed her by her woollen jumper and lifted her out of the chair, her looking at me defiantly, my fingers disappearing into the wool, my fists clenched and the wool of the jumper in and around my hands, her looking at me defiantly, as though she despised me, in silence, as if she were saying I was nothing, I was nothing, I was worth nothing, and I pulled her by the jumper, turned her around, her body taking steps, turning in front of me, and only her defiant look, not a word, not even the beginnings of her voice, and all the contempt, I could feel the air that came in through my nostrils, it was thicker than air, I felt my lips pursed, merged, I felt I could pull her body, push her body with just one arm, but I let go of her, her wool jumper keeping the same shape it had in my hand, she tried to fix her jumper, to give it the shape it used to have, but it was ruined for ever, it had the holes from my fingers and it was stretched wide, there was nothing that could bring it back to how it was, she sat down and looked away, the contempt, all the contempt, in silence, as if she was saying I was nothing, I was nothing, nothing, I was worth nothing, I held her face with my two hands and forced her to look at me, I felt her neck straining, I saw her eyes not wanting to cry, but the tears, but, but the tears break through her will. I let go.

Simão, a little man, months from losing his sight, had two living eyes and was watching me from the half-open door to the hallway.

It was still day, there was a breeze that came from some cool place and across my dust-covered face, it was peace, conciliation, it was a transparent silence that fell over the last sounds of the afternoon, when I came out of the workshop, left my uncle at the *taberna* and walked home on my own. The whole city was starting to relax. On that short walk, I knew exactly what I'd find the moment I went up to the front step and opened the door – my wife's face, flushed, smiling at me – locks of hair falling over her forehead, crossing her gaze, touching her cheeks – my wife's body standing in the middle of the kitchen – her belly growing bigger every week. I'd approach, we'd embrace sideways on, and I'd place my hand on her belly. I'd mould the round shape of her belly with the palm of my hand.

That afternoon I went up to the front step of my house, opened the door and she was already waiting for me. She wasn't smiling because she was holding a shoebox with both hands and it seemed to be too serious an object. Before saying a word, she held the box out to me. Only then did she say:

'Have you seen this?'

My wife had begun to tidy and clean the house even before we'd been married. She left her godmother's boarding house with a single suitcase, her eyes filled with hurt, believing that she would never see her again. We spent that day in each other's arms. We slept that night in each other's arms. When I woke the next morning, she already had a kerchief on her head and was cleaning dust from the shelves that no one had touched since my mother died. For two months it was like this every day. The mesh-door cupboard in the kitchen, where there were pans covered in spiders' webs, went back to being the colour of wood and the aluminium pans could once again be distinguished from the enamel pans; the heaps of dust that had blackened the corners of all the rooms disappeared; the china of the plates hanging on the walls gleamed again in the Sunday light; at the back of the wardrobe, my mother's dresses, covered in hairs from the cats who came in through the yard door, reappeared. In the months that followed, she stretched out in the sun, washed and sewed the sheets that were folded in the trunk of the bedroom or in dresser drawers, where there were ancient mouse nests and dry mouse skeletons; she scraped the kitchen floor with a knife to unstick crusts of bread, mackerel bones, entrecôte bones; she swept the ceilings, unblocked the pipes; put the curtains to soak for three days before washing them in the tank; and scrubbed the walls with a thick brush that she dunked in the almost full bucket of water and soap. When her belly began to get too heavy – pains in her kidneys and her back – all that was left was to clean the attic. We had to put up a ladder and go through a hole in the bedroom ceiling. The first time she went up, sure-footed on the ladder, her arms stretched right out because of her belly, she couldn't put so much as the tip of a toe in the attic. The entire surface, even the wooden beams, even the tiles, was covered with things in piles, broken, useless, buried by dust. Every day, slowly, bit by bit, my wife went up into the attic, and bent under the slope of the roof, sweating, she pulled out chairs missing a leg, cracked tubs, boxes and all kinds of bits of furniture, which she burned in the middle of the yard or organised into piles which on another day she would carry to the dump. It was in the nearly empty attic that my wife found the shoebox that she held out to me.

I put the box on the table. My wife's face was waiting for a reaction. With the tips of my fingers, I lifted the lid. I put my hand in the box and pulled it out full of medals. They were copper medals, attached to faded, soiled, worn-away ribbons – rags losing their colour. They were medals with images of little men running inside circles made of carefully sculpted laurel leaves. On the reverse there were letters engraved, which read: 'First place, marathon.' Later we would find some for second or third place. I had no answers. I lifted my eyes to my wife's face, and without words I showed her that I didn't know what those medals were either, nor what they were doing in the attic. That evening, over dinner, and after dinner, and as we fell asleep, we tried to invent explanations for that box full of medals – probably, probably, probably. In moments of silence, I tried to remember something my mother had said, something I'd seen and which would help me to understand. But nothing I remembered and nothing we were able to invent seemed to explain that shoebox filled with marathon victories.

'There's got to be a simple explanation.'

In the dark, lying in bed, I decided I'd ask my uncle. He had to know something. He'd have stories to tell. There had to be a simple explanation. I fell asleep, relaxed.

In the morning I walked with the box under my arm. And time passed as I sawed laths on my own, I nailed nails on my own and could think without anyone interrupting me. In the mid-morning my uncle appeared at the entrance to the carpentry shop, and from afar, excited, wanting to speak but saying nothing, he gestured me over. As soon as I'd put down my tools, he disappeared. I hastened after him, and as I came out of the shop I could just see him going into the piano cemetery.

At the open door, Marta is blocking the entrance with her body. Maria puts Íris down on the floor of the yard. In the morning, in the light, it's already possible to see the invisible spots where the heat will grow. Ana and Íris squeeze in through a chink between Marta and the doorframe. They run into the kitchen – they're looking for Elisa and Hermes – they look in the hallway, they look in the sewing room, and when they find only silence they return muted, but slowly, to the kitchen. Maria with her face downcast, hurt, walks towards her sister and the two go into the kitchen.

My wife appears with her hair in disarray, in her nightdress. She's surprised to see Maria, but can't say anything because Ana and Íris surround her, pulling her and giving her little kisses. When they stop, Maria is sitting in a chair, unable to cry, and Marta is beside her, standing, a hand resting on her shoulder. My wife approaches. Maria, her hands on her legs, her sad gaze on her hands, speaks weakly:

'This time it's over. This time I'm not going back.'

My wife and Marta have already heard these words many times. Through the window the morning is picking up strength. Marta tries to console her sister, caressing her shoulder. And my wife asks her questions. Maria replies with the same weak voice. In a corner, Ana and Íris, alone, have conversations all to themselves in a place where there is no one else. My wife – concern on her face – listens to Maria and keeps asking her questions: –

'And what about the neighbours?'

And Maria keeps replying:

'What do I want with the neighbours? . . . This time it's over. Really. This time I'm not going back.'

The china tureen that ornamented the middle of the kitchen table had been bought by Maria and her mother at the

Luz market. It was afternoon, it was Sunday, and it was September. It had been years since my wife had gone to buy items for Maria's trousseau. Every birthday, every Christmas, Maria had received gifts for her trousseau – sets of bedsheets, sets of towels. Sometimes, on late Saturday mornings, my wife would get back from the market, and from among the thin bags of lettuce, of carrots, among bags that had fish scales stuck together, she would take out saucepans, boiling-pans and aluminium jugs.

These purchases were made with the money my wife saved. She bought glasses and cutlery, salt and pepper pots, cruets for oil and vinegar, gravy boats, napkin rings.

That afternoon, Marta was already married and still living in the house close to the workshop. My wife and Maria were walking through the Luz market. It was clear as a September afternoon. They smiled, they analysed objects they wouldn't think of buying, and they asked:

'How much?'

They crossed the street with the shoes and clothes to look at the fashions. Maria had a shoulder bag. My wife had a napa bag on her arm. They stopped beside a merry-go-round to buy a *fartura*, and while they ate, with oil and sugar around their mouths, they watched the children throwing tantrums and listened to the shrill music being distorted by the loudspeakers.

They passed stalls selling chairs and wicker baskets. My wife held up a wooden spoon and asked:

'How much?'

And they reached a stall that sold all kinds of chinaware. There were china dogs, painted as Dalmatians, sitting, with gentle eyes. It made them want to stroke the chilly ceramic heads. There was a china fountain with multicoloured lights that worked with a mechanism that meant it never stopped pouring out water. There were decorative plates for hanging on the wall, and there were plates for everyday. There were dishes. There were tureens.

Maria's gaze was immediately attracted by that tureen. She lifted the lid to look at the inside and to hold the china ladle whose handle was sculpted with flowers. The grip of the lid was three roses with ceramic petals. The handles of the tureen were also made from roses. At various points on the tureen, and on the dish on which it sat, there were small roses and rosebuds sculpted and painted in tiny detail.

Maria looked at my mother as though she didn't dare to ask. My mother looked at her, turned towards the stallholder and asked:

'How much?'

And she asked if he couldn't knock the price down, he said he couldn't, she asked the same question again, he knocked the price down and my wife took her purse out of the bag.

The man wrapped each piece of the tureen in sheets of newspaper, saying:

'You've done very well out of this.'

The lampposts were already lit, but it wasn't yet night. Late afternoon was a sky that darkened to its own particular shade of blue. The stallholder was enjoying himself, wrapping the tureen dish in a piece of newspaper and fitting it into a plastic bag. He was enjoying himself repeating lines he'd already said a thousand times. My daughter smiled, and my wife gave clever answers, casually.

This was the tureen that Maria's husband picked up with both hands. He held it by the dish, held it up to the height of his chest, and with all his strength threw it to the ground in a moment of absolute silence. The pieces of the tureen were spread, useless, across the kitchen floor; also spread across the floor were the buttons, pins, pencil ends, pieces of toys and all the purposeless objects that were kept inside.

I went into the piano cemetery. I walked through the dust until I came to my uncle, at the back, his chest leaning over an upright piano, looking at something that was happening over the other side. I approached. Looking at me with his enthusiastic left eye, he pointed me towards where he'd been looking. Inside a piano with no lid, no legs, sitting on the floor, a bitch was lying, with a resigned and tender expression, with four newly born puppies.

'They were born last night,' my uncle whispered.

Under the mechanism of the piano – the strings stretched out – there was a torn old tangled jacket covered in dog hairs. On this jacket was the body of the bitch, surrounded by her children. They were small like mice, they had their eyes closed, stuck closed, short ears, and they moved slowly without knowing where they were going. They made a constant noise, made up of many thin squeals. They opened their mouths and stuck out their tiny tongues. They opened their mouths and from time to time hung on their mother's thick teats. When they moved away – waddling or dragging themselves on their little paws – the bitch grabbed them with her mouth and brought them back, putting them down close to her.

With a smile, my uncle stared at the bitch and her pups. When something happened, when the bitch chose one and began to lick it, my uncle smiled wider. As we walked together to the carpentry shop, we had no words to say. We had thoughts.

Leaning over my workbench, I went back to work and only later remembered. I interrupted a story my uncle was telling and that not even he was listening to. I opened the shoebox and called him over. I didn't have to ask him any questions. Amazed, suddenly sad, he held some of the medals.

That was the morning I learned that my father died far away from my mother, exhausted, on the same day that I was born.

After hearing my uncle at last, my father and I were even more strangers. My father revived in words that had the light coming through them, and the smell of wood, and everything I didn't know about myself.

After spending all the days making doors and windows, benches and tables, dreaming about pianos, my father would close up the big workshop doors and run through the streets of Lisbon, running and tearing the streets of Lisbon. Then he'd arrive early at the races that were held on Sunday mornings. He took trains at Santa Apolónia, and travelled alone second-class to the suburbs where, at a tranquil pace, he ran to different parts of the city. When there were marathons, my father would arrive and the other runners would look at him from a distance. There might have been fear in these looks, or disdain, but fear is what there was and that was why they feigned disdain. My father ignored them, just lived within his own light. When he ran past them people would call him by his name. Before he arrived people would comment:

'Here comes Lázaro.'

As he ran past them, the people would say:

'Come on, Lázaro!'

As though he could hear them, he ran across kilometres that were left as marks on his face. Close to the finishing line other runners would arrive, who with their final strength might pull him by his vest, or thump him in the back, who might knock him over, but he always arrived out in front, and perhaps limping, perhaps with the palms of his hands grazed, perhaps with blood trickling down his knees; he was glorious and infinite. When he received his medal, he would lower his head. People applauded him, admired him, and spoke his name. They would never forget his name.

It was on the day that my father ran with the best in the world. He travelled by boat to Stockholm and every little detail was new. The sea was how you'd imagine death to be, or unconditional love. My father had a great deal of hope. On that day he ran along the streets, against the streets, until the moment that he began to lose his place, began to fall back, to run in disarray, muddling his legs and his arms. He fell after thirty kilometres. He was surrounded by people who didn't know him. He was taken to hospital. And he died. He stopped breathing and thinking. He didn't stop being my father.

It was on the day that I was born.

My uncle said that, when the news was heard, there were some people who thought he had found death while fleeing from it, and there were some who thought that he had escaped from death while seeking it.

I couldn't understand why my mother hadn't told me – all those years, summers and winters, all the times we'd sat at the kitchen table eating cake halves and drinking tea, all the times I sat on the earth floor of the yard while she washed clothes in the tank, sitting by the fire, sitting on the yard steps – I didn't understand where I'd been born from. This black ignorance spread itself inside all my years, it moved ahead, it ran, till it touched me there, at that moment, standing opposite my uncle and a shoebox filled with medals.

The light, the smell of wood, and my uncle, almost voiceless, almost as if he was breathing, spoke to me of my aunt.

'She's the one who can explain it to you better.'

The times my mother spoke to me of my aunts they were light words in her voice, they were like breezes. Along with my uncle, my father had had two sisters. The younger died tragically, so tragically, gravely, in a way that no one dared speak of it, in a way that just to think of it demanded a lowering of the eyes and a conspicuous silence, as though everyone was to blame for her death. The older lived outside Lisbon. When my aunts saw me, I was very small, I'd just been born. After the younger died, the older never came back to Lisbon.

My uncle, as if breathing, spoke to me of my aunt. He told me that she'd kept newspaper cuttings. He told me that she remembered everything.

As of that moment – me measuring laths, my uncle varnishing doors and telling stories that never ended – I could only think that I wanted to go, ought to go, needed to go to my aunt's house to talk to her and listen to her.

It was Simão who started the game, who invented it. Marta was still living in Benfica. Elisa was small; Simão would open his arms and say to her:

'Hug me as hard as you like me!'

Elisa smiled with her eyes, she started running and stood, her arms wide, very far from Simão. He pretended to cry, with the pretend crying of a child, pretended to be rubbing his eyes.

Once Elisa believed that he had cried enough, she would run into his arms and squeeze him as hard as she could. Simão felt Elisa's little chest squeezing him. She squeezed him until her throat started making a noise signifying great effort. At that moment she'd stop and Simão would kiss her cheeks noisily.

I knew that Simão visited Maria. I didn't talk about this, but I knew. Simão played this game with Ana too. Francisco started playing this game with Hermes, and later with Íris. Whenever Francisco comes into Maria's house, he looks for Íris, opens his arms and says to her:

'Hug me as hard as you like me!'

In the kitchen, after lunch, Maria remains seated at the table, her gaze lost. Sometimes she gives a jump inside because she thinks the phone is going to ring. She believes her husband is going to call to ask forgiveness, calling for her – please, come home, please. At other times she raises her face, looks all around her, because she thinks the phone has rung. Noticing that her sister remains indifferent, running plates under the tap, realising that her mother hasn't stopped putting away the food that was left in the oven, Maria goes back to losing her gaze, and returns to her sad thoughts.

In the corridor, the afternoon begins to pass across the objects. There is no one to see them or hear them, and so their silence is not real. Perhaps a speck of dust falls on to the table under the mirror. Perhaps the mirror doesn't show any reflection at all. Perhaps time has stopped.

In the sewing room, on all fours on the carpet, Íris, with her bandaged hand, is gripping a doll by the waist. Her fingers go round its waist. She tilts the doll one way and the other, one of its little plastic feet touches the floor, and then the other – tap, tap, tap. Wobbling, the doll walks, making its way across the pattern in the carpet.

Sitting at the other end, completely hunched on the floor, Hermes is holding a fire engine.

Íris's voice, reedy – a child imitating a child – it's the voice of the doll:

'Hello, neighbour. What are you doing?'

The fire engine, in Hermes's hand, has the thickest voice he can manage:

'Hello. I'm having a rest. I was just putting out a fire.'

'Oh, a fire, that's very good. Where's your mummy?'

'My mummy's to work. She comes home at ten o'clock.'

'She's to work? But . . . but she told me she would come home at thirty-two o'clock.'

Hermes opens his eyes wide, opens his mouth in pretend amazement, in pretend shock, and says:

'At thirty-two o'clock?'

'Oh, no, I'm sorry, sir. My mummy's coming home at seventy-forty o'clock.'

As though marvelling, Hermes opens his eyes and his mouth wider still. From deep within this surprise he says:

'At seventy-forty o'clock?'

For a moment Íris says nothing. She waits. Her narrow shoulders tremble as she laughs. Ana and Elisa know that they're more grown-up and they're talking, sitting in little chairs, under the brightness of the window. Hermes gets up, pulls his sister's arm and says:

'She says her mother's coming home at seventy-forty o'clock . . .'

Íris laughs to herself. Ana and Elisa look over towards her and smile. Ana says:

'Oh . . .'

Íris, in the middle of a laugh, says:

'She's coming home at a thousand o'clock.'

Ana, laughing, looks at Elisa and rotates her index finger against her forehead. My wife, without coming in, calls Íris. She is coming to fetch her to have a siesta. Hermes starts a tantrum. He wants his cousin to keep playing. My wife starts to scold him. He is about to cry, he's really going to cry, when he picks up the fire engine and throws it on the floor with all his strength.

Íris is nearly three years old. She comes up to him, puts her finger to her lips and very seriously, so that only Hermes can hear her, she says:

'Don't cry. I'll go and sleep my siesta with Granny, but I'll come back yesterday. All right? I'll come back at seventy-forty o'clock.'

And she gives him a kiss on the cheek.

My wife was talking about how much the baby had kicked between the fifth and seventh months.

'There were nights when it wouldn't even let me sleep.'

About how it became absolutely quiet in the last month.

'I ended up being worried.'

I, however, thought only of my uncle's words. I thought of my older aunt and of everything her eyes had seen. I thought of my younger aunt, dead, and of all her eyes had forgotten. I thought of my father and all I didn't know about him. I thought of my father, my uncle, my aunts, alive and together in the same room, without knowing that one day the future would arrive.

At Easter we always had a picnic in Monsanto. At home my wife would fry cubes of pork and fill a tub with rice. She took fried potatoes. She took tomatoes and lettuce leaves to make a salad. I arranged everything on the truck, putting in a bottle of fizzy water, another of orangeade, a flagon of wine, and placed the blankets over the top.

With some patience we were all able to fit in. Marta was still thin and she went on Maria's lap. Then came my wife, squeezed between Simão and Francisco. Then me – driving with my elbows drawn in. A few years later Simão had already started going on the bicycle he'd bought with what he'd earned as a stonemason's assistant. He'd head off before us and we'd pass him on the road. My wife, seeing him from behind, would get anxious because she thought that Simão, being blind on one side, might more easily fall and break his neck. As we passed him our daughters, one on the other's lap, would lean out of the window, waving their arms and shouting.

The rope we used to attach door frames, or anything we were carrying, was always in the truck. When we arrived I'd tie it to the strongest limb of a tree, always the same one, and make a swing. My wife spread the blankets on the ground. We ate pork on enamel plates painted with flowers, and we were together. There was a moment when, all at the same time, we attached some value to being together.

When we finished eating, our children would head off in various directions. Simão was always the first one up. Marta was always in charge of looking after Francisco. Maria almost always hid herself away to read romance novels. I lay on a blanket under a pine tree. I closed my eyes. Once she'd cleared away the plates, my wife would come and sit by me, craning her neck to try and see our children.

On one such afternoon, I'd already fallen asleep and woke up to a shrill whining. Maria came pushing Simão's bicycle, and she was crying. The birds fell silent in the trees. Marta stopped pushing Francisco on the swing. My wife got up:

'So what is it?' asked my wife.

Maria didn't stop crying. From closer up, we could see that her face and arm were grazed. She approached us slowly, fearful. I was sitting on the blanket and asked her, my voice firm:

'How did you fall?'

Under my voice, she trembled.

'Simão didn't tell me the bicycle doesn't have brakes . . .'

I got up suddenly. I tore off a pine branch that was above me and went to look for him.

Not much light on our faces. It was earlier than my usual time to go and sit in the kitchen, but I was sitting there already, drinking coffee. My wife, between the things she was doing, held her belly with both hands, looked at me and understood. Later, out on the street, it was still the gloom of early morning. It was colder than my usual time to go out to the workshop, but I took long steps, I thought, and I noticed nothing. There were indistinct, distant people on the pavements, continuing along their way. As I reached the station, as I bought my ticket, as I waited for the train, as I went in, as I sat to watch the landscape passing in the window, I kept imagining all the things I didn't know.

The moment arrived – solid and real – when I was standing there, in front of my aunt's house – the address written by my uncle on a piece of paper, and written on another piece of paper kept amid old envelopes in the drawer where my mother's documents aged, the written remains of her life. I opened the iron gate, went in, stopped at the door – a solid, real moment – and knocked three times. I waited. Birds perched on the electricity wires. I waited. I knocked three times again. The door was opened to me by a hunched-up woman with startled eyes. We remained in silence. I learned later that she was my cousin.

I told her my name, told her who I was. She moved away to let me in. We took some steps along a darkening corridor. A mirror hung on the wall, over a table. For a long time it had reflected nothing but shadows. As we approached the end of the corridor, there was a revolting smell, getting worse. It was a smell that was inside the walls, inside the floor, the roof – it was in every object because it was a smell that filled the air, turning solid. As we went into the room my cousin didn't break the silence, but stopped to look at me. My aunt was sitting on the bed. Her body was enormous. She was leaning up against pillows. She had her sheets tangled at the foot of the bed. She smiled at me with four or five rotten, worn teeth and a paste of food that covered them. Fine networks of veins branched across her round, swollen, fleshy cheeks. Her eyes shone. Her belly was a heavy bulk, tall, overflowing its sides. Her breasts were the same bulk. Her legs, full, stretched out, weren't the shape of legs and ended in two gigantic thighs that squeezed against one another. Her arms were two arches of flesh, thick at the shoulders, thick at the wrists, ending in a thick hand, ending in narrow fingertips.

When I made to introduce myself, my aunt's voice, uneven, weak and strong, interrupted me:

'I know very well who you are.'

And she reached her arms out to me. I made my way across the carpet. I leaned over, and against my instincts turned my cheeks towards her. As I was giving her two kisses her arms held me. She pressed her rough, warm cheek, her hard, dishevelled hair, against my face. The smell that filled the room, born from the creases of her skin, was a mixture of hot food – soup – and sweat. It was a body lying for years on the same sheets – a brown stain around that body. It was an enormous night shirt – metres and metres of fine fabric – covered with stains under her chin – oil, grease, sauce. When my aunt's arms let go of me, I took two steps back and kept my expression unchanged.

Her eyes shone. I answered her questions. I told her there weren't many weeks left until the birth of my first child. An even bigger smile spread across her face; she congratulated me and told me that it would be a girl. She told me she was quite sure it would be a girl. I talked to her, then, about the workshop and about Benfica. Her gaze was frozen on the space in front of her as though in this invisible air she could see images of what I was telling her. After a moment, she was the one who was talking to me about the workshop and about Benfica. She was a child, and she'd take her father his lunch; she'd go into the carpentry shop and sit with him in the piano cemetery. And then later she was a girl who set her elbows on the window ledge and, as people returned home from work, waited for her boyfriend. Then she was living close to the workshop, she was married and her oldest daughter was born – the woman who was there with us, who kept her eyes on the floor, perhaps because she had already heard these stories many times. Her name was Elisa.

I took advantage of a moment of silence to talk about my father. My aunt's expression didn't change. Time. I told her that I'd only learned a few days earlier that my father was a marathon runner. She showed no surprise, continued to listen to me, and when I finished she turned to my cousin and said to her, naturally:

'Elisa, go and fetch me the drawer from the living-room cupboard.'

We waited together for my cousin's footsteps, the sounds of the drawer opening in another room, time. And my aunt's gaze fixed on me. My gaze not knowing where to stop – the pile of dirty plates on the bedside table, the bedpan on a stool, the flies changing direction in sudden angles over the bed. My cousin came into the room, holding the drawer between her wrists and her chest. She passed in front of me. It was a drawer filled with papers. She put the drawer down on top of my aunt's belly. My aunt lifted out pieces of paper and postcards with writing on them, and took out a stack of folded papers tied with a piece of string. For a long time she pulled at the ends of the bow. She held out a yellowed newspaper cutting to me. I approached the bed, held the cutting in both hands and began to read.

My father. Dead too early, and too far away. Dead and exhausted on the same day I was born. Time. As I returned the cutting to her, my aunt examined me. After a pause, she showed me other cuttings. Before the day I was born – they described races my father won. A deserving winner. Going through a spell of really good form. An example to those who were starting out in this event. As my aunt folded the cuttings at the creases, as she arranged them, she began to talk about my father. Her face wanted to break into a smile that never came, and that remained balanced in a limbo of almost existing and not existing. In her voice my father was a human being, and living again, he was a man, he was a young lad. He might perhaps have passed me in the street, I could have noticed him, could have looked at him and imagined his strengths and weaknesses. And then, silence. The light came through the damp-stained curtains. My aunt's nails scratched the bottom of the drawer. She was holding up a photograph. She looked at it a moment, smiling at it as though smiling at a person, and held it out. I took the photograph in the palm of my hand – its weight. And I don't know how old I was at the moment I saw my father's face for the first time.

Time. I held the image of his face looking at me, and believed with sudden impressions which stuck into my skin like needles that he could see me. My dead father was younger than I was, and he was looking at me. Sudden impressions, skin, needles; I didn't know if it was me looking and seeing my father in a dead time or whether it was my father, alive, looking and, for the first time, seeing me.

My aunt insisted I keep the photograph. I refused and wanted to give it back to her. She kept insisting. It was as though the photograph were burning my fingers. I tried to give it back, following her hand. She evaded it with brisk gestures. Slowly I placed the photograph inside the drawer. On top of letters, pieces of paper, my father was still looking at me.

With the tips of her fingers my aunt chose one of the envelopes and took out another photograph. Seeing it, her

face saddened. She remembered the story that was too sad to tell. She held the photograph out to me and said it was her late sister, my other aunt.

I handed the photograph back to her. She took it and placed it in the drawer without looking at it again. Her silence was real.

When I began saying my goodbyes, my aunt asked me to stay a little longer. I continued to say my goodbyes. Then, amid the words, she said: 'This bed.' And they were eternal words. My cousin Elisa said nothing, but she lifted her face. I left my aunt, the centre of that room, and went out, thinking I would never see her again. At the door I said goodbye to my cousin with a gaze deep into her frightened eyes, and I thought I would never see her again. I never saw them again.

I walked to the station. The whole of the walk, and later, too, through all the streets that took me home, I remembered my father – the shape of his face, what he was thinking – and I remembered my aunt – lying there, waiting for nothing – and I remembered my cousin taking care of her mother – afraid, alone, waiting for nothing.

I went into the house and found women from the neighbourhood walking back and forth. My wife was about to give birth. I moved chairs out of my way, shoved widows aside and went into the room. My wife stopped writhing on the bed. Her face drenched in sweat, as though reflecting a fire, she turned to me and smiled at me just exactly as I was smiling at her.

On Saturdays the nights take longer to fall. Marta's husband comes into the house. It is early at night. He sits at his place at the table, rests his head in his hands and Marta's movements get faster. My wife greets him, her voice faint. Maria doesn't move.

With all the speed she's capable of, her legs alternating very quickly and her body hovering slowly, Marta does the calculations of the number of plates and begins to lay the table. Maria, seated, is her own shape in stone, and thinks that her husband will choose dinnertime to phone her, to ask her to come back, to tell her he misses her. My wife is leaning over the stove. I know her face. Marta's husband is sitting at the table and he is too far away, all he has left here is his body and his silence. Wanting to call the children to dinner, Marta shouts into the hallway.

My wife moves away from the stove, holding a pan which she puts down in the middle of the table. Slowly Marta's husband fills his plate and begins to eat. There is a calendar on the wall, there is a fruit bowl with wizened peaches, there is a lit lamp hanging from the ceiling. Marta begins to get impatient as no child has yet appeared. My wife fills Maria's plate and asks her, wordlessly, to eat. Marta goes to call the children from the sewing room.

She opens the door and the four of them are sitting on the rug. Íris is talking to her sister:

'Now you've grown up and you're a lady.'

Marta, her cheeks red, starts to say something and only Elisa looks at her. She says to clear up the toys and go and have dinner. Turning to Hermes, she says:

'Get a move on! Your father's already eating.'

As though still muttering, Marta returns to the kitchen. My wife puts the bread on the table. There is the silence of small sounds, there is age, there is light. Marta notices that the children aren't coming and asks my wife to go and fetch them.

My wife goes into the sewing room. She rounds up the grandchildren and starts pulling them up under their arms. Íris objects with her knotted eyebrows. My wife continues to hurry them. They go down the corridor. Elisa is in front. Behind her, Íris allows herself to be pushed along by my wife. They go into the kitchen. Marta's husband has already eaten, and he has already gone out. Maria hasn't yet brought her hands up to touch her cutlery.

It was almost the end of summer, and Marta was just a few months old. My wife was breastfeeding her. Marta closed her eyes, and she was innocent. I was on the other side of the kitchen, watching them. It was almost the end of summer, I was alive, I was so utterly alive, but my heart was apart from me, breastfeeding and innocent, on the other side of the kitchen.

Maria has said a couple of things. Having given up on waiting for her husband's call, her arms stopped weighing her down and, at last, she was able to breathe. Inside her, she repeated the certainty she had that her husband will call tomorrow. Or it might be that her husband will choose the moment when she arrives at the workshop, that he wants to say sorry in person, wants to look her in the eye to show her he's sincere. Maria has convinced herself of these certainties and, lighter now, freed from the need to wait, she has said a couple of things.

Marta approaches and answers her. My wife looks up. It's time. The three of them walk to the sewing room. They don't have time to think, but there is serenity in their faces. It's not the same serenity in each one's expression, but in all of them it's genuine – the same truth in different illusions.

When Elisa, Ana, Íris and Hermes see them, they already know bedtime has arrived. The end of Saturday is a warm feeling that the children know how to accept.

Elisa is the first to get up off the carpet. Without saying anything, any shouting, Ana, Íris and Hermes get up immediately after her. They follow my wife out. On the bedroom floor, between the beds, my wife will arrange folded blankets and sheets for Hermes to sleep. Ana and Íris will sleep together in his bed.

Marta and Maria, sisters, tidy away the toys that are spread around the sewing room. They tidy away the final remnants of the day. Marta bends down with difficulty, places the palm of her left hand on her knee, and sweeps her other hand in an arc across the floor. The blankets are piled up on the bench in front of the sewing machine. These are the blankets, folded, which my daughters will arrange as mattresses. On top of the blankets, on the bench, are the sheets and the pillows. When they finish arranging the beds, Marta will walk to her room and get ready to sleep. Her husband won't have arrived yet, but Marta will know it's Saturday and it's not worth waiting for him. She will think of other things. On the sewing-room floor, their heads on the pillows, their bodies covered by the sheets, Maria and her mother will keep breathing – the silence, the darkness, their breathings. My wife will think of Francisco. Maria will think of her husband and she will be sure that he will ask her, tomorrow, for forgiveness, and he will ask her, please, please, to come back. My wife will be asleep in minutes. Maria will fall asleep later. On the black floor of the sewing room she won't know whether moments have passed, or hours, since she lay down to sleep.

I was lying in my room. I wasn't sleeping, and I wasn't awake. I was lying in my room – windows closed, darkness. I had the covers over my head, but I didn't feel them. I was just breathing in the rotten smell of illness. I existed in a world that was made up of nothing but hopeless pain – constant pain, bones bending, bones coming away from the flesh and no hope that I'd go back to walking the streets, unworried, light, unaware. My wife, shadowless, took steps across the kitchen floor and boiled pans of water when she didn't know what to do.

I held my voice in, within me, I tangled it up with my black pain. It was deceiving my whole body. I held out against the sharp pains like death itself before crying out. I called my wife's name. It was morning, or it was afternoon. Bits of my voice went through the bedroom door, landed on the floor of the hallway and some of them made it to the kitchen. Maria spent her days with my wife. The two of them came into the room. Hanging in the middle of the ceiling, the lamp lit its yellow light – the glowing filaments, the image of a red-hot heart. In the first months my wife tried to follow the timetable for my medication. Later, in silence, the doctor told her she could give me my medication whenever I asked for it; it would no longer do me any harm.

Maria went back home when Francisco arrived from the workshop. She made her way down the streets, holding on to Ana, her little steps, and a basket with dinner already prepared. Morning and afternoon dissolved along the way, but they never disappeared, they never disappeared. At all times there was the weight of a closed fist squeezing her heart. Even when she thought about other things, when she almost forgot, there was always the weight of a closed fist squeezing her heart.

It was one of those late afternoons. The night was beginning. Maria went into the house and let go of Ana's arm. Her husband had already arrived, he was leaning on the sink, and when Ana rushed over to him he didn't bend down to caress her, nor to smile at her, nor to speak to her in that voice people use to speak to children. Maria went into the kitchen, spoke a syllable and he didn't reply, didn't look at her, didn't ask after me. They remained silent. Maria took the pan – the lid tied down with strings – from out of the basket. Her husband was still leaning on the sink, closed in the impossible thoughts he had, which covered his face. Ana put down the doll she was carrying and sat down next to a chair. Time seemed to be just like on every other day.

Cutting through time, Maria's husband, crossing the kitchen, knocked into her with his elbow.

'You hurt me . . .'

'It wasn't on purpose, was it?' he said rudely.

Maria was going to reply to him in the same manner, when he – shorter than her – stopped right in front of her, chin raised, lips pursed and eyes burning. After a pause, Maria saddened, and said:

'You don't love me any more.'

Her husband repeated this phrase until it became ridiculous, even more ridiculous, until it was just those words and no longer that phrase. She kept looking at him, with the same sadness. He raised his voice even further:

'Don't look at me like that. I know where you get those ideas . . .'

And as though stuttering, nervous, as though giving up

halfway through what he was going to say, as though not giving up right after that, he held her wrist, squeezed her wrist and began to talk, as though talking to himself, in phrases he interrupted and resumed and continued and interrupted.

He pulled Maria by the arm. And took her down the corridor. And they went. Into the room. Where they slept every night. And he pointed. At the bookcase. Filled with romance novels. That Maria had kept since. Childhood and which she organised. In alphabetical order and. All the stories. She knew by heart and which she. Could have recounted in every detail and. He pointed at this full bookcase. Clean and dustless. And said:

'Because of this. This rubbish. It's because of this. All of it. Because of this rubbish.'

And nervously. Choking on. His words. And as though. Stuttering. He threw an arm against the bookcase and knocked it over. All the romance novels on. The bedspread and as though. He was crazy and as though he was. Crazy. He began to tear them with. Both hands while he repeated.

'Rubbish. It's all because. Of this rubbish.'

On the bed a heap of torn pages and torn jackets, titles – dreams of, passion wedding in, spring the heart's flames stronger, than prejudice triumph, of destiny in love with the man, a certain girl and woman loving for the first, time and unkn, own irresistible flo, wers to, o late be, yond de, sire cru, el smi, le da, wni, ng o, f em, o t, i, on, s.

And at last Maria's husband stopped his arms. His quick breathing filled and emptied his chest.

And through the tears that hung from Maria's eyelashes, the heap of torn pages on the bed – torn Sabrinas, torn Biancas, torn Júlias – was a shapeless, dazzling mass.

And leaning on the doorpost, her doll hanging by the end of her arm, Ana was watching. Her eyes were huge.

My uncle was saying every word that came into his head. It was morning. My uncle interrupted a word after the first syllable when my neighbour came running in:

'Da . . .'

I dropped my tools on the bench, gave the workshop keys to my uncle and went out past my neighbour. The way home was quick and it was slow. The front door was ajar. In one corner of the kitchen, Marta was small, sitting in a chair, serious, feet in the air, and there was a woman taking care of her. The other women walked past one another, muddled with one another, tangled with one another. I passed through their shadows – the steps of my boots digging into the floor. The bedroom walls were the opposite of vast, eternal fields, they were the opposite of landscape. My wife with her eyes closed. She opened her eyes when I touched her hair, closed them again when the pains submerged her. I tried to go into that world beneath her eyelids. I had her head in my arms. A time passed that was made up of pains that moved away for moments that were shorter and shorter, and that returned ever stronger. All the women gathered round her. She began to push. All the women encouraged her to push. I held her hand and felt all her strength. Her face turned red, and then purple. Her face was strong, and at the same time it was fragile. The whole universe stretched, all life, and it was about to burst. Like an elastic that stretches, stretches, and when it snaps will hit us in the face. Then the women's faces were lit up by a miracle. The midwife put two fingers to the roof of the baby's mouth and pulled it out in one go. It was in her arms, a girl covered in blood, beautiful, attached to an umbilical cord. She passed her into my wife's arms. Together, inseparable, we looked at her and it was impossible to control the tears that burst on to our faces. Maria had just been born. Something vast had just been born in our hearts.

My wife – waking up one Sunday morning she remembers that it was on a Sunday that I died. The hospital. The telephone ringing in Maria's house. Earlier, Sunday mornings had been the time we all woke up together, we all got up together. It was sunny every Sunday morning. Our children. Even earlier, Sunday mornings were when her godmother would open all the windows of the boarding house, they were sun.

Marta – on Sunday mornings she's the first person to get to the kitchen – nightdress, slippers – makes breakfast so that the children feel all is right with the world. Her husband didn't sleep at home. Earlier, when they still lived in Benfica, Elisa was so small, she'd go into the bedroom, jump on to her parents' bed, stumble across their bodies, lie down between the two of them and, together, they'd laugh, they'd laugh because it was Sunday. Earlier, Marta was just a girl, she'd help her mother to make lunch and she laughed, too, she laughed because it was Sunday.

Maria – there are Sunday mornings, like this one, when she feels a thin pain inside her, like the cold, when she cannot smile; and there are Sunday mornings when she believes in a solar certainty that fills her up. On those Sundays, all her ages mingle together. She is a child, playing with Simão in the yard, she's a girl reading romance novels in the piano cemetery, she's nearly a woman, dreaming of her wedding day.

Today she thinks only that her husband is going to phone her, that her husband is going to ask her forgiveness, and she feels a thin pain inside her, like the cold.

Elisa – Sunday mornings are already lots of things. When she was small, in the Benfica house, she'd walk barefoot along the hall runner and climb on to her parents' bed. Her mother told her to keep still, and at the same time she tickled her. Elisa laughed a lot, and under the sheets she'd push out her thin white chest with its many ribs just perfect for tickling. Now grown, she no longer goes to her parents' bed. She gets up when Hermes starts pulling at her arm. Hermes wants to play. When she gets to the kitchen her mother asks her if she's done her schoolwork yet.

Ana – Sunday mornings are a matter to which she gives some thought. Ana thinks about what she feels. She thinks, 'Now.' And she thinks that now is, mysteriously and concretely, now. Later, time will make her forget what she feels. Later, years later, she'll find it strange that anyone could consider Sunday mornings a matter to be given some thought, still less a matter worth talking about. She will never talk about this. No one will ever talk to her about this. She will never think about this. Now, this is what she thinks about.

Hermes – he is beginning to discover Sunday mornings, just as he is beginning to discover everything. He doesn't remember many Sunday mornings. He remembers days when his mother or father doesn't go out to work. He remembers days when Elisa doesn't go to school. Hermes knows what it is, this word 'Sunday'. He knows it's a word. There are words like it. There is the word 'anyway', there is the word 'seventy'. Sunday, anyway, seventy, are words Elisa and his mother use. Hermes doesn't really know, he really doesn't know what they mean. He knows they are words. This is enough for him. On Sunday mornings, Hermes goes to wake Elisa. He asks her to play. Elisa goes to do her schoolwork and Hermes goes to play alone in the yard.

Íris – Íris has happiness. When it's Sunday morning, Íris wakes up and the house is full. Not just her grandmother trying to persuade her to eat, not just her mother having to go to work and chivvying Ana along. There's her father, too, and there's a lot of time. Íris wanders the house in her pyjamas. She chats with her father, her mother, her grandmother. She goes into the living room, approaches Ana and suddenly grabs her and kisses her on the cheek. For a moment Ana smiles, bites her tongue and makes an awkward face. Then she continues to focus on what she was doing. Íris grabs hold of the toy box, lifts it in the air and tips it on to the living-room floor.

It was only much later that I realised something in my uncle's face had changed. It was only much later that I realised that from a certain moment all his gestures and all his words were fragments of a goodbye.

My daughters were small. There were not many months to go before Simão would be born. When my wife went to the grocer's or to the market, she'd take Marta by the hand, she'd push a buggy with Maria watching everything, and carry Simão in her steep belly. All the neighbour women who passed her shared their hunches. Many said she would have another girl, many said she would have a boy. Standing in the middle of the carpentry shop, my uncle was very serious – his left eye open, the absence of his right eye covered over by the smooth white lid, fused with the skin of his face – and told me that a boy would be born. He told me he was quite certain a boy would be born. And he followed me with his good eye and his blind eye to be quite sure I had no doubts.

I had no doubts. I had no silence or peace for any secret thoughts. There were two girls waiting for me when I got home, and in a few months there would be another child, too, boy or girl, crying in the night, needing everything I could give. That was what I thought about. I wanted to finish the work that came in every day because I wanted more work. Each hour life began, and there was no limit to what my body could take. I didn't feel the splinters of wood that stuck into the palms of my hands, just as I didn't notice how, in the mornings, my uncle would arrive at the workshop before me, how I didn't get angry when he'd disappear for two hours and then came back smiling. I said nothing to him. Deep down I thought he went to the *taberna*.

He didn't go to the *taberna*. It was only much later that I realised that for those hours my uncle would go to the piano cemetery.

My wife, Marta, Maria, Elisa, Ana, Hermes and Íris all woke at the same time. They remained in bed, each thinking themselves the only one awake. Minutes passed. When Íris got up and sat on the bed, Hermes suddenly got up, too. Ana and Elisa got up, too. When they started playing with the pillows, jumping on the beds, shouting, Marta got up, and in no time at all her slippers were echoing on the hall floor. In the sewing room my wife got up, clutching her back. Right after that, Maria got up.

The morning passed. It is Sunday. There's a week until Francisco runs in the marathon at the Olympic Games. Marta's husband has just gone into the kitchen, walked across it in silence, gone into the living room and sat down in silence. Marta follows him, and the moment he sits her body is there standing in front of him – hands on her waist. She whispers that they're going to go out to Lisbon after lunch. Her husband tells her she can't go. Marta tries to settle herself, she breathes, and still whispers:

'But you promised.'

Her husband tells her she can't go. Marta, irritated, whispering loudly, says that her mother is counting on the lift back, that her sister is also counting on the lift; she says again that he promised, he'll need the bits of wood to burn in the winter. Her husband tells her they will go to the workshop the following Sunday, he promises her, he says her sister can keep her mother company on the train. Marta asks if he's already forgotten that next Sunday Francisco runs in the Olympic Games; she gets angrier, whispers ever louder, gets angrier.

In the kitchen my wife finishes making lunch, turns off the stove, and Maria is sitting waiting for her husband to call her, and the sound of Marta's voice, whispered in the living room, comes in like razor blades cutting through the air.

My daughters and my wife haven't seen Simão since the first weekend Íris spent at home, just after she was born.

Sunday. Sun. My daughters' husbands almost dropped Marta when they were helping her down off the back of the truck. Maria was watching them from the window, my wife was in the hallway, Hermes in her arms, next to Elisa, and they jumped at the shock. Hermes started to cry. It was Marta herself who comforted him, as they came up the stairs, hand in hand, very slowly. Hermes, ever so small, thin, scrawny, and Marta.

When the two sisters saw one another there was a soft, embarrassed smile on their faces. In each other's eyes they were girls. In the middle of Maria's living room it was as though they were in their room at our house and another summer afternoon was drawing to an end and their voices and dreams were mingled together. They were girls, suddenly grown. Marta had her best dress on, a cardigan and a shining pin. Maria was in a nightdress she had bought before going into the maternity ward. And they embraced quickly, amid nervous laughter, bumping their clumsy bodies, when what they wanted was to embrace and stay in that embrace for a long time.

That day my wife smiled, too. Ana ran to Elisa – holding hands. Excited, speaking loudly, she was about to say something about her sister when her mother made a sibilant sound – then they took careful steps to the bedroom door. Maria went ahead and opened the door very gently, avoiding the tiny noises of the hinges and the latch. Behind her, my wife held Elisa's and Ana's shoulders. Behind them, Marta occupied the whole doorway. The shadow, which was the colour of the whole room, covered them. Maria stopped at the head of Íris's crib, and, proud, happy, she waited for them to come closer.

Íris's body, covered by a pink blanket, was an even, perfect shape. In her sleeping face there were her little lips, her baby's nose, her serene skin. She had one hand open, abandoned beside her head – the fingers of a doll. She had the serenity that's only possible in absolute innocence, in absolute purity.

When they came back to the living room they were laughing, wanting to speak loudly but restraining themselves, covering their mouths with their hands. The husbands, sitting with legs crossed, watched them come in. Hermes, on the ground, was moving a piece of paper around, worrying it. My wife, satisfied and silent, went into Maria's kitchen to make some tea.

They were sitting at the table, talking, drinking tea, eating slices of the cake that Marta had brought, when they heard a knock at the door. Maria made to get up, but her body was worn down, pained. Marta made to get up, but her body was huge, heavy. My wife got up and walked towards the door. She thought it was Francisco. She opened the door. It was Simão.

He had washed his face. He came in, not knowing what to do with his hands. My wife hadn't seen him since the night when that thing happened that we'll never forget. What little news she received came from Francisco, or, before that, when Marta still lived in Benfica, she knew about the afternoons when he'd go to visit Elisa. My wife held back in her throat the lightning flash she felt when he said:

'Mother.'

Simão was wearing a clean shirt with old faded stains. He was wearing worn old trousers. He was wearing boots that took a couple of embarrassed steps. Marta and Maria got up to greet him with a shyness of being his sisters, his actual sisters, and also strangers, almost strangers.

Simão stroked Elisa's head, but it took her a time to recognise him. Maria, managing to speak normally, gestured him towards Ana, who was looking down at the ground. Simão smiled. Then he bent down and held his hand out to Hermes, but the boy remained fearless, staring at his uncle's blind eye. Maria said:

'You know I had a little girl?'

'Francisco told me.' Simão's voice was soft.

Maria offered to go and fetch her.

'Leave her. I don't want to be a bother.'

'It's no bother. It's time for her feed.'

And there was silence. My daughters' husbands had stopped their conversation and looked at him. Marta offered him tea. He said no, and thanked her. My wife wanted to see him. She wanted to make up for whole years of missing him, of loss, of anxiety, of hurt. She wanted, in a single moment, to recover her son. Our son.

Maria came in, with Íris in her arms. Elisa and Ana clustered around her legs. Marta leaned herself on the tabletop, stood up and walked towards her, saying incomplete words, with soft consonants. Maria smiled with her whole face and put the girl in her arms. Marta, looking only at her, continued to speak with the same little voice, tilting her up so that everyone could see her. Marta put the girl into my wife's arms – her face tender now – and it was my wife, with an exaggerated gesture, who put her into Simão's arms. She was so small in his arms. He smiled. He looked around him. His sisters were smiling at him. My wife was looking at him tenderly. He lowered his face to kiss Íris's cheek, but pricked her with his beard. As though shocked, she started to cry, inconsolable. Simão tried to rock her, to calm her, but she cried more and more. Then he passed her into Maria's arms, who also tried to calm her, but she shouted, cried more and more. Simão, embarrassed, put his hands in his pockets and took them out again. Maria sat down to breastfeed Íris, but she didn't want it. She only wanted to cry. Her face was round and red, getting ever redder.

'There now, all gone . . .' Maria said again and again.

Íris, wrapped in a shawl, was a small, compact body, a single solid shape that cried. My wife and Marta tried to calm her, but she cried, shouted as though tearing her voice in the air. Her sister and cousins looked at her, marvelling. Simão began saying his goodbyes. Íris was gathering in strength, as though she didn't need to breathe.

'Wait. Don't go yet,' said Maria, under Íris's distressed, shrill cries.

But Simão, embarrassed, hastily saying his goodbyes, as though fleeing, left.

The morning Simão was born, a lad appeared at the workshop, panting, addressing me as sir, with the message that I ought to go home right away. I stopped looking at the half-sawn piece of wood that was held in the lathe, wiped my hands on my trousers and went up to my uncle to give him the workshop keys. He held my arm, sent the lad away, telling him I wouldn't be long. I looked at him, not understanding, but I didn't speak because for the first time there was peace in his face, there was calm – his serene face.

The lad's footsteps moved away across the floor of the carpentry shop, then the dirt of the entrance hall and then the road. The sounds of the birds in the roof-beams returned. The endlessness of the specks of sawdust returned, specks of sawdust that hovered in the air, floated and came to rest on every object, on our skin. My uncle started walking towards the piano cemetery without needing to tell me to follow him.

What stretched out ahead of us was time. At the end of one of the passageways of dust, my uncle stopped in front of an upright piano that was cleaner than all the others. I realised that this piano was shining. My uncle's voice was soft. He told me that over the past months he had been trying to bring this piano to life. He'd looked for the parts that were missing, replaced the parts that were damaged, rotten. His face showed that it knew sadness. My uncle had tried to repair the piano to give it to the boy who would be born, but he hadn't been able to finish it in time. There was so little left to do. Then he asked me if I would finish sorting it out myself. He asked me to look for the final parts. I didn't altogether understand at that moment what it was he was saying to me, which was why I smiled. I smiled. I put my hand on his shoulder and said we'd have to fix the piano together. He made me promise I'd fix the piano, made me promise I'd give it to the boy who would be born. I replied yes, yes of course, and I smiled. I smiled. In the silence that followed those words and that smile, I wanted to give him the workshop keys, but he told me he'd go out, too. I was already thinking about my wife, about my child about to be born. I went out with my uncle, closed the big workshop door, and as I ran I said goodbye with broken words.

When I reached the house, when I went into the bedroom, my wife already had Simão in her arms. Our daughters were round her and I approached the happiness. I held the happiness in my arms.

The following day my uncle didn't come to the workshop in the morning, nor did he appear mid-morning. He didn't come the next week, nor the next month, nor the next year, or ever again. Time passed. For the rest of the whole of my life, for all the days that would pass until that Sunday when I died in that hospital bed, I never saw my uncle again.

The piano he had started to repair was the part of me that still waited for him. I never repaired it. Dust covered it, making it indistinguishable from all the other pianos beside it that had temporarily died.

Later I remembered the hours, I remembered the goodness that shaped my uncle's blind, dirty face, standing watching me or talking, talking – the stories that flowed from his body as though there were no end to the stories to be told. Later, too late.

In the truck, Marta's husband is driving, annoyed. He doesn't speak, he doesn't hear, he looks straight ahead and he drives. Beside him, Maria and my wife have Íris and Hermes on their laps. On the back, wrapped in the noise of the engine and the wind, Marta travels in her armchair, and Ana and Elisa hold on to the bars of the truck. Up in front, Íris and Hermes are making up words to say when they get to Lisbon. In the back, the wind is making their hair into unusual shapes and doesn't let them speak, but occasionally Ana brings her lips to Elisa's ear and says words that no one else hears and that no one remembers.

Marta tries to see all the streets before they reach the workshop. She turns her head this way and that. They arrive at the workshop. Marta gets up from her chair and remains still, waiting for her husband to go into the *taberna* and come out with a few men. My grandchildren wait leaning on the wall. Maria and my wife surround the men, as though their stretched-out arms or their anxiety served some purpose. Two men hold Marta under her arms. Slowly. Slowly, the husband and another man receive her and with the care of something heavy and fragile deposit her on the ground.

Marta's husband returns to the *taberna* with the men. My wife chooses the right key and opens the big workshop doors. Going in, the children run on to the dirt floor. My daughters and my wife don't run, but their faces are rejuvenated, and as they go into the carpentry shop they are children, too. There are squares of wood on the floor, there are pieces of laths – so many possibilities. My work bench is arranged as Francisco left it. The bench which was my uncle's, which Simão uses when he arrives in the morning asking Francisco for a few days' work, is covered with scattered tools. My daughters know, as my wife knows, that nothing bad can happen in the workshop. As they walk their voices are simple and free. They are children. Maria opens the big patio door and goes down, followed by Marta and my wife. My grandchildren grab pieces of wood, they make houses and swords. Íris goes out of the carpentry shop on her own, she crosses the entrance hall and makes her way alone into the piano cemetery. Elisa, Ana and Hermes are being kept occupied, they don't see her and think she's on the patio with my wife, Maria and Marta. My wife, Maria and Marta notice little things, weeds growing between the pine shavings; they don't see her and they think she's in the carpentry shop with Elisa, Ana and Hermes.

Íris walks through the piano cemetery. She looks all around her. She can make out the edges of the shadows. She lifts lids off keyboards. She presses down on keys that make dry sounds, wood against wood. She sits down on the lid of a piano without legs, on the dust. She is so small. She lifts her face, looks at me and says:

'Who are you talking to?'

Silence.

'I'm talking to the people who are reading these words in a book.'

'Maybe my mum will read the book, won't she?'

'Maybe.'

'What are they called, these people who're reading the book?'

'They have many names. Each of them has a different name.'

'Maybe there's one of them called Íris, isn't there?'

'Yes, maybe.'

Silence.

'And you – what's your name, sir?'

'Me?'

Silence.

'I'm your grandad.'

Íris smiles. Her voice:

'Grandad . . .'

I smile.

'What are they like, these people reading the book? Are they Grandma and Auntie?'

'They are, but they are other people, too.'

'Where are they, the other people?'

'Only they know where they are. We'd have to ask them to take a look around them. We'd have to ask them to shut their eyes.'

Íris shuts her eyes, tightly as she can.

'See? These people are just like that. They close their eyes, and they still exist. They close their eyes, block their ears, and they still exist.'

Íris opens her eyes. She gets up. She stops looking at me. She approaches the keyboard of one of the pianos. With her bandaged hand, she sticks out her index finger and presses down on a key. She presses down on another key. It is as though a long time has passed, but only a moment has passed. She looks at me again.

'How do you know, Grandad?'

'I've been one of those people.'

'But have you already read this book the people are reading?'

'No. It's not finished yet. The story isn't over yet. There are still a lot of words before it finishes. On the blank pages there's space for all those words, only they haven't been said yet. They haven't been heard yet.'

'So how come you've already been one of those people? Have you already lived the life these people are living?'

'No one can live someone else's life.'

'That's not true. You didn't just live your life. Have you seen Grandma? You wore her down. You made her old before all the other women her age. Say what you like – the light clouded your eyes, you didn't see, there was some force that carried your movements, you couldn't feel – say what you like, but the truth will still exist – the truth.'

'You're not even three yet, you can't talk like that. No three-year-old talks like that.'

'I can't? I can't? You're sure of that? You're dead. You should be the last person to talk about what I can and can't say. What are you afraid of? I don't believe you've forgotten the mornings you went out and left Grandma losing hope of receiving any affection, nor the evenings when you got in late, with the smell of the *taberna* embedded in your clothes

179

and your skin, nor the week after week when you just went out in the morning and got in at night and nothing else. The conversations during and after dinner getting shorter and shorter, until they were nothing more than the soup sipped from the spoon and the shadows in the kitchen – until they were nothing. And if the soup was too hot, if it was raining outside, if you were annoyed, you might throw the bowl on the floor, you might push Grandma, knock her down, make her cry and pretend not to hear, pretend it didn't bother you, that her sadness meant nothing. You don't want to hear, but you have to hear. And my mother? And Aunt Marta? You taught them that their father, their only father, can grab their mother by the arm, look at her with disdain and push her against a wall.'

'I taught them many other things. I always liked my daughters. I always thought about them. I always wanted them to be happy.'

'That's not enough. You never really listened to them, you never really looked at them. You were afraid. You're still afraid. The saddest thing isn't that you're lying to the people who are reading the book, who don't know you and won't ever know you. The sad thing is that you're lying to yourself. The sad thing is Uncle Francisco getting ready to run in the marathon at the Olympic Games without any memories of you ever, at any time, telling him that you were proud of him. Everything he has achieved has been without you, against you. And Uncle Simão? You can't have forgotten all the harm you did to him. You didn't lose him on that night that you'll never forget. You lost him long before that. And me, too, my sister, Elisa, Hermes. You died, you're dead, but your mistakes remain alive. Your mistakes remain.'

'Not everything is my fault. Or is it?'

'I'm the one who's not yet three years old, or have you already forgotten that? You were the husband, the father, the grandfather.'

'Yes, but I wasn't only the husband, father and grandfather, I was other things, too.'

'You were what you always were, and still are: an egotist.'

She walks towards the piano where she had been sitting. She sits again. There is a moment of silence that brings back the afternoon light, Sunday through the little dirty window. Maria's voice is heard calling Íris's name. Hearing her mother call her, she lifts a finger in the air. They have noticed her absence. Now she has to go. She looks at me, smiles, gets up and with clumsy steps she leaves. She is nearly three years old.

The air in the piano cemetery is clear.

Francisco came up to just above my knee. He walked back and forth in the kitchen and in the yard. His little legs, in their little trousers, didn't stop. Francisco was like a serious, animated doll. I called him. He didn't come. Marta, or Maria, or Simão called him. He didn't go. There always had to be someone walking behind him to make sure he didn't get caught on doors, climb chairs, knock over brimming saucepans. His hair grew and became unruly. His hands were small, holding on to the pieces of crust his mother gave him. His eyes were the size of everything they saw. His mother called him. He ran towards her and held out his arms for her to pick him up.

Everyone, even Íris, can imagine the end of the afternoon. There is a constant breeze. It comes down the road and makes scattered grains of earth shine, like stars. It makes specks in Maria's eyes shine. My wife and Marta shake sawdust from their clothes. There is a pile of pieces of wood arranged on the back of the truck, next to the armchair. In the winter Marta will pick pieces out and burn them in the fireplace. Birds are becoming calmer in the air, like the branches of the trees, like voices or stones. Time is dull in Maria's gaze. Her husband hasn't arrived, doesn't arrive, hasn't arrived to ask her forgiveness, come home, no, no he doesn't say – come home. Hermes runs round the truck. My granddaughters are delicate, they start their goodbyes with little gestures, tender smiles. Marta's husband comes out of the *taberna* with the men who've come to help him. They come, laughing. They lift Marta up, take two steps back, two steps forwards, and deposit her on the truck.

Maria has to go back home. My wife, Ana and Íris are at her side. The truck moves away. Marta, sitting in the armchair, waves. Hermes leans out of the window. The truck moves away. And disappears. They are alone outside the workshop doors. Maria takes the first step. She has to go home. She walks ahead. Behind her, my wife gives our granddaughters her hands. Every step for Maria is another defeat. The afternoon moves away, beaten. There is a week to go before Francisco runs in the marathon at the Olympic Games. It is still Sunday. As she passes the end of our road, my wife cranes her neck to see the façade of our house, the deserted space in front of it, to imagine it inside. Maria knows that the world's roads are endless – veins spread across the surface of the world. You could walk down roads your whole life, until you have no more strength in your legs, you fall to your knees and die, transform slowly, with the rain, with the years, into the stones of the pavement, dissolve between the stones, like dust, like water, disappear.

Ana and Íris know other things. They don't notice the shock that shakes the body of their grandmother, my wife, when she recognises the gypsy who two days earlier knocked on her door and handed her the blouse which she had been hanging out and which she had dropped. He's leaning on a corner, his knee bent and the sole of his boot against the wall. He watches, though keeping his head down. His eyes between the black hat and the long white beard. His eyes buried in the wrinkled, burned skin. My wife hurries her steps, pulling our granddaughters by the arm. And they continue to make their way down the streets, after Maria. And they arrive, together, at the door to the building. Time is dull. My wife, Maria and my granddaughters, before going in, they think they know everything that is going to happen.

Kilometre sixteen

the sun inside a fire. Running between flames, crossing ruins that sag over flames that move as though dancing, happy at the destruction, and finding in the centre of this fire the sun, the sole emperor, immense, serene, witnessing the consummation of his work, the inevitable dissemination of the evil he has created, that he wished to create

in search, search of the wind. Because my will is as big as a law of the land. Because my strength determines the passage of time. I want. I am capable of launching a shout within me that tears up trees by the roots, that bursts veins in every body, that pierces through the world. I am capable of running right through this shout, at its own speed, against everything that hurls itself to stop me, against everything that rises up in my way, against myself. I want. I am capable of expelling the sun from my skin, of defeating it once more and for ever. Because my will regenerates me, gives me birth, rebirth. Because my strength is immortal.

like the night. I didn't have to say anything to Simão, because, even without having seen each other for months, even without having heard anything – anything – from him for months,

I understood his expressions. We walked like that, through deserted streets. There was a certainty that was clear and confused, sharp, limpid and hazy, obvious and unbelievable, evident, sure, and impossible. I was going to have a child. She and I, we were going to have a child. There was so much to say, to ask, but she went into the house and closed the door. She closed the door. I walked through deserted streets, my brother accompanied me, and I thought about what I could have said, what I could have asked. There was nothing to be said, nothing to ask. In the heart of the night, the cold entered me through the sleeves of my jacket, under my sweater, under my shirt, against my skin. We arrived at Benfica. Soon we would be arriving home. Simão stopped, and before saying goodbye asked if he could work with me in the workshop for a few days. Yes, of course. I never knew whether Simão asked for days in the workshop when he really needed the work, needed to make some money, a little, or when he missed being my brother. He explained to me where he was living – the house where he rented a room – and before he moved away, as he was saying see you tomorrow, I wanted to hug him, to tell him I was going to have a child and to cry – not out of sadness or out of happiness but because at that moment I was a child. Instead I continued my walk home, like the night, like the hours

through the July heat, the afternoon

through the December cold, the night

through the July heat, the afternoon – this afternoon – I remember those moments when I'd come running out of the workshop, alone, training for being here, alone, and when I imagined what might happen when I was here, never believing that I'd remember what I imagined I would think, never believing that I was already thinking what I'm thinking now.

and I had taken a decision. There was nothing to decide, I couldn't change what was set, but just let my arms and legs lose their strength on the bed, just let my body rest, accept the night, when, in the darkness of my room, I convinced myself that I had taken a decision. I was going to have a child, and so I would be another person. I didn't know, however, that the next day was going to be so long, and in the morning when I arrived at the door of the workshop and saw my brother – the white lid of his right eye, his cracked lips – I was able to smile sincerely. After explaining to him what there was to do, I leaned over my bench to continue the work I'd begun the day before. It had been some weeks since my brother's voice had sounded in the air of the carpentry shop. It had been some weeks since the specks of sawdust – rising, hovering like a universe – had been touched by my brother's voice. It happened slowly, it was nearly mid-morning when he spoke a few words. From these loose, spaced-out words – just their syllables, almost – phrases grew. Piled up like a muddled tower, stories grew. Slowly, my brother was the lad who told me endless stories. My brother was still coming back. But I had other stories, divided up into phrases, divided up into words, trembling inside me. Distress. When lunchtime arrived, I told Simão that I wouldn't be long. There were a lot of people on the streets, too many – solid shapes. I arrived at her house and knocked at the door. The lady – her smile – the corridor

– the music from the piano – invisible cornucopias – the pictures on the walls – the door to the hall. Behind me the lady disappeared. I opened the door. She stopped playing and looked at me. Her skin was even lighter, under the brightness of her eyes. Her smooth hair followed the straight line of her back. Her hands. Her white, thin hands taking off my clothes as my hands took off her clothes. My hands running over the surface of her skin. Her hands squeezed against my back. My hands gripping her arms, wrapping around them. The palms of my hands wrapping round her arms. Her hands digging into the nape of my neck. My hands opening, losing all their strength, grabbing at the air. Her hands stretched out over the rug. Our hands' forgotten time. And her hands, alive. Her hands, animals – cats, birds, wild animals – on the piano keys. And the music stretched over the whole hall, the whole air, the whole world, inside my naked body, inside the ribs arched on the rug – music being breathed. And again, reality – the cold, strange clothes on my body. The streets – my body a stranger to myself. The afternoon passed within my brother's monotonous voice, his monotonous enthusiasm, within time that repeated itself. I closed the big workshop doors. My brother went into the *taberna*. I was ready and I started to run. I ran as though I wanted to, as though I was able to overtake the wind, as though my body didn't exist and it was only my will that ran, that was fast, fast between the houses one after another, the streets, and everything I didn't want to see. I arrived home. I washed. I walked across the city. At the entrance to the hospital, as I waited for her, my decision became more solid within me. There were night-time noises, the branches of the trees moving over the nocturnal imprecision of the cold, the lit-up windows of the hospital, and me. Ruled by time, utterly, I waited for her and my decision became

Kilometre seventeen

evening falling. Another summer afternoon comes to an end. Marta is already a woman, she's sixteen years old. Maria imitates all her gestures awkwardly – she is fourteen years old. In the kitchen our mother is doing something simple, superfluous, and another summer afternoon comes to an end. The lightness that comes in through the bedroom window, that touches the folds in the curtains, is yellow and sweet – honey. Beyond the window, the sun comes down on buildings and for a moment turns their edges incandescent. The lightness touches the face of my sister Marta, sitting on her made bed, and touches the face of my sister Maria, sitting on the floor, sitting on her feet, knees bent in front of her, leaning against the wall. Marta has a boyfriend, and no one knows, no one must know, except for Maria. Sometimes at dinner Maria and Marta exchange a look because something has reminded them of their secrets. Maria dreams of the day when she too will have a boyfriend, she dreams about him. For a few moments, like a lightning flash, she believes she can see his face: every detail, the eyes, the lips, the lines that are so real. Marta and Maria's voices and dreams are mingled together. Marta describes everything she feels, she describes a thousand times all the little encounters she has with her boyfriend, everything she believes, everything she under-stands. Maria describes the stories she has read in romance novels, she describes how they end, she says, 'If this hadn't happened, and if that hadn't happened, if he hadn't been jealous, if she hadn't been proud.' Maria listens to her sister as though she has finally met a heroine from a romance novel. Marta listens to her sister, imagining herself having the same dilemmas as the heroine from a romance novel. Their voices are feminine, and luminous. The afternoon draws to an end slowly. Simão arrives from work, comes by me and my mother. Time is calm over the objects of the world, and in the motion of the world. My father will arrive later. Until then, the evening falling, like torn paper raining down from the sky.

my decision within me. They were shadows. She approached, coming out of the shadows. When I noticed she was there, she was already very close, she could almost have touched me if she'd reached out an arm. She took three steps, and she could have touched me if she'd reached out an arm. The words I'd chosen, and repeated, and memorised to say to her, were lost. As though I knew no other words, I just looked at her. Her voice, rescuing me. A chasm hadn't opened up into the centre of the earth, the rivers hadn't run with blood, night hadn't frozen over the city. Her voice, in simple words, telling me that everything was all right, the universe was still going, I could breathe. I breathed. And it was there, in front of the hospital where my father had died, on that strangely real night, that I held her hands and said to her liquid eyes, 'We're getting married.'

by one another. Groups of runners pass me. I don't know what wind it is that's carrying them along. The sun presses me against the ground. The sun bends my back, the ground pulls at my chest, but I am stronger, stronger, bigger than the exhaustion. I've long known that moment when the body starts repeating: give up, give up, give up. My legs don't give up. Give up, give up, give up. But I am still alternating my arms ahead of my body, as though punching the air, as though fighting the air and it was getting ever weaker, ever closer to giving up. And my body is heavier than the ship that brought me out of Lisbon. Give up, give up, give up. I don't give up. Groups of runners pass me now, the wind carries them along, but I am bigger than the exhaustion. The sun, defeated, will leave me to the silence. On my skin the special grease that covers me will be cool again. I'll stop hearing the voice that repeats in my head – the sun. I'll keep hearing the voice that exists in my core – my will. The sun will stop to torture them and I'll overtake them in triumph, the air will be light again, I will thank the wind that brushes my cheeks to cool me. I haven't given up. I'm not giving up now. My wife and my son are waiting for me. My son will wait for me before being born. When he is born I'll have this, this will, to give him. His face, small, unimaginable, will look at me and understand that he has been born out of an energy that is greater, more incandescent, more intense than the sun. Feeling himself protected in my arms – these arms – the same arms that now alternate ahead of my chest and which are like two worlds – day, night. Two lives separated by a moment that doesn't exist. Two lives that alternate, that repeat and follow one another, endlessly, after everything, endlessly, endlessly

never, the night when that thing happened that we'll never be able to forget. I was ten years old, and I knew it wouldn't be long before I'd start accompanying my father in the mornings when it was time for him to go off to the workshop. It was a November which had rain every day. There was no difference between Mondays and Tuesdays. Wednesdays, Thursdays and Fridays were all the same. I was sitting at the end of the kitchen table. I had a pencil in my hand, my exercise book in front of me and I was finishing an exercise of casting out nines. When I made a mistake I didn't have a rubber so I'd rub out with little pieces of bread. My mother would say, 'The bread's not for ruining.' My sisters, when they walked by, would lean over the exercise book and scorn the dirty pages – grey charcoal clouds. It was getting dark early, and when Simão arrived I could imagine the opaque night in the yard, over the branches and thick leaves of the lemon tree. Simão smiled at our sisters and our mother. Simão liked talking to me. When we were alone he'd spend hours telling me all the words his head could think of, but with our mother and our sisters he could manage no more than a little voice of embarrassment. That was his way of adoring them, of looking at them from a distance, of being happy at their happiness, of hiding an absolute feeling behind his face, as though hiding a well, a mineshaft. And with our father, not even a smile, not even a meaning that was only imagined. Only silence. Deep and opaque like the night. Life went on in the kitchen, with my mother and sisters, organised, getting the dinner finished – their steps around the table. After washing his arms and face, Simão sat down, his palms turned up towards the fire. The wick of the oil lamp and the fire undid the shadows that fell against the walls, cleaned the shadows in the most hidden corners. Maria began to lay the table. No one found it odd that Simão had sat down. His place was at one end of the table. I finished up my schoolwork and sat down at my place. When there was nothing left but to set down the tureen in the middle of the table, my sisters sat down at their places. As though the gaze from each of us were a ribbon reaching out from our bodies, we followed our mother's path with the tureen until she reached the table. Marta served us all. My mother went to fetch the bread, a knife, and went to do other things, because there were, after all, still things to be done. Marta, Maria, Simão and I had already started eating when we heard the front door bang clumsily, not closing, banging again, staying closed. We all knew then that

Kilometre eighteen

our father had just arrived. When he opened the kitchen door and came in, bumping into the doorpost, no one looked at him. He had been at the *taberna*. When he spoke, we recognised the voice he spoke with. It was a wet, rounded voice, sometimes slurred. It was a voice that hesitated on random syllables, as though falling asleep in the middle of a word, as though it wasn't going to finish it. It was a voice that alternated between serious and seriouser. Words pressed themselves against one another in this voice. Our mother didn't reply to him. Marta, Maria, Simão and I kept eating. Our father's sweater was rough, it prickled. I recognised its touch. It was brown, stained, with little holes in the knitting, elbows worn, with dust, sawdust, wood shavings. Our father. We recognised the voice that he used to speak to our mother, and to nobody, a voice with which he complained that we hadn't waited for him to start our dinner. Underneath his dragging, badly articulated, repeated words, silence. After a moment, our mother pulled out his chair, and as though speaking to a child, told him to sit. Our father ran his fingers through his hair – dust, sawdust, wood shavings – muttered some incomprehensible grumblings, turned his head one way – his voice muffled – turned his head the other way and sat. Our mother filled his plate with soup and continued on towards the things she had to do. He was serious, his expression frozen. And suddenly he woke up. He looked for his spoon. Grumbling, he waved his spoon in the air, eventually bringing it down into the soup. He lifted the spoon again, and again brought it down into the soup. He lifted the spoon again, opened his mouth, but once again brought it down into the soup. My brother and sisters and I kept eating. Our father asked our mother why we hadn't waited for him. She didn't reply. Our father lifted his full spoon, waited and threw it back down into the plate. And he asked why we hadn't waited for him. Our mother didn't reply. Getting angrier and angrier, his eyes changing, he asked again why we hadn't waited for him. Our mother didn't reply. He stood up suddenly, and the chair fell on to its back. He took two steps towards our mother and grabbed her by the arm, squeezed her arm. He turned her towards him. There was a wall of hell in his eyes. Again he asked her the same question. She didn't seem very scared. Again he asked her the same question. A moment of still-ness – breathing. And he gave her a shove in the back. Our mother fell to her knees on the kitchen floor. Simão got up from his place. Our father turned to face him. He touched him with his rage. And he turned to face our mother. He came closer to her. Again he asked her the same question. She again didn't reply. Our father raised his hand to strike her, letting the blows fall wherever they might. Maybe her face, maybe her back. He had his arm in the air, when he felt a hand holding his wrist. It was Simão. His lips were pursed and his eyes were also burning. As though unable to believe it, in his hate, our father turned towards him. Without anyone noticing, our mother got up and leaned against a wall. My father's gaze and Simão's, meeting one another, were a single iron bar. But our father wasn't afraid of anything. His strength was invincible. He tugged his arm free. My brother continued to look at him with all the strength of his left eye, challenging him. Simão was a man of sixteen. He wasn't afraid of anything. For a moment, our father understood whole sentences in that gaze, and wanted to shut them up, and wanted to silence them for ever from out of that blind gaze. The thick palm of his hand came through the air. A quick movement by my brother held his arm. Our father didn't want to believe it. Our father's strength against Simão's strength. Blood flowing in their veins. Our father. Fury, rage, unable to do anything. With both hands my brother pushed him. Our father was down where he'd fallen, humiliated, incredulous. He got up, ran to Simão and was pushed again, and fell again. He got up, wary, his voice blocked by something he wasn't able to say, and he shouted, 'Out!' He pointed at the door, his arm shaking, and called him names, every kind of name, and shouted: 'Out!' My brother, over his voice, shouted, 'You'll never see me again!' The words stabbed into our chests, tore our skin, through our ribs, stabbing like knives one after another into our hearts. Our mother's face, begging. Our sisters' faces, frightened, hurt. My face invisible. And the voices of Simão and our father the voices of men. Simão shouting: 'I'm never setting foot in this wretched house again!' And our father who didn't stop shouting, 'Out!' Not stopping: 'Out!' And Simão, taking nothing with him, not even a jacket, went out – the night – and slammed the door. Our mother, in silence, took two steps as though to follow him and stopped at the thundering of the door. We were still, under the cloak of wretchedness that covered us. Our father lost all his strength and was transformed into his own shadow. After that night Simão never came into the house again, and he never again saw our father.

Kilometre nineteen

forgive me, little girl. Please, forgive me. I know how your hands saved me. I can still remember your skin, your whole body, your eyes watching me through the darkness, your eyes shining. I want your voice, little girl, sweet little girl. We can dream together. We can sit together and share a thought. Forgive me. The days will go back to being the size they were when we walked across gardens hand in hand. The sun which illuminated us then must always exist to illuminate us. Forgive me. The same weightlessness continues, like light, like light, that filled us up. I ask you – forgive me. We are everything, again – we still believe. Time hasn't passed. The days will go back to being the surface on which we dream. The afternoons

alone. We married without witnesses and walked the streets hand in hand. Because I wanted a life that was just ours, I had replaced some things in the house. I'd built a new bed. I'd bought a mattress. I'd made a table and four chairs.

I'd bought a stove. My mother and my sisters only learned that we'd got married two days later, when I told them. My mother understood. My sisters didn't understand, but after ten minutes they'd forgotten their inability to understand. And they wanted to know what she was like. They wanted to meet her. They wanted to imagine our child. They smiled. Five weeks had passed since the night she told me she was pregnant. It was a Sunday afternoon, January. She had a three-month belly, her skin slightly raised. When we were alone I would run the palm of my hand over her belly. My mother was carrying Íris, Maria came holding Ana's hand, Elisa came holding Hermes's hand, Marta came alone. They arrived and occupied all the chairs we had. When we began to talk, Ana started playing with Hermes in a corner. My mother was happy at the house's being brought back to life. My sisters stared at my wife. They tried to talk to her, but it was hard for her to reply. At that time

sun that blinds us. I've just crossed a bridge and I pass a runner, stopped at the side of the road, hands resting on his bent knees, who has lost control of his breathing. The air, like a stone, goes in and out of him, the world goes in and out of him. He closes his eyes and his whole face grimaces. A small distance away there are people who don't get any closer but who watch him, fearful. I don't give up, I don't give up. The sun stabs needles into my eyes – needles made from lines of light. But still I go on, still I go on, still

go slowly past. My mother and my sisters said nothing, but were shocked to find the house almost empty. From that afternoon, whenever I went to Maria's I'd leave with something my mother had hidden to give me. No need to tell your sister. And she'd give me packets of biscuits, or bags of pears, or jars of fruits in syrup. She'd give me all kinds of things she'd hide under the iron couch where she slept, set up every night, dismantled every morning. When she took the train to visit Marta, she'd return laden with bags of spring greens, sprigs of parsley, oranges, salted bacon, *chouriço* sausages. I'd accept everything, ashamed because I thought they felt sorry for me, they thought I had nothing, I was the little boy who had nothing, unprotected. Because it was easier, I'd accept everything, and quickly leave.

reflected in the stones of the pavement. Lisbon is the sharp clarity that comes through the air. Lisbon is the stained colour of the walls. Lisbon is the new moss being born over the dry moss. Lisbon is the pattern of cracks, like lightning flashes, slipping down the surface of the walls. Lisbon is careful imperfection. Lisbon is the sky reflected

in the stones of the pavement. It was cold, the last week of January was beginning. There was ice on the weeds – blades – that grew between the stones of the pavement. My ears were frozen. My nose was frozen. My hands were in the pockets of my jacket, frozen. When I arrived at the road of the workshop I didn't expect to see Simão. But I reached the top of road, looked ahead and there, almost leaning on the big doors, was a shape beset by sharp movements. Each step I could make him out more clearly. When he noticed me he stopped still to wait for me. It was my brother – his blind face. I couldn't understand his smile. I understood the dirty skin of his face. I didn't understand his eagerness. I understood his hair spiky in stuck, solid, hard locks – dry oil. I was two steps away from him. We didn't greet one another. Not a good morning, not any word, not any syllable. I took two steps and, standing beside him, opened the door. Together we walked across the entrance hall of the workshop. My brother wanted to talk. There was some news he couldn't hold back. I was used to his news, his enthusiasms about nothing, which was why when we reached the carpentry shop, when we stopped, I was the one who spoke and told him I'd got married. Simão made an expression as though he were saying the appropriate phrases, he waited for a beat and then, when it seemed to him that he could speak, he said

Kilometre twenty

he'd found a piano for us to repair. And he waited for the reaction I didn't have. I breathed. Then he told me that one of the men in the *taberna* had told him about a piano he wanted to sell, that no one had played for years, covered in a sheet. I asked him if he thought we didn't have enough old pianos, if he thought we didn't have enough ruined pianos, gathering dust in the piano cemetery. My brother's face lost the shape of his eagerness. But then he immediately said we could repair it, make it as good as new and then sell it. I smiled at his naivety. I knew that even if we managed to fix this piano – which might be rotten, might be irreparable – we'd never be able to sell it. Because I felt sorry for his childish expression I told him that when could we'd go and see what condition the piano was in. Maybe the following day, maybe the following week, maybe never. I didn't want to make my promise concrete, but it was enough for my brother to set about sawing, sanding, starting his endless, disconnected, incomplete, incomprehensible stories with enthusiasm. Not listening to him, I had a single thought – it filled my whole morning – all the possibilities of a single thought. There was a long time before lunch and I looked at my watch, looked at my watch, again looked at my watch. The hands moved too slowly. When I stopped being able to bear it, it was the beginning of the end of the morning. I put down my tools, told my brother I wouldn't be long and went out. The streets. Benfica, they were the birds that came down from the sky to settle in front of me and to take flight as I passed. The people, disorientated. Benfica, they were the puddles of water that reflected me for an instant. January. Benfica, it was the cold wind that moulded me. I knocked on the door. How long did I wait? The lady opened the door to me with the same smile as the other days, but to me, that late morning, it was as if she were another lady with another smile. I followed her down the corridor. The doors to the hall. The details of the shapes – curved, straight, angled – were too sharp, they seemed to be wanting to speak to me, they seemed to be wanting to dissuade me. There were times I closed my eyes, and there were times I forced myself to keep my eyes open. That was how it was when I went into the hall and saw her sitting at the piano. The keys – the strings – the notes all hurling themselves towards me and piercing me. Threads of blood flowing from my wounds like signs, traces that showed my guilt of a crime I had not yet committed, but which was inevitable. I hid my uncertainty behind a firm gaze, a mask of feigned determination. When she finished playing, the lady had disappeared behind me. When she finished playing, seeing me, her face changed because she understood at once. Then, suddenly, the words I had thought of all morning at the workshop, the whole way over, the words I'd woken up with. Suddenly looking at her face, I didn't know how to say anything but the rough, single, impossible words, words worn away from being so often repeated in my head, endless, like thorns, like spears, made of stone, made of night, made of winter, each syllable as though final, inevitable once spoken, separating flesh from bones, dead, dead, dying, killing, covering the whole world with the absolute darkness of their own death. The last time we'd see one another. I told her it was the last time we'd see one another. Her expression was wounded with the hurt. Silence. After disbelief, tears – liquid, limpid, glassy clarity. She walked to the window, turned her back on me and stood facing the cold white remains of the morning. Her body in her dress slipping across the rug. I walked over to her. I put my hands on her shoulders

last time will never come

and I didn't say anything to her. I waited for my hands, just the weight and the touch of my hands, to tell her everything that was true and couldn't be named. The last time we'd see one another – each gesture, each moment. She turned back towards me and we looked at one another with a strength of believing for a moment that there was no god that could part us. Then straight away, with a certainty that stabbed against us, much greater than a single moment, we knew that we really would be parted. It was the last time we'd see one another. Everything was the last. She fell into my arms. I squeezed her body, crushed it. We rested our heads on each other's shoulders – our cheeks touching – hot tears. Time passed. We drew away to look at one another. We exchanged glances. I took off her dress. I removed my clothes. Our bodies. And the white light on us. And my body against hers, my body beating, beating, beating against her body, crushing it. And my fingers. Lightly. The points on her skin that my fingers touched. Gentle. And the repeated clash of flesh. And the disfigured faces. And the light, intense, from everywhere, permanent, constant, blind. We lay there on the carpet, side by side – our heads under the piano. We had no words. We had silence. We had our breathings, and what we could see, suddenly real. We had time bringing truth and sadness back to us. She didn't get up, didn't walk naked, didn't sit at the piano. She stayed lying there, without strength, without life – her gaze undone. I got up. I dressed, slowly. My clothes didn't heal the wounds on my torn body. The last time we'd see one another. I walked over to the door to the hall, leaving her lying on the carpet, without looking back. I reached the hall door and looked back. Her face believed I was going to go back, I was going to take steps back to her arms, to her naked, abandoned body. I didn't go back. I opened the hall door and ran through the quick impossible maze of the corridor. I opened the door to the street and ran, lost, destroyed, through the Benfica streets.

weight, my legs, my arms alternating. Or perhaps it's the blood in my body weighing me down, draining me. The vest and shorts stick to the grease. The sweat I'm not sweating is boiling me under my skin. Maybe it's the sweat weighing me down, draining me. The houses are further and further away. The houses beside me. The people in the windows. I don't look at the runners passing me. I look at my legs – their perpetual movement. Feet touching the ground, lifting me up, moving me onwards. Legs. I trip over myself. I fall on the palms of my hands

Kilometre twenty-one

and get up. I mustn't stop. I rub my hands to get the memory of the stones, the loose grains of sand, off my skin. The stones burn – embers. The sight of Stockholm wavers. The façades of the houses contort. Blisters the colour of the houses rise up, holes

because it might have been an afternoon in June. I can't be sure. It might also have been an afternoon in late May, or even July, but it wasn't very hot. It was a quiet afternoon. My father didn't mind me going out on to the patio, didn't ask me where I was going. Some thoughts were distracting him from me. Perhaps he was thinking about pianos. My steps crunched over pine shavings until I reached the big patio doors. I was still a lad. I was thirteen, fourteen years old. Marta still lived in the house near the workshop. When I went in, Simão was already there. He'd gone to see Elisa who was still so little but already walking, already running, and at that moment she'd just awoken from her nap. Simão was playing around with her. Marta was smiling. Their voices mingled with the pleasant lightness that came in through the half-open windows. I went in, to those smiles and those voices. That afternoon, like many others before and after it, Simão's presence was always clandestine because we couldn't tell our father we'd seen him, we couldn't mention him. There were other times when my mother would hide and ask us about him in a whisper. We'd reply to her, hidden, whispering. Discreetly, so that Elisa wouldn't notice, Marta told us she was going to the workshop, that she wouldn't be long, that she was going to fetch a hammer and nails, which she needed for something unimportant – hammer a nail, hang a picture. Marta's husband had gone out to deal with a few things including borrowing a hammer and nails from the workshop, but hours had gone by and he still hadn't got back. Perhaps he'd been occupying himself in the *taberna*, Marta said. Simão and I distracted Elisa so that our sister could go out without the little girl noticing, without her crying, without her insisting on going, too. My brother and I made little kiddie voices, saying words that didn't exist – and the sound of the front door, almost imperceptible, opening and closing. Marta, surrounded by that afternoon that might have been June, walked down the street – her steps unconcerned – she walked down the earth road of the workshop. There were birds, sparrows, flying overhead. There were the distant sounds of the city, within the distant sounds of nature. Marta walked towards the workshop, and although it was close, because she left home so little it seemed a great distance, an excursion. As she passed the *taberna* door, she leaned in to see if her husband was inside, having lost track of time. He wasn't. There were only

the heat – the fire – the heat – the flames – the heat – the embers – the heat – the heat – no escape – I run, run away – no escape from the heat, the fire

two men, asleep. One was standing, his whole weight leaning against the counter; the other was sitting in a crooked chair, his elbows digging into the dirty tabletop, his head on his hands. There was no one behind the bar. Inside the *taberna* it was a different month and a different time of day. Marta left this suspended image behind her, and went on. She took slow steps, making the most of her freedom. I think she was smiling. Not an open, obvious smile, but a gentle touch to her face. It was a time for breathing deeply, for filling your whole body with clean, new air. Marta went into the workshop, through the big doors, and she still hadn't got used to the shadows when she noticed the sounds that were coming from the piano cemetery. She thought it might be our father and she took a silent step, about to call out to him. Suddenly she stopped, turned to stone, when in the space between two piled-up pianos, behind a wall of pianos, she made out half the face of her husband. Her husband's shirtsleeves were rolled up, his arms were around the back of a woman. The eager breathing of the two of them as they kissed. Her husband's mouth fixing itself to a woman's neck. Her husband's mouth seeking out a woman's mouth. In silence, Marta took two steps back. In the entrance hall of the workshop, her body, covered by a dress in a flowery print. That moment something came down from the sky, came from the centre of the earth, went through her. She touched her face with both hands to make sure she existed. She didn't have to wait long. Her husband came out of the piano cemetery with an expression of feigned casualness, looking vaguely left and right. He could easily have seen her. Marta was behind a few pieces of pine that leaned upright against a wall. Her heart was beating. A good deal of her body was in view. But he didn't see her, he walked across the earth, between the stones, and into the carpentry shop. Marta heard her husband's voice, the other side of a wall, muffled, distant, greeting our father. It was only later, slowly, that she saw the woman who came out of the piano cemetery. It was Maria. As she walked she was adjusting her blouse, wiping the dust from her skirt. Without noticing a thing, she hurried out through the door.

Kilometre twenty-two

on the new table I'd made. As soon as my wife's belly began to be noticeable, two weeks before we were married, she stopped working at the hospital. She was sent home. That night, when I came in, she was sitting in a chair, she was still, looking at the door. She had nothing to do. The dinner was ready. The house was tidy. But the look in her eyes wasn't simple, there was hurt in it that I wasn't able to understand completely, that made me feel guilty. It was as though the look in her eyes, in mine, touched me with guilt. I smiled at her, nervously. She didn't smile back. Her face, lit up by the oil lamp, remained serious. I said some word to her – 'So?' She didn't reply. As though I was unaware of the hardness of her gaze because there was no reason to justify it, I went towards the washroom. I had my back to my wife when I heard her voice. She asked, 'Do you still like me?' I lowered my eyelids over my eyes to feel the weight that dropped within me – lead. I opened my eyes and turned towards her, smiling. I approached, then put my hands – thick, coarse, rough hands – on her shoulders. I bent down to kiss her, but she pulled her face away and asked me again: 'Do you still like me?' There was a moment when we looked at one another, and when I bent down again she didn't move away and we kissed. My wife's lips were strange, for a moment. And only slowly they went back to being familiar. After that her gaze and her silence were beseeching. As though I didn't understand, I managed to smile at her again. Trying to reduce the importance of her beseeching, I turned my back on her and walked towards the washroom. However much I tried to avoid it, I carried with me the image of her body, naked, lying on the hall rug. As I took my steps, I could hear her in my head still playing piano. I could make out the smell of her body on my skin. I filled my hands with water

fill my hands with fire, flames, embers

because you know the unnameable. And you will go on, with me always, escaping the names that are not you, you'll go on eliminating the distance of years and time. When dying, you'll dream you're still alive. Who could say that, being dead, you'll dream of still being alive, or still being alive you'll merely be dreaming that you've died? Today, now, you exist in me, you are beautiful in my heart. We are once again

to throw it over my face, to be reborn. I held the towel with both hands and wiped myself down. We had dinner. The night passed at the speed of the oil lamp on the table, slowly. That day I hadn't done any training, but I lay down in bed and felt more exhausted than after my Sunday marathons. I was more tired than I am now with the sun trying to kill me. I was tired inside. Covered by a sheet, I rested the palm of my hand on my wife's belly, on our child. And that was how I woke up the following morning, with courage again, with strength, my own master. In the bedroom, as I dressed, my wife watched me. In the kitchen, as I had my coffee, my wife watched me. In the street – the light. A neighbour said good morning to me through the cold. It was as though his voice

the sun aims all its strength at my eyes, I run against the sun, I enter it

was coming through a pane of glass. I replied, but didn't hear my own voice. I didn't stop. Icy wind came into me through the sleeves of my jacket, my sweater, my shirt, in through the bottoms of my trouser legs. Between my clothes and my skin I had a layer of cold, a second skin. The workshop's earth road. The *taberna* was open, but there was no one there. It was a deserted marble counter, a table and two empty chairs. I didn't stop. The bunch of keys in my pocket. I opened the doors. My everyday steps, my everyday gestures, so different, so unknown, because these moments were present, and solid. They were moments of my solitude. I had learned to touch them, breathe them, to exist completely within them. Like when I ran down the streets and Lisbon was every month of the year. Like when I ran by and all the seasons of the year were the colours of my solitude. Deep and filled with unshareable meanings. I had known my solitude for a long time – all the thoughts I had above the silence, words pursuing an echo they never reached. It was within the difficulty of my solitude – a black path of statues – that I built myself up. That morning was made up of moments that belonged to that time. The sawdust that covered the floor silenced me. I went over to one of the windows to see winter on the patio, the sky clean and cold. I entered that endless picture. I disappeared. I came out of that endless picture. I walked over to my carpentry bench. The smell of the inside of the wood. I was holding the plane with both hands when the lady came in. Her face

Kilometre twenty-three

wasn't smiling. Frightened, hurt, concerned, she was a different person. A gold pin on the collar of her black jacket, and she was a different person. Small, thin, a different person. She asked me to go and look at the piano. When she noticed my surprise, or my discomfort, or my shyness, she begged me to go and look at the piano. I looked at her, not understanding. I had seen the piano the day before. I had been lying down, naked, underneath it. I couldn't understand how after just one night the piano could have caused such distress. I invented a thousand possibilities – perhaps it was a desperate subterfuge to make me come back, perhaps she needed me, or, more likely, perhaps there really was some problem with the piano, perhaps, perhaps, perhaps. All these ideas were accompanied and overlaid by the memory of her look when I told her it was the last time we'd be seeing one another, when she remained lying there for ever, naked; they were accompanied by the weight that sank my heart in my chest, in a well that I had inside my chest. I couldn't understand how something could have happened to the piano, but I told her I'd go. I didn't ask her what had happened, but I told her I'd go. I told her I had to wait for my brother, and that as soon as he arrived I'd go and take a look at the piano. Satisfied, but still frightened, still hurt, she went out. My head was filled

came into the carpentry shop without a word, extinguishing an uninteresting conversation. Her husband, who had been in the piano cemetery with Maria, looked at her and became annoyed. Our father looked at her without curiosity. Her husband asked her, 'What are you doing here?' Marta's voice was the voice of a clear, almost invisible shadow, and she said in a voice that was very worn, 'I've come to fetch a hammer.' And she was interrupted. 'Didn't I say I was coming? What's the hurry?' And with the same aggressiveness, the same disdain, he asked, 'And you left the girl on her own?' Marta made herself look him in the eye. Her voice, pale – 'She's stayed with Francisco.' Simão's name couldn't be spoken. Set apart from it all, it was only then that, without fretting, without saying anything, my father noticed my absence. In such a brief moment of silence, less than the space between words, Marta felt herself tremble inside. Her husband, severe, said to her, 'I'll get the hammer, I'll be right home.' Marta made herself look him in the eye. She wanted to see his cruelty. Mute, silent, she walked home. The world, within her and without, was a construction of blades she couldn't touch. At home she didn't see my face, or Simão's face. We talked about something or other, and we didn't really see her. Elisa got excited at her arrival – Mummy, Mummy, Mummy. Marta picked her up, and with her in her arms gave her a hug, her eyes closed, that lasted a long time. I said, 'I've got to go.' Simão came out with me. At the door to Marta's house, I went back to the workshop, Simão went off in the opposite direction. The afternoon was fragile over the city, over the distant vegetable gardens, over the streets and over the workshop road. The afternoon aimed its brightness at things. The afternoon came in through the windows of Marta's house and hurled itself in a torrent on to the floor. Elisa's short legs went round and round the kitchen table, her little hands looking for something they didn't know. Though no one knew it, without thinking about it herself, that was the day that Marta began to get fat. With slow movements she opened the door to a cupboard, took out a tin of lard cakes, hard and dry and covered in cinnamon and sugar, and sat down to eat them. Her gaze misted up in the empty air. She couldn't think about Maria. It was unbearable to her. Still chewing the last lard cake, she took two steps to the bench under the window and picked up an enamel plate filled with cold roast bacon. She took a knife from the cutlery drawer, got the bread basket and sat down to eat. When she started feeling full, she struck her closed fist against her chest.

with possibilities and contradictions. My brother arrived mid-morning. No sooner had I heard his steps on the earth of the entrance hall than I put down my tools and moved away from the carpentry bench. When he reached the carpentry shop I was shaking the sawdust from my trousers and the sleeves of my sweater. As he took three steps into the carpentry shop, opening his mouth, before he'd said a word I was past him, saying, 'I've got to go out, I won't be long.' He turned his whole head to watch my back with his wide-open left eye. Benfica was alive. Carts and motorcars passed, people passed, pigeons passed.

as though I had brought my hands too close to the fire, almost touching it, as though my whole body, this body, was my hands

passed by my sister Maria's street. It was late afternoon. There weren't many days left before I was off. My mother was at the window waiting for me, holding Íris in her arms, and as I passed she held her little hand at the wrist and they waved to me. From my mother's face, from her smile, I could tell that she was proud of me. It didn't take me long to reach São Sebastião de Pedreira. I was still taking it easy when I turned back. As far as Benfica, high on hope, I overtook every motorcar I met. I passed my sister Maria's street again. I couldn't make out any movement in the light beyond the window and the tulle curtains. I wanted to imagine that on that day my sister wouldn't fight with our mother, nor with her husband. I could remember when Maria and our mother started fighting about something or other. They'd begin by saying casual words, things that they didn't feel, hurting one another. Then they'd put on their tearful voices, accusing one another, and they might bring Maria's husband into the argument or they might bring in the children, Ana and Íris, who were also crying or who stayed together, hand in hand. I could remember when Maria and her husband started fighting. She might – or not – say two or three things that insulted him, or accused him. He'd start pushing her, or throwing plates on the floor, throwing glasses. Once, using his two hands, he split the porcelain tureen that had always adorned the centre of the kitchen table. Ana and Íris cried, or just stayed together, hand in hand. As I ran past I imagined that, on that day, neither Maria, nor her husband, nor our mother would fight. Two or three times a week I used to stop by, drink a glass of water and see if everything was all right. But that wasn't a day for stopping. That was a day to run and not stop.

Kilometre twenty-four

didn't smile. She had the frightened, hurt, worried expression that she'd shown me at the workshop a little over an hour earlier, but she was still distant. A distant lady. I followed her along the corridor. I'd known the way for a long time, but there was a pattern that we couldn't change, it was too late. For her I'd always be the image that I myself didn't know, millimetrically exact. We snaked our way along the hall in silence. Our steps were quick, there was a breeze that passed us, that we passed through. We reached the doors to the big hall. When she opened them in front of me, there was what I'd expected to see and there was what I saw – the piano, burned, destroyed, without legs, set on the floor. The walls near the piano were black with soot. The ceiling above the piano was black. The carpet around it was burned. I walked over, incredulous, and bent down to look at the piano which was almost completely burned up, its grey insides crossed by pieces of blackened metal, the sheets of wood that were still cooling off as embers, the surface of the varnish deformed by blisters where the wood hadn't been incinerated completely. Behind me the lady was a small, thin, old statue, and I didn't need to ask her any questions. I could imagine the moment when she hurled the lit oil lamp on to the piano. I could imagine the despair. I could imagine her standing there, her face turned to the piano in flames. The white skin of her face lit up by the flames. I could imagine the strings snapping inside the fire. I don't know what the lady expected me to say. I said nothing. I walked along the corridor alone, knowing that somewhere in the house she was there – the body I loved, the skin I knew completely, that I still know. The streets of Benfica didn't exist. I arrived at the workshop, went into the carpentry shop and Simão, absorbed in his thoughts, was startled at the speed of my return. Without letting him catch his breath, I asked him, 'Can we go and see the piano you were talking about yesterday?' In wonder, he looked at me with his left eye as if to say yes, as if not to say no. I grabbed him by the arm and we went out. I closed the big door and we walked together. He explained to me what it was like, the piano, the condition it was in. I didn't hear him.

the air boiling as it comes into me. I breathe boiling air

night was beginning on all the streets. In the kitchen my wife had her arms stretched out over the pan. Her pregnant belly meant that she had to keep this distance to shred parsley, coriander or any kind of herb. Having lost track of time, she said to me, 'You're here already?' I walked towards her to kiss her. As my lips approached and my chin ran along the skin of her shoulder, she shrugged her shoulder against her neck and with words broken by giggles she repeated, 'I don't want any sweaty kisses here, go and wash first.' But I kissed her, I kissed her again, and my kisses reached the surfaces of her skin that while she laughed she couldn't hide.

and I see the other runners in the distance. Like me, they're being punished. I know that they also used to be children who ran without fear. They were young lads, and they believed. In other places time has stopped for them, too, when their lips met lips. All over the world, in squares, on staircases, in tunnels, on bridges, the simple gesture of lips getting closer, skin that begins to touch at the threshold of its outlines, that joins, slowly and completely, and remains, skin against skin, lips lips; all over the world, under many, so different trees, under the ringing of so many bells, on the banks of rivers big and small, locks of hair that touch a cheek, the strength of a face felt by another face, the taste; all over the world, people of all sizes and all races, houses of wood and stone, gardens, the warm weight of eyelids over eyes, breathing that touches skin, lips lips, morning or afternoon or night or now, fields, cities, people, two people, the whole world frozen for two people all over the world. In the distance, the back of a runner. Now it's as though it were simple

love you too much, almost too much, I love you too much, almost too much

sisters. Marta never spoke to Maria about that afternoon in the piano cemetery. There was a single Sunday lunch at our parents' house when Marta, angry and hurt, ignored Maria. Then straight away they went back to being as they had always been. Marta knew how to forgive, and she made herself forget. When Maria arrived to see Elisa, who was still small, Marta smiled at her and they were just sisters, ever sisters. It happened sometimes while Elisa was taking her nap, or when she was spending the evening alone, that the memory of that afternoon came to her. For a moment the image of her husband's face, between pianos, behind pianos, and her sister's back. For a moment, again, the image of her husband's head sinking into the neck of her sister. Marta, alone, grimaced and fled from this image, ate a whole pan of boiled potatoes, roasted a pork sausage. With no one else there she would walk through the house's enormous afternoons. Her husband would come in, and go out. Maria would follow him with her eyes, go after him, try to talk to him in a sweet voice, but he wouldn't stop, wouldn't wait for her, didn't see her, didn't hear her. In the morning, when her husband had already gone out, when Elisa was still asleep, Marta would stand in front of the mirror. With the tips of her fingers she would move aside the straps and let her nightdress drop to her feet. And she would look at her body – the thick skin enveloping shapes of stone that grew in extravagant ways. In a few months her body was deformed. When I arrived, I was able to make her laugh. Between our conversations, between the little games with Elisa, I witnessed the changes to her body. My mother would arrive to see her granddaughter and witnessed the changes to her body. Simão, when he turned up to see her, witnessed the changes to her body. My father, Maria, all of us witnessed the changes to her body, but we said nothing. On Sundays, when Marta arrived bringing Elisa by the hand, when her husband arrived a few minutes later and we all sat down at the table for lunch, no one commented on the way Marta held blocks of pork and gnawed at them, quickly, one after another with her lips greasy and her eyes getting smaller and smaller, sunk in her round face.

the springs of the cart. Simão and I and three men from the *taberna* unloaded the piano. Earlier, at the man's house, standing at the piano, when he named his price, my brother came up to my ear and whispered, 'Take it.' I remained silent, as if thinking. I looked at the piano, I looked at the man, I looked at the piano, I looked at the man and said half the sum he'd asked for. He accepted at once. As we crossed the entrance hall of the workshop with the piano – a weight crushing us against the floor – I could see that the men couldn't cope. We stopped. We had a breather, and started again. We put it down in the carpentry shop. We went to the *taberna* and drank two glasses of wine. As we came out, it was January. In the carpentry shop, the upright piano, varnished, with secret scratches. Simão was talking, telling stories, making up futures. I walked round and round the piano, I concentrated. Then, at a given moment, I stopped and put my index finger on a key – a lame note. With that note began a whole week of me and Simão spending all our mornings and all our afternoons around the piano. Hours followed one another slowly, I thought about her, my brother would go to the piano cemetery to look for parts and would come back satisfied with pressure bars, hammers, rods. I felt a tenderness towards Simão's blind, smiling face, my brother, my brother. Then I'd leave him at the *taberna* and go to train. I ran in a time that was constant combustion, a flame blowing inside me. Like blood I ran through the veins of Lisbon, touched its heart, penetrated its heart, and then, more slowly, extracted myself, undid myself and came out. A secret from myself. I'd arrive home and find a place held in suspension. My wife under the oil lamp, her belly, our child forming, slowly growing, waiting for a moment. Like now

a given moment in time. Now. Now is a stake, driven into the surface of time, just as it might be stuck into the earth. All the cords of time are supported by this stake and they can hold up a tent as huge as the sky. The gardens around the entrance to the stadium have been left behind a long time or short time or long or short time ago. With each step, a different now. I run, carrying time. I take a step, now, another step, another now, and on I go – now, now, now. I'm not scared any more. I'm alight with my certainties. I can accept naturally that, now, my father has just died; just as, now, my sister Maria has fallen off the bicycle at the Monsanto picnic; just as, now, my niece Elisa has just been born; just as, now, I am here, frozen in this moment, at this step, replaced by the next, replaced by the next. Wherever my wife is, that moment exists. It's so different and it's just the same, the same moment. Wherever my mother is, there's this moment which for her lasts much longer or much less time. Where I am. Here, on this road. Here, where I could be if I closed my eyes. All time, the years and decades I've lived, that I've not lived, that I will live and that I won't live, it all exists in this moment. I fall – my cheek to the floor, the sun pushing my shoulders and not letting me get up, now, time, my knees burning, the palms of my hands on the ground, an incandescent sheet, red-hot, the heavy boiling air that fills me up

don't leave me

and I get up. Slowly. Slowly. The weight of my body – a mountain – on my arms. My knees – the trunks of the plane-trees in the garden – bend. I go on

together. We looked at the piano proudly. Once again we were aware of being capable and of being endlessly brothers. We were made of the same impossible, unpronounceable words. Simão left me to go and fetch the man with the cart. When the sound of his steps had disappeared, I put a stool down in front of the piano, sat down, and played a piece with notes spaced out, that I made up, and that I felt. Time. Afternoon. My brother came back, already with a few men from the *taberna*. I was seated facing the silence. I sat down next to the cart man. He held on to the bridle, I had my hands resting in my lap. People were frozen on the pavements to watch the piano, tied up, solemn. Behind us, my brother went with the men from the *taberna*, on foot, chatting about nothing, their phrases left unfinished. The lady stood amazed when she opened the door. The lady stood amazed as she followed us with her gaze. In the corridor we huddled so as not to knock off any pictures, so as not to scratch any furniture. When we came to corners we'd manoeuvre back-wards, forwards, backwards, forwards. In the hall, the place of the grand piano was empty and clean. The burned part of the rug was covered by another rug, like a patch. The walls around the piano were clean, but worn down from having been scrubbed. We put the piano up against the wall next to the window. The lady's eyes shone. She stood there, arms down by her sides. The men left, led out by Simão. The lady looked at me for another moment, and went out. She came in. Her hair was still long and smooth, her lips perfect, her skin white. Inside I was slowly trembling. I was about to tell her I still wanted her, I still felt the same way, but my will was stopped in its tracks

Kilometre twenty-six

because I heard the front door open and close, because I could make out the silent footsteps along the hallway runner. And the lady came back into the hall, followed by the tuner. He knew I was there, and said my name – Francisco. His voice disappeared into the air. The tuner, blind, couldn't see our serious faces, and maybe that was why he smiled. I gave him my hand to lead him. Suddenly it was me, her and the tuner. She had her hands on her stomach and she was beautiful. I remembered the first day I saw her. I tried, struggled to think of other things, but I looked at her and all I could remember was the first day I saw her. And at that moment there was so much I wanted to tell her. I wanted to tell her everything I thought, I had been, I still was, but I remained silent, passed through by each isolated note that the tuner played, by the cry, almost inaudible – but unique, unique – of the piano strings being stretched – the groans of flowers dying. At the sudden moment when I walked out of the hall, the tuner turned his head, not understanding. She – hurt, wounded – didn't look at me. And I, wounded by myself, continued to walk, to flee, continued along the corridor, along the streets until I was even more lost to everything, until I had lost myself completely.

through the sun. The ground tilts under my feet. In the distance a whole garden that wavers, trees going up and down. I put one foot down on the road and I feel it escape, I feel it tipping. I put down the other foot and it's already tipping the other way. At the same time the ochre façades fade into every luminous colour – white, yellow. And they move away, and they move closer. They waver within their outlines, they transform themselves into smudges that burn like poppy petals, oil-lamp flames, they waver

father

before being born. The child

the hall mirror. And Marta, proud of her nearly new house, filled with nearly new things. A plaster doll on a bookcase. Its arm broken on the trip, but I'll glue it back. And she was smiling. Proud of the copper pans hanging in order of size, of the porcelain penguin, of the large wall clock that lost ten minutes a day, the hall mirror that already wasn't big enough to reflect all of her, a new pan, washed cutlery. Looking at me. Proud of the discoloured frame where she kept a photograph of our sister. Her holding it, giving it to me, showing it to me. Maria

with Maria. Just like when they were girls and they locked themselves away in their room. Our mother would forget to call them. Just like when they knew exactly the same secrets. They were girls, sisters. They laughed, just the two of them, at the same jokes. They were the only ones laughing. My father would look at them, straight away giving up trying to understand them. Simão didn't get close. I was the little boy. I handed her back the frame. I looked at her again. She

smiled, and her face wasn't at that moment, it was at a time that only for her had not been lost, in a past that only she still recognised. She put down the frame when Elisa woke up. Uncle, Uncle. Cheeks flushed. And Marta smiling, showing me the bedroom. Proud of the little bedside tables, the chest of warped drawers. Returning to the kitchen, Elisa snuggled in my arms. And Marta: 'Do you want to see what we've got here? Go and show your uncle.' And me putting Elisa down on the floor, a little girl. Her walking barefoot towards a photograph of me, resting on the lowest shelf of the cupboard, holding it with both hands, almost dropping it, holding it and giving it to me. The two of them looking at me, smiling, proud. I

Me: in a photo, immobile, seeing the living reflection of myself, maybe wondering at what I have become, frozen and watching myself closely. I smiled at them as they'd expected,

put the photograph down on the same low cupboard shelf, and there, in a time I shall never know, a time that has stopped in that photograph, I remained, still looking in some direction in that room, eternally looking in some direction in that room

Kilometre twenty-seven

oh Mother, don't, don't cry, purest queen of heaven, help me for ever

tear of blood from the sun, boiling in the corner of my eye, rolling down my cheek, clouding up my sight of what will always be unknown to me, death

not yet born

yet. The music she played as I lay there, naked body on the hall rug, broken-apart, aching body. The music tracing a path in eternity, a road supported by liquid trees, by reflections of trees in the breeze. The slow, lingering music, over everything that was beginning to exist – transparent worlds

cold. That night I arrived home later. My wife knew. I was sure of it. The oil lamp lit up the curves of her body – her belly. Our child was – is – there, not yet born, maybe mingled with earth, with sky, with sun. Maybe next to my father, maybe watching me through him. My father's eyes being his, his eyes being my father's eyes – the same darkness, the same incandescent light. That night, falling asleep, we met. Then, the morning. Close to the mornings of the previous days, and different. I opened the workshop door. In the cold, I was completely awake. It was a clear time of day. Time passed, with me on my own. I resumed old jobs, which had been left since the day the lady came in and showed me the burned piano, the day we went to fetch the upright piano from the home of the man from the *taberna* and started fixing it up. Later, in a moment within my thoughts, I thought I heard footsteps in the entrance hall. My attention. I wanted Simão to arrive. And silence. I said his name. My brother's name dissolving into the silence. He didn't come. He didn't come in the afternoon. He didn't come the next day, or the next, or the next, or the next.

my father calling me

in my body as it lost the shape of running; in my elbows no longer a right angle, now uncoordinated outlines, each of my arms, on its own, standing out from my body, trying to survive, trying to cling on to some invisible image that supported them; in my legs falling on to the road with each step, digging into the road under my own body's unbalance

a weight that never goes away. I was still small, the boys of my age only thought about little games, they hoped it wouldn't rain, and there was me, always, always carrying this black weight in my chest. For just a moment, Maria saying something funny, our mother happy, me happy, and right afterwards – or at that same moment – I'd remember the black weight – lead – which never left my chest. Perhaps in winter, night-time, the kitchen, Marta talking about something purely good. Our father in a contented silence. And me, almost well except for the weight that never left, that I was sure would never leave my chest. And it never left, that late afternoon never left, under the branches of the peach trees, my brother arriving home – Simão, Simão – and me blinding him for ever. After that day it happened only twice. I was nine years old, he was fifteen. In the bedroom we were fighting, he'd tired of pushing me, he threw me on to the bed and said, 'You made me blind.' And there was nothing I could reply with, I couldn't get up and call him names. I was twelve years old, he was eighteen. In the piano cemetery we got angry for some reason and I accused him of not wanting to work, I said to him, 'You're a parasite.' He stood there looking at me with his firm, iron eye and he said, 'You made me blind.' Those words went right through me, words he said to me only twice but every day since that afternoon, when I was still small, when my voice had changed, when our father began to be ill, when he died, when I met my wife, during and before and after each marathon, repairing a piano, at each piano note played by the tuner, when I learned I was going to have a child, falling asleep, waking, now, I never forget, and in remembering always, always I have a black weight

Kilometre twenty-eight

that never leaves my chest. The guilt. I've thought so often about what it would have been like if I had been the one blinded in one eye and not Simão, I've thought so often about how much I'd have wanted me to be the one blinded. Later on, I think about how ridiculous I am, that I don't really feel that, that I'm an egotist, and, more ridiculous still, I feel sorry for myself for not even being able to feel sorry for myself. Many times I believed I'd got used to this weight, I believed it had become a part of me, like my arms, my legs, but every time I saw my brother turning his whole head to see something that was happening to his right, each time I remembered how he moves his head, I realised that I'd never

a child

on the day he died

in the yard, with my mother's weeding-hoe. I had a tin full of worms by the end of the afternoon. When I showed them to my father, he said: 'Tomorrow you wake up early and you'll come with me.' We went to the workshop just to fetch a bucket, my father's fishing-rod and a small rod he'd made for me from a very thin lath. My eyes shone when they saw it — it had a coconut-fibre thread tied to one end of it, and at the end of the line two or three round lead weights and a hook. My father put it in my hands and said, 'It's yours.' He waited, in his contentment, and with a father's voice said, 'Be careful with the hook.' We went out together and it was still early. I carried my rod in one hand, the tin of worms in the other, and I was proud. My father carried his rod in one hand and the empty bucket in the other. There were not many people out on the street yet, but as we walked I'd have liked them to have looked at us. A father, a son. We reached the park and went round behind walls of boxwood, under flowering trees, through the green smell of trimmed bushes, through the sweet smell of flowers. When we reached the lake, our reflection in the water was my father, big, my father, and me, small, beside him, boastful, happy. Then I looked through the water, fresh and green-tinged and thick with slime over a bed of dust that was liquid, almost liquid, light, and I saw the fishes slipping, bending their red, yellow, orange bodies. I saw the fishes slipping, serious, serene. My father pointed to one of them and whispered, 'It's a pompano fish, see?' I replied in my child's voice, in my eagerness, but he put his index finger to his nose and said, 'Shhh.' He whispered, 'Don't startle the fish.' We were up against a barrier that came up to our knees, between a bush and the little house for the two ducks that slept and floated adrift in the lake. I chose a worm from the tin – it twisted itself between my fingers – and I felt sorry for it. It was my father who chose another and taught me to put it on the hook. Then it was him who taught me to dip the hook in the water and to give it a light tap, a light tap. When a fish came close, my father put his hands over mine and taught me to pull it in. When my father took the hook from its mouth and put it in the bottom of the bucket

I watched it until my father caught another and another. He caught two more. In a short time we'd filled up the bucket. It was still early and we were already heading home. It seemed natural to me that it was still early, just as it seemed natural to me that we were returning by the same way we'd come, behind walls of boxwood, under flowering trees. My father had the bucket hanging from one arm. I watched him admiringly. He made his way contentedly, father, my father. He had his work clothes on, his sleeves rolled up, his strong arms. I had a hat wedged on to my head, but it was only then as we returned that the sun

burns

was starting to warm up. Our steps were the scraping sound of boots on grass. We were just about to leave when a man came running towards us and held my father by an arm. It was only much later that I learned he was the man who looked after the park. At that moment I just looked at my father, I looked at the man and didn't understand. I came up to just above my father's waist. I raised my head and saw him apologise. I saw the man grab him by the arm, without looking at him, as if he couldn't hear him. And my father asking him to let us go. And the man gesturing to a lad who was passing and telling him to go fetch a policeman. And my father asking him not to do that. And the man not looking at him, not hearing. And my father putting the bucket down on the ground. And time held back by silence. And me, little, my fishing-rod in one hand, the tin of worms in the other and a hat wedged on to my head.

the sky comes undone over Stockholm

child

the sky comes undone over Stockholm

not yet born

arms lighter, because they've stopped existing. And I can't feel my legs. In my body, there's some other thing that sacrifices itself in place of my body. Maybe it's what I'm thinking. Like when I close my eyes and I still exist. When I close my eyes, cover my ears and I still exist. Maybe it's this shapeless matter that's burning up, this shadow. Hands hurl themselves out to touch it and to pass through it, like passing through flames. Words hurl themselves out to name it, but they don't stop, they go right through its infiniteness. And there's peace in the chaos of my movements, my legs, my arms, unbalancing, free, lost, desperate. And there's silence in the roaring that surrounds me, grave and constant and deafening. There's silence in the voices, in the applause, that are thrown towards me from one side of the road and the other, that I pass through as though breaking through fine tangled bushes, as though passing through a cloud of birds. I no longer have any doubts. I am strong and serene and immortal. I no longer have any doubts.

child. I feel you in the palm of my hand, under the skin of your mother. In her eyes, I see yours.

on the road. My running shoes land crooked on the road. Feet to the side, crooked, unable to recognise the surface of the road.

wooden steps. Maria opens the door for me. My mother. Ana. Íris. Maria saying to me, 'My little boy.' Me looking at each of their faces.

notes played on the piano, now heaped up inside me, and us, lying on the rug, our bodies

my mother, mother, my mother, proud of me running in the Olympic Games, but silent, only her face. Ana and Íris around me, happy – happy children. And Maria, my sister, like when she was young, like when our father died, saying to me, 'My little boy.'

father

father

Kilometre thirty

fall over myself – stones – my cheek to the road, the world cloudy through my eyes, my breathing inhaling dust, my legs burnt, embers, my arms burnt, my heart, my chest breathing

time passes in Benfica, silence passes over the piano cemetery

I must go and meet my father.

PIANO NOTES COME OUT of the wireless. Who is there, far away, playing them? The white shining surface of the refrigerator. The white shining surface of the tiles. My wife knows this time of day through her own skin. The afternoon is drawing to its close, as it does every day. It's Monday, maybe this is why my wife remembers 'every day' better. Monday is a day my wife associates with 'every day'. If someone in a conversation says 'every day' my wife thinks of an infinite succession of Mondays. Friday is the eve of the weekend, which is why it's a different day. Saturdays and Sundays are different days. Tuesdays, Wednesdays and Thursdays are particular days on which things happen that are particular to Tuesdays, Wednesdays and Thursdays. Mondays are regular, anonymous days. They are every day.

This is why my wife, even if she doesn't remember, knows, recognises this time of day, without having to look at the clock on the kitchen wall, without having to pay any attention to the sharp whistles that interrupt the piano notes on the wireless. It's why weeks, months, seasons exist. It's why my wife knows this time of day by seeing it and feeling it and breathing it every day – an infinite succession of Mondays.

Perhaps. My wife doesn't know if Maria will be the first to arrive, holding Ana's hand, the voices of our grandchildren meeting and shouting, with her work problems and talk, with the life and moods of the six, seven women who work around her, chained to their sewing machines; or whether Maria's husband will arrive, dispirited, the silence of the house almost unchanged, Íris walking barefoot along the hall runner and meeting him without surprise.

My wife knows. Leaning on the kitchen sink, she dries her arms with a cloth and thinks. Yesterday they arrived from the workshop. Yesterday: Maria, defeated, coming up the stairs – her feet heavy on the steps – her body hoisted up by her arm on the banister. Yesterday: our granddaughters, vaguely understanding everything. Yesterday: my wife there, but far away. Her body there, her presence if requested, but the words that populated her, the images she shared with no one, very far away.

And when they opened the door, Maria's husband was a ghost amid the shadows of the house. He didn't greet anyone, didn't speak, didn't say sorry to Maria. My wife put down the suitcase she had brought and went into the kitchen. Ana and Íris went to play in the living room. Maria walked the corridors and the rooms as though it were a necessary thing to do, as though she were doing something other than trying to give her husband a chance to talk to her.

At the dinner table he seemed sad. He didn't look at anyone. His face was a memory of other days. Then between one moment and the next Maria said something to him. She spoke naturally, as though nothing had happened, as though she no longer remembered, as though she'd forgiven him, as though it didn't matter. Her husband replied with a syllable. She spoke again – a question about his answer. He replied with two syllables, a pause and then another syllable. She spoke again – another question. He replied calmly. And so the evening went on. The children laughed when they found some detail funny. Maria was the same daughter and wife and mother as on other nights. As though nothing had happened. They were already all asleep when my wife, alone, set up the iron couch in the dining room, stretched out the sheets, put the pillowcase on to the pillow, lay down on to a groaning of springs and, after some time that she doesn't remember, fell asleep.

Íris is in the living room. Leaning on the sink, my wife wipes her hands on a cloth and she knows this time of day through her own skin. The surface of the windowpanes. The surface of the tabletop. My wife hears the sound of the key going into the lock. Piano notes come out of the wireless. Who is there, far away, playing them?

'Grandad is loveliest of the world,' said Elisa, sitting on a piece of wood on the carpentry shop floor. It must have been summer, because the sun had been very hot and the cooler time of day was slowly beginning. I stopped what I was doing to look at her with a smile. Elisa was three, four years old. My Marta still lived in the house near the workshop and she was out on the patio doing something with a straw hat on her head. It was Saturday.

'Grandad is loveliest of the world,' said Elisa, when I was not yet sick and I didn't know that my time was seeping away. Elisa was three, four years old and she'd wanted to come and be with me. I was making a door frame or a window frame or something when I saw her come in, so very little, her body still unsteady from climbing the stairs. For a moment her body was sketched by the sunlight. She sat down on a piece of wood on the carpentry shop floor.

'Grandad is loveliest of the world.' I took her in my arms and went to the patio door. Marta was still living in the house near the workshop. She had a straw hat on her head and she was sitting with Francisco on the bottom step. They were eating oranges and talking. In front of them, wagging its tail, was a dog. I went down the stairs, and as I approached them Elisa was playing with my ear. I put her down on the ground and she began to run around on the pine shavings. I stayed a bit to make the most of the cool. I peeled an orange. We talked about something that was more or less important at that moment. But that was a long time ago. The sky was loveliest of the world.

I'd just arrived back from the workshop. The gentle voices of my children were gliding. As I dried myself with the towel that was hanging in the washroom, Francisco ran around my legs. It was the last moment of lightness. Someone knocked unhurriedly at the door. From that moment the light began to transform into the shadow that was the colour of the sky and the streets, the shadow which would turn black and come in through the night. I had already arrived back from the workshop. I opened the door.

The wrinkled, distressed face of a woman looking at me from down there, who hadn't yet come up to the front step. She looked away. She looked at me again. She asked if this was where my wife lived. She said my wife's name. She said the name, solid but light, white, a single white shape; the unpronounceable name which exists, but which is impossible, because it is a name whose meaning is from a time before there were words, the first name, like a spot in the universe that's still empty, waiting to be filled up with life, illusions, possibilities.

233

Francisco, small, shy, leaned silently on the half-open door, watching the woman with his huge child's eyes. My wife walked alone to the door and for a frozen moment she was frightened, her lips had no words, the palms of her hands on her skirt. She told the woman to come in. Marta, Maria and Simão fell silent when she entered. Francisco ran into my arms.

The two of them sat at the table. Dimly lit. The woman chose the words and the moment to say them. She chose the voice to say them with – serious, firm. They weren't merely words. My wife's godmother, who'd had a boarding house, glasses, who opened the door to me that first time I saw my wife, who closed the doors and the windows when my wife told her she was going to have a child, who'd brought her up since she was small, had died.

That night, there was nothing for us to do but sit at the kitchen table, after putting our children to bed, me listening, my wife telling all the stories she remembered about her godmother, about how she was sometimes tender, how she always laughed at the same jokes, how she invented enemies from among the women who lived next door, how she treated the plants in their pots, how austere she was and innocent. I know what my wife was thinking that night before she went to sleep.

In the morning, dressed in black, she went into the morgue accompanied by the gentleman from the undertaker's. At the end of the morning she opened the door to the chapel while the priest and the gentleman from the undertaker's talked next to the coffin. She sat in a chair, her hands between her knees, and spent the whole afternoon looking at the same spot, and she was there the whole evening, the whole night. At the same time, at home, I was trying to tell Francisco not to make so much noise and filling Maria's plate, and Simão's, and using a gruff voice to tell them to eat it all up, and playing with them, and stopping playing with them, and saying to them:

'It's time for bed.'

The nieces of the woman who had raised her only arrived the following morning. They passed through the incandescent light that flooded the open door to the chapel. They had black jackets over their shoulders, they were tired, pulling their husbands' arms.

Tuesday went by, with nothing happening. She darned socks. She took off Íris's bandage. The man from the butcher's talked to my wife about Francisco. He told her he was certain that next Sunday there was no doubt about it, Francisco would win for sure.

'Oh, that would be good,' said my wife.

'For sure!'

'Well, it would be good.'

'For sure!' the man repeated.

Wednesday went by, with nothing happening. My wife was almost about to telephone Francisco's wife. The morning came to an end, but it wasn't yet the time Maria arrived for lunch. My wife was almost not going to wait for Maria, almost not going to ask her if she could make a telephone call. She would have to tell her afterwards. As soon as she arrived, she'd tell her. But right then she couldn't wait. She had to know if there was any news from Francisco. But she didn't want to give our daughter the satisfaction of letting her know that she'd made a call without asking. The last time they'd argued about this, my wife had sworn to herself that never again, never again would she use the telephone without asking first, a proud woman. But she had to know if there was any news from Francisco. Something inside was telling her, something inside was telling her. She couldn't wait. But it wasn't long until Maria's lunchtime. But it was still a bit of time. But she didn't want to give her the satisfaction. But. But. She was thinking these thoughts when the telephone rang. My wife took a breath, answered, and wasn't surprised to find it was Francisco's wife, talking quietly and telling her that everything was all right.

'But is he liking Sweden?'

'He didn't say.'

'Is it cold or hot there?'

'He didn't say.'

'Do you think he might need a jacket?'

'He just said that everything was all right.'

Francisco's wife didn't even begin to answer my wife's questions. Slowly, with each phrase, as though making her way down a staircase of phrases, my wife began to give up. At the same time she could imagine that perhaps Francisco's wife had become accustomed to using that lifeless tone, that voice, when she still worked at the hospital, when she walked the nurses' corridors pushing trolleys of trays or holding a capsule between her fingers. Having given up on asking about Francisco, my mother asked her about the pregnancy.

'I'm getting on.'

It wasn't worth asking anything else. They said goodbye. When Maria arrived for lunch, my mother recounted the entire telephone call with Francisco's wife. When Maria arrived home at the end of the afternoon, before they sat down for dinner, she told her again.

It was on Thursday, after the tantrum thrown by Ana as she awoke, after holding Íris in her arms to say goodbye to her mother and sister down there, that my wife changed her skirt, put on an ironed blouse, put a bag on her arm and went out with Íris. They went down the stairs and reached the door to the street.

Morning. The sky is absolute and it exists because it is July. The walls of the buildings are light from the same light that lightens the bodies of the people, the windscreens of the parked cars, the worn scratches on the pavements, the rubbish on the side of the road and the pavements made of stones in rows, of yellowed weeds and earthy holes. Íris wants to let go of her grandmother's hand, wants to run on her own, with her little legs, her little knees below the end of her frilly skirt. My wife takes two steps, grabs her by the hand again, scolds with words that Íris pretends not to understand and on they go, the two of them, just so, together, along the pavement. They are going to market.

My wife is thinking about what she's going to buy, what she might perhaps buy. In her bag she has a closed purse; in the purse, coins and well-folded notes. Sometimes Íris starts to tire, walking more slowly, and my wife has to pull her by the arm. They reach the market.

The sun is dazzling, reflected by the loose plastic bags dragging along the ground. Around the market there are stalls and noise. Inside, in there, are the vegetables and fruit. Out here there are clothes, plastic toys, stakes stuck into the ground and cars passing by slowly, steering round the people who choose and look and ask for prices. Íris starts crying because she wants a toy – a clothes-iron made of plastic, a set of little saucepans made of plastic, a hairbrush and mirror and hairpins made of plastic. My wife tells her that if she behaves, if she behaves, when they've finished looking at everything she will come back and buy her a toy.

My wife, dressed in black, and little Íris, continue on, hand in hand, making their way between people, looking at everything. And then, after a mixture of people and sun and colours yellowed by the sun, they reach a stall that displays sweaters, trousers, shirts and blouses and shorts and socks. My wife looks over the clothes and immediately sees only the black ones. Black smocks for the summer, plain black blouses for the summer. Íris, gripping her grandmother's arm, sees only the two little gypsy children sitting on the clothes table, playing, naked from the waist down, barefoot, mouths circled with dust. My wife and Íris are surrounded by the remains of phrases spoken by the people passing by, by bits of a voice shouting into a megaphone that reaches them on the breeze, the dogs fighting, down over there, by the motorcars that slowly pass, steering round them, and occasionally sound their horns. It is now. My wife lifts her eyes from the clothes and sees the gypsy who came last week to bring Íris's little blouse. She sees the cold – icy – eyes of the gypsy who on Sunday, as they returned from the work-shop, was out on the street, leaning up against a corner.

He's maybe sixty. Gypsies never know their own age. It's as though they were born at the beginning of time. He's smoking a cigarette. When a breeze comes past, it ruffles the smoke and his beard. He looks at my wife. She's at his stall. He's leaning on his wagon. He straightens up. This move-ment, and what he says with his eyes, calls my wife over. Íris goes with her. And it's all natural, with no hesitations – the gypsy lifts Íris up from under her arms and hands her to the youngest gypsy, who's leaning on the clothes table, standing waiting for customers; this gypsy puts Íris down next to the two children who are playing on the clothes table, who are throwing socks at one another; my wife gives her hand to the gypsy so he can help her through the back door into the wagon – the door closes.

Inside the wagon's little storage room my wife is sitting on a heap of sweaters, still wrapped in thin shiny plastic bags. The gypsy is kneeling in front of her. This moment clashes with the moment in which they throw themselves at one another and kiss – the hard lips, rubbing, struggling, squeezing together. The gypsy's hands are dry – dry veins in his skin – and they have gold rings on their fingers. The gypsy's hands squeeze my wife's chest, the black blouse, the thick black bra. One of his hands goes up under her skirt. Perhaps I no longer know her body. Years have passed since the last time I touched her skin – my hands feeling the small of her back, the shape of her waist. The gypsy draws back. His gaze and my wife's gaze don't draw back. He undoes his trousers. The quick, heavy breathing, only gradually calming down. And once again the gypsy throws himself on my wife. There is a moment of silence as he enters her. And there they remain, indifferent to the world, in the wagon's little storage room, on a heap of nighties in plastic bags that make a noise with every movement, fitted together – my wife's arms and legs wrapping around him.

My wife emerges quickly from the wagon, arranging her hair. The gypsy emerges slowly, as though returning the movement to each leg and each arm. Abruptly my wife lifts

Íris off the clothes table. In the air, Íris waits for her astonished face to be able to say goodbye to the children who played with her and who are still on the tangle of nighties, watching her move away. My wife takes her in her arms and makes her way between the people who cross her path.

She stops, breathes, puts Íris down on the ground. She straightens herself up, breathes, keeps walking. At a given moment the stretched-out strings turn concrete, the knots at the end of the stakes turn concrete. My wife's face is serene. She doesn't think about stopping, but she feels Íris's tugs and, looking at her, she remembers. Together they reach the toy stall.

Íris, holding her grandmother's hand, falls back as she looks at the plastic case she's holding in her other hand – hairpins, a mirror and a hairbrush for dolls. Which is why she pays no attention to the way they are going, and is only surprised when they reach the workshop, when my wife is already putting the key into the lock of the big workshop door.

The nieces of the woman from the boarding house come back from the cemetery alongside my wife. They had nothing to say, but they asked questions just so they could be saying something. My wife wasn't afraid of silence, she needed it, and she didn't answer them. Sometimes she'd change the expression on her face, as though these slight changes had some meaning, but she didn't answer them. When they were saying their goodbyes, friendly, they told her that late that afternoon they would be going to the boarding house to deal with some matters relating to the sharing-out and they'd expect her there.

My wife kept on going, without any sleep. She spent the afternoon dealing with our children, with Marta's help.

When she managed to sit down, she stopped to enjoy the rays of light that passed through the windows and came to rest diagonally on the floor.

After the streets, she reached the pavement outside the boarding house, the wall with the ivy leaves that she'd climbed so many times to meet me. We were young on the nights of that summer. That evening my wife was still young, but she knew she had lost something for ever. In her thoughts, her godmother's face, dead, lying in the chapel, mingled with all the years when that same face, alive, another face, would smile at her, would become angry with her, would explain everything to her. And she'd say:

'Daughter.'

She'd end her requests with that word. Often, in the middle of a sigh, within some phrase, she would say just that word:

'Daughter.'

My wife remembered a great deal – everything. Too many winters, Christmases, too much time when it was just the two of them, together and alone. One of the nieces of the woman from the boarding house opened the door and wrapped her in a voice that feigned familiarity. The walls were strong – they were eternal, one might say. My wife went into the house, that house she never thought she would enter again. In every corner she saw herself, little, enchanted by some mystery, or sad. In every corner, in the empty space of the open doors, in the corridor, she saw the face of her godmother – smiling, angry, explaining everything to her, just straightforward.

In the living room the other niece took some steps towards my wife to speak to her as though they had lost the same thing.

'Leave it,' she said.

The nieces' husbands, rather bored, remained seated in their armchairs.

On the table there were tea services wrapped in news-paper, open boxes of cutlery, rows of goblets, piles of folded doilies, copper ashtrays, orphaned figures in porcelain.

Then, after a moment that the nieces deemed sufficient, they sat my wife down in an armchair and said to her:

'We've called you here because we want you to accept something.'

And they looked at her, expecting gratitude. And the fake enthusiasm of their own expressions prevented them from noticing that my wife's face remained immobile. Trying to preserve the surprise, they moved almost in silence, clumsily. With their bodies they were blocking the thing they wanted to give her. They looked back at her over their shoulders. One of them walked backwards towards her. When she turned, she held out to her the thing they wanted to give her. And looked at her, expectant.

It was a teaspoon that my wife, as a girl, had bought to give to her godmother. It was a delicate, simple spoon. At the end of the handle she had engraved a single small word: mother.

Simão never wanted to know. My wife always worried. He never wanted to know. He was still small when my wife and I said to him:

'Your sisters are going to be someone, and you'll be nobody. Your sisters are going to be ashamed of you. Two sisters who're going to be someone with a brother who will be nobody.'

He turned his back on us. And went up to his room. My wife and I would be left there, saying nothing. At other times he would be harsh. He'd shout:

'Leave me alone!'

And turn his back on us. And go up to his room. I'd say:

'There's something wrong with that boy.'

At other times I'd follow him up the stairs and go into his room. He'd open his left eye wide and almost lifted the lid off the right. I'd squeeze his arms and shake him as I said:

'Is that any way to talk to your father?!'

Íris is nearly three, and she knows it's different going into the workshop now, just as it was different last Sunday, as it was different in those days when she would arrive at the workshop with her grandmother, with her mother, to visit Uncle Francisco. Today the workshop is empty – the little birds, the little birds in the roof beams – and her grandmother hearing every step she takes on the earth floor of the entrance, she's thinking about something, but there's only the empty workshop – the objects alone there, the solitude of the tools, of the pieces of wood, of the pianos.

My wife knows it's different going into the workshop now. On Sunday there was something in her that was soothed by the voices of our daughters, of our grandchildren. At times it was like those afternoons when I was still alive, when she would gather all our children together and together they would all come into the workshop. Now, everyone knows, it's different.

My wife stops at the threshold of the carpentry shop. Íris lets go of her hand. My wife doesn't have the strength to hold on to her. Íris moves away slowly. Stumbling twice on loose stones, she reaches the entrance to the piano cemetery. My wife's tired voice:

'Don't touch anything.'

After a moment when she's listening to her grandmother, Íris's smile and her eyes – light or shadows on the surface of the sea – and the curls that roll down on to her shoulders and her little body disappear into the piano cemetery. For years my wife has known about the blind passion that children feel for the piano cemetery. Before now it has been Marta, Maria. It has been Simão, Francisco. My wife knows that no harm has ever come to them. Which is why she doesn't worry, and returns to her thoughts. She returns to her body, ruffled, untidy under her clothes, as though her clothes have stopped being quite right for her, as though her arms are no longer the same length and are longer or shorter than the sleeves, as though her torso has turned around itself and its shape will no longer fit the shape of the blouse. My wife returns to herself, and takes a step into the carpentry shop.

I don't know what she's looking for. Perhaps she needs some empty time.

Íris hits the keys of an upright piano with both hands – a confused noise; the noise of her hands hitting the keys mingles with the noise of the detached or crooked mechanisms against the old wood, and mingles with a shy note, forced against its will to be heard. And again. Again. And she's had enough. The walls of the piano cemetery are cool. The light comes in through the dirty little window and is lost. Íris is so small. Her sandals accompany the movement that her body makes as it turns around itself. She finds the lid of the same legless piano where she sat on Sunday. In the dust surface there are still traces of that passing. She sits. She looks at me, and says:

'Are you still talking to the people from the book?'

'I am.'

Silence.

'Are you tired?'

'Not yet.'

'You really could be by now. Don't you ever rest, Grandad?'

'I can't. I have to tell this story to the end.'

Silence. Íris puts the plastic hairbrush down on the piano lid, puts down the hairpins and mirror. She has her back to me as she leans down to rummage around in a pile of keys. In her hands each key seems too big. She has her back to me. She says:

'When I'm big I can read the book, too, can't I?'

I smile.

'Yes, of course.'

Silence. She turns her face towards me.

'Grandad, tomorrow I'm going to be big, aren't I?'

'Yes, Íris, tomorrow you're going to be big.'

We smile together.

'When I'm big I might even know how to play the piano, right?'

'Yes, but you'll have to learn at school.'

'That's all right. Teacher will teach me and then I'll play a piano for my mother.'

'Do you think your mother will like it?'

'She will. She'll even get so happy that she'll ask me to play another song. One of those songs . . . A love song.'

She turns her face towards me. She covers her mouth, waiting for my reaction.

'But don't be sad, Grandad. Then I'll play a song for you, too. Except that I'll play a grandad song.'

'What's that like, a grandad song?'

'It's a song with words from the little girls who are the granddaughters and the mothers singing them.'

'So will your mother sing, then?'

'No, it's the music that has the words. When I play a piano you can hear the words that are inside the piano.'

She moves towards an upright piano, and away. She takes little steps, marked in the dust, her gaze fixed as though she were filling up with ideas. She freezes in the middle of a step. Slowly she puts the sole of her sandal down on the floor. She smiles. She says:

'I went with Granny to the market.'

'I know.'

She sits back down on the piano lid.

'Granny bought me a brush for me to brush my hair.'

'Yes, I know.'

She puts the brush and the hairpins in the folds of her skirt, on her lap. She holds up the mirror in front of her face, and in the little reflected circle she sees skin, lips, an eye.

'Then you also know what happened.'

'Yes, I know.'

'And what are you going to do? Will you hate all gypsies? That would be easy enough to do. Whenever there's a conversation that relates even vaguely to gypsies, with markets, with fairs, you'll take advantage of the moment to spread your poison. And underneath everything you say, hidden away, buried away, there will be that feeling you have. That's something you're good at. You know how to hate. You know how to impose your opinions and not let anyone contradict you. You know how to bring conversations to an end. If, of course, you weren't dead, if you could still have conversations.

'But we're having one, aren't we?'

'We are?'

'Again you're talking as though you weren't a little girl who's not yet even three.'

She continues looking at herself in the little mirror that she's holding in front of her face. She has the hairbrush in her other hand, and she starts brushing. Slowly.

'What is it you're afraid of, anyway? Are you afraid that I'm going to talk about Uncle Simão? It's nobody's fault that you can't forget the image of a little boy, your son, up against a wall, blind in one eye, terrified, knowing he can't run away, and you walking towards him, closing your fists, burning inside. Are you afraid that I'm going to talk about Uncle Francisco? It's three days till he runs in the marathon at the Olympic Games, on his own, always on his own, thinking that you never valued all the things he did just to please you. And, just the same, trying everything he can to win. Even knowing that if you weren't dead, if he got home and showed you the medal for first place, you'd turn your face away, uninterested.'

'I always did the best I could.'

She drops the mirror on her lap. She gives up on the brushing, her wrist limp. She looks right at me.

'Maybe the people reading the book will believe you, but you can't believe yourself. You know. You can still see Granny's face when you threw her to the floor, after squeezing her arm or striking her in the face with your hand. You can still remember all the times they looked at you with

247

disappointment, with pity. You're afraid that they'll take away from you something that was never yours, but which for a moment you believe belongs to you just because you're you. You've disappointed yourself, you feel pity for yourself, and for a moment you believe that other people should be the ones to pay for everything you did wrong and for everything you couldn't do.'

She looks at me. Silence. She gets up, still looking at me. Her footsteps on the dust. She skirts around pianos, parts, piles of keys, makes her way down passageways and leaves the piano cemetery. Her child's steps knowing and not knowing. She meets her grandmother standing at the carpentry bench where I used to work and where Francisco works. Íris approaches and gives her her hand. My wife feels Íris's little hand between her fingers, holding them.

Even without any pianos to repair, there were mornings and afternoons when I'd go into the piano cemetery to be alone. There were mornings when, summer or winter, the same light always came through the window, the same shade of dirty brown. The previous night I might have spent hours at the *taberna*, I might have argued with my wife. Slowly threads of the previous night would pass through my head – mists of alcohol dissolving, words or images of my wife that rose up suddenly. There were afternoons when I'd change my mind, when for a few moments I'd give up, but when, suddenly, straight afterwards, I'd believe with all my strength that I could change everything. And I'd look at the pianos, and I'd think.

I'd look at the dead pianos, I'd remember how there were parts that could be brought back to life inside other pianos,

248

and believe that all life could be reconstructed in just this way. I was not yet ill, my sons were growing up and turning into the lads that I had been myself not long ago. Time passed. And I was sure that a part of me, like the parts of the dead pianos, would continue to function inside them. Then I remembered my father – his face in the photograph, the box of medals, his stories told in my aunt's voice or my uncle's voice – and I was sure that a part of him was still alive in me, revived each day in my gestures, in my words and in my thoughts. A part of my father revived when I saw myself in the mirror, when I existed and when my hands continued to build all the things that he – secretly, so close and so far away – had started. Then I thought there was a part of my father that would remain in me and which I would hand on to my children so that it should remain in them until one day they begin to hand it on to my grandchildren. The same would happen with what was only mine, with what was only my children's and what was only my grandchildren's. We repeated ourselves, and moved away, and we moved closer together. We were perpetual in one another.

One of those afternoons when I was sitting in the piano cemetery, alone, thinking, I heard the footsteps of the postman on the earth floor of the entrance hall. I came out, as though busy, quite normal, and received the letters in my hand – bills and an envelope with the name of my cousin: Elisa. The postman was talking about the weather, complaining about the cars. I looked at him, I replied only with yeses, I said:

'Yes, right.'

I wanted him to leave, wanted him to leave me alone. I had never received a letter from my cousin before. I looked at the postman. I replied only with yeses. I squeezed the pack of letters in one hand. And I held my cousin's letter carefully in the other.

Me, Marta, Elisa, Hermes, Íris, Ana, Maria, Simão, Francisco, Francisco's wife, the son who would be born, Hermes – the weight of the gypsy's body, the perspiration, the hot smell of the gypsy's body – Íris, Maria, Marta, Simão, Elisa, Ana, Maria, Francisco, me, the son who would be born, Francisco's wife, Francisco, Simão – the touch of the gypsy's eyes, the fire in the gypsy's hands, embers, flames – Maria, Marta, Elisa, Ana, Hermes, Íris, the son who would be born, Francisco, me, Marta – the gypsy's skin slipping, the smooth skin – Maria, Simão, Francisco, me.

On the way from the workshop to Maria's house, my wife wants to escape from remembering the gypsy and she thinks about us. Our faces and our names mingling with flames. She goes faster. It's not long until Maria's lunchtime.

I was left alone. I waited, until after a few quick footsteps, and went into the piano cemetery. And I didn't breathe. I opened the envelope. I unfolded the sheet of paper. I ran my eyes over the lines that my cousin Elisa had written to me – straight lines. And greetings, and the signature, with broad round shapes – Elisa. Then, slowly, I put the sheet down on a piano and looked at it from a distance. I imagined my cousin sitting there, the corner of the sheet aligned with the squares on the tablecloth, the ballpoint pen the worn colour of objects that are valued but old. I held the sheet of paper again, as though I wanted or needed to confirm what was written there – she passed away last week, peacefully. I put the paper down again and thought about my cousin's choice of words – passed away, peacefully. I compared the words with the images I recalled from the day I took a train more to learn about my father than to meet them. My aunt, who looked at me, who held photographs out to me, was dead now, passed away, peaceful. And I couldn't help but imagine how that fat woman, that immense woman, stretched out in a dirty bed, had been washed, dressed in clean clothes, and finally presented with dignity. In just the same way I couldn't help but imagine my cousin, beside her, standing, all alone, in clothes she had bought to wear for the special occasions she never had. I held the letter again, and read it again. Those written phrases were the only visible part of all the phrases that my cousin hid inside herself. They were the only evidence of her voice. I folded the sheet of paper and put it away in the envelope. As I did it, I discovered that my aunt truly had, in days gone by, been a little girl. My cousin, too, in other days, she had also been a little girl. And that was how I saw them – dead and abandoned little girls. That would be how I'd see them again, later, whenever I remembered them in my thoughts.

In the kitchen, a memory makes Marta smile. Everyone in the world recognises the sun. July. In the living room, Hermes is sitting with his hands resting on his legs. Without any help he is trying to understand mysteries. Elisa is tidying up the toys that Hermes has left disordered in the sewing room. It is Friday. The afternoon is taking its time to end. July – luminous calm.

The dogs bark. The dogs bark. Afternoon. Hermes, Elisa and Marta wait. Someone knocks at the door. Elisa goes into the hallway. She walks, with a thought suspended. She opens the door. A woman with brown eyes, made lighter by the dusk. A woman who is too straightforward. Marta comes into the hallway. She walks towards the door. Hermes comes into the hallway. Marta stops beside Elisa. Hermes walks towards the door. He stops beside his sister and mother.

The three of them look at the woman, who looks only at Marta and asks after her husband. She says his name. The first time I heard that name was in the kitchen of our house. At that time Marta's husband was her invisible boyfriend and I was thinking about things that have stopped mattering. Marta has her arm resting on her son, but she doesn't have the weight of the arm on him. Marta has a blue smock on her body. She has slippers on her thick feet with their thick toes. The woman is wearing a skirt and a fine blouse. Her hair is well coiffed. Marta looks at her and is surprised that she never imagined her like this. She is a woman like other women. She has eyes and a voice and dreams. She is concrete. She lives with the same fear. Marta feels a small shudder that she's sure can't be seen. Her voice is faint when she says her husband isn't in.

The woman looks at her with a pity that Marta understands as being for them both – for her, and for the woman herself. Perhaps this pity also includes the children and even the whole world – the yellowing weeds, the cracks that cover the walls of houses, the dry moss on the surface of fences. The moment is brief. The woman looks at her and they are almost speaking to one another in a limpid language that has no words. The woman's face is preoccupied when she says thank you – the skin – and when she moves away. Hermes comes out from under his mother's arm and walks down the hallway. Elisa is a shape that moves into the sewing room. Marta remains, watching the woman making the movements that open the big door and heading away along the pavement, without looking back.

Marta closes the door slowly. Her body occupies almost the whole corridor. She walks past the entrance to the sewing room where Elisa is, she walks past the entrance to the living room where Hermes is, and reaches the kitchen. She sits down on a chair. There's water boiling on the stove. A moment. The clarity is the night as it remembers something that has died.

A moment. Hermes, in the living room, recognises the sound of the engine of the truck. Elisa, in the sewing room, is almost big, she's almost a young woman, and she knows. The sound of the truck's engine stopping in the street. Night has fallen over Marta. Are there breezes within the night? Marta waits for the sounds of the door opening, the dogs, the footsteps, the kitchen door. Her husband comes in and is surprised to find her sitting in the gloom, but he says nothing. It is his eyes that ask. They ask Marta. So small inside herself – a speck of dust. His eyes. Marta's voice bears all the sadness she feels, but she merely says:

'A woman just left who was here asking for you.'

Her husband doesn't stop looking at her, but from that single sentence he looks at her differently, because suddenly, too quickly, he understands everything. He doesn't worry about inventing some excuse, he doesn't reply, he doesn't say anything. Perhaps angry with the woman who has come looking for him, he turns on his heel and goes back out.

The kitchen door, the footsteps, the dogs, the street door opening. Outside, the engine of the truck starts to work, it can be heard further and further away and disappears around a bend. In just the same way Marta's heart disappears within her.

She gets up and turns on the light. She calls Elisa to lay the table. She calls Hermes for dinner. She will go to bed early. She knows her husband won't come back tonight. She is sure that, at last, she has made a decision.

'Once there was a little fart, who was called . . .'

And he paused.

'Little pink fart!' said Elisa and Ana in unison. Simão pretended to be surprised, and went on:

'One day she was at home when she heard a knock at the door: knock, knock, knock. "Who is it?" asked the little fart. "It's me, the little green gas," she heard from the other side of the door.'

And the story went on. The story could go on for ever. When they were together, at Maria's house, if Marta had come to Lisbon, Simão would go and put his nieces to bed for their nap and told them stories about the little pink fart. They were stories that always smelled very bad. If the little pink fart fell over, she smelled bad; if she played, if she gave little green gas a kiss, she smelled bad. The little pink fart was beautiful and pink, but she was a fart, which was why she smelled bad. Simão told the stories very seriously and each time the little fart or the little gas did something that smelled bad, Elisa and Ana would laugh with their little girl laughing voices. The mother of the little pink fart was called the yellow fart, her father was called blue gas.

Sometimes Marta would come into the bedroom and say:

'Don't tell the children such things.' But as she said this she would be laughing, too.

Sunday – Sunday. Sitting on the yard steps, my wife was peeling potatoes that she dropped, raw, into an enamel basin. I was at the top of a stepladder, pruning the vines that grew up the trellises against the wall. Francisco was holding on to the ladder with both hands, and when I told him to he'd move away to collect clumps of branches that had fallen in tangles on the ground. Then he would throw them on to the pile of firewood. The morning passed.

Marta was the first to arrive. My wife was no longer in the yard. She'd gone up the steps with the potato skins in her apron folded up over her belly and she had come back to fetch the basin. She had gone through the ribbons of the door. Marta arrived laughing and talking loudly. Behind her came Elisa, little, saying:

'Oh, Uncle,' and she ran to Francisco.

Behind them, slowly, came Marta's husband.

I came down the ladder to greet them, and because I'd finished I put down the pruning shears. Francisco was playing around with Elisa. Marta's husband and I talked about nothing. Marta said things we didn't hear and tried to get into the conversation. The morning passed.

At a certain point Maria arrived with her husband. Marta's voice faded. Her expression turned heavy. As they approached we could see the husband, and Maria's face behind him, taller. In greeting we spoke mingled words, diluted words, words that were whispers, grunts, that were not words. When Maria made as if to approach Elisa, Marta rushed over and picked her up in her arms:

'Go on now, let your uncle rest.'

But Francisco wasn't tired and he didn't need to rest.

There was a silence in Maria's footsteps, that lost their meaning and stopped. Our daughters' husbands didn't interrupt their conversation; Francisco made the most of it to fold up the stepladder, but I noticed. I wasn't sure what, but I had no doubt that I'd noticed something.

My wife appeared through the ribbons, at the door, at the top of the stairs, smiled gently, spoke some childish syllables to Elisa and called our daughters to help her lay the table. Maria went up the steps and into the house. Marta, with Elisa in her arms, kept looking at us, as though my wife hadn't spoken to her, as though she was ready to continue with the conversation we weren't having. We stared at her, uncomprehending. She held out for a moment, but ended up putting Elisa down and, thwarted, went into the house.

As we had lunch, I had the flagon of wine at my feet. I'd lift it up to fill my glass. Sometimes Maria's husband or Marta's husband would hold out their glasses and I'd fill them, too. Discreetly, head down to my plate, I lifted my gaze to confirm that Marta wasn't addressing a single word to Maria. I made the most of a moment when everyone was distracted by something funny that Elisa had said – sitting on a chair on two cushions, bib tied round her neck – to touch my wife's arm with my elbow; I pointed at our daughters with my chin and raised my eyebrows in a question. My wife, as though surprised at my silent question, said in a low voice:

'Just leave them be.'

And there was a moment of loose phrases, unconnected. Someone said:

'Elisa's already becoming a little rascal.'

Or:

'We should have set the table out in the yard.'

Or:

'It's good, the cod.'

There was a tragic moment. We had already finished eating when my wife sat down. She stuck her arm out to reach the cruet and knocked over my full glass. A lake of wine spread across the tablecloth, over the napkins, between the plates, and ran in red threads over the table's edge.

Still sitting, I moved myself away, dragging the chair with an abrupt shove of my legs, but I still got stained by the wine. I said:

'What a damn mess!'

My wife got up, went to fetch an old cloth, rags. My voice became thick and harsh. My voice was used for asking her questions that she didn't answer. She kept cleaning, as though I wasn't saying anything, as though I didn't exist. I got up, stood behind her and shouted into her ears as she twisted the cloth over the sink. Still she was impassive. I grabbed her by the arm. I shook her.

'Don't you hear me? Don't you hear me?'

As I let go of her, she gave up on eating and began to clear the table. The plates piled up in her hands. The top plate had the cutlery and the fish-bones, tipped from the other plates. There was silence. Still she didn't look at me, as though I didn't exist. I waited for her to approach the sink, and with a slap knocked the plates from her hands.

Elisa began to cry. Our daughters' husbands looked at places that didn't exist. Francisco looked at his mother. Our daughters got closer to one another, sisters again, as though whatever had separated them had lost any significance. In Marta's face, next to Maria, I could see that she had forgiven whatever secret had hurt her, she hadn't forgotten, but she had forgiven. And she was looking only at me. My wife, crouched down, was gathering up dirty cutlery and shards of broken plates.

I had only been ill a few months, but already I wasn't working. At the workshop I'd sit on a pile of planks of wood. Francisco was slowly ceasing to be a lad and starting to be a man. His age was like that diffuse time of day when afternoon begins to mingle with night, it seems like it's afternoon, it seems like it's night, and it's no longer afternoon, and it's not yet night.

There was one day I left the workshop to make my way slowly homewards to rest. I stopped at the *taberna*. I drank. Weeks had passed since my last glass of wine, the doctor forbidding me, the doctor looking me in the eye and forbidding me. I drank three glasses, four, and for a moment it was like when I still had a future. I arrived home, avoided my wife, and went into Francisco's room because I knew no one would come to look for me there. I lay down on his bed. The pillow was too low.

When Francisco arrived, after his run, he found me sleeping. He woke me, and from my breath or my voice, or from what I said to him, he knew right away that I had been drinking. Against my grumbles, he helped me up. And he seemed to be already a man, because he said to me:

'Are you afraid of dying?'

And he seemed to be still a boy because, when I was up on my feet, he wanted to hug me. I said to him:

'I don't really hug.'

We stood there facing each other, still in conflict, with our arms out, impossible to make out which of us was the man and which the boy, almost hugging.

Even Íris, little, concerned with her dolls, knows that a day that moves as this one does towards evening can only be a Friday. She doesn't know the word 'Friday', but she knows what it means. It is the end of the afternoon – the apotheosis. Maria has arrived, with all the strength in her body fading. Standing under my wife's arms, Ana takes off her smock. Ana has her exercise books on the kitchen table to solve some divisions. On top of the refrigerator, the wireless pours out piano music. It is like an open tap, forgotten, losing a thread of water that isn't noticed, that can barely be seen. Maria's husband has arrived, short and angry, enemies watching him from all directions. He has enemies on top of the kitchen cupboards, he has enemies behind the plates drying over the sink, he has transparent enemies that mingle with the tulle curtains and tremble with them, passed through by the breeze that the windows let in – the end of the afternoon.

It has always been like this. For some incomprehensible reason, my wife doesn't like – has never liked – to talk about what she's got heating up in the pans on the stove. Maria, with her thin voice, asks:

'What's for dinner?'

My wife replies:

'Look, it's food, all right?'

Maria says nothing, because she knows it has always been like this. She forgets about it. She walks over to some place she knows in her thoughts. All through the kitchen there is the smell of food being made. She remembers. She approaches the stove, lifts the lid off a pan, and without any expression looks inside.

Íris is leaning right up against Ana because she is waiting for her to finish her homework so that they can play together. Her father, passing her, trips, and shouts:

'Leave your sister in peace.'

Maria is startled by the shout, but she says nothing. She raises her eyes, and lowers them. She walks towards the door and pulls Íris by the arm. She wants to take her to the living room. Íris is small and stabs her buckle-shoes into the floor, she objects and flails around. On the other side of the kitchen Maria's husband raises his chin and his voice gets thicker:

'What is it you're doing?'

It has begun.

Maria could have told him with all sincerity that she is taking her to the living room, which was what she understood he wanted, but she is unable to because his voice has wounded her. This is why she also has to reply to him rudely, she has to hide the fact that she has been hurt and she has to hurt him, too. This is why she replies with some haughty phrase, rudely, to provoke him, to strike him.

Piano music fills the few empty corners of the kitchen. Maria's husband, as if threatening, says:

'Well, well, well.'

The piano music changes colour. It turns red. Maria doesn't let it rest.

'Well what?'

Ana gets down from her chair. The exercise book is left open on the table. She takes her sister's hand and the two of them leave the kitchen.

Maria's husband has blood flowing through the veins in his temples. He is alive. As if trying to restrain himself:

'You're not talking to your father now, you know.'

My wife can't keep silent:

'And what does her father have to do with anything?'

He turns his head the other way:

'Now it's both of you? You keep quiet! No one's talking to you.'

My wife can't, she demands a reply, pulls him by the arm:

'What does her father have to do with anything?'

He frees himself:

'Ai ai ai . . .'

My wife can't, she approaches him again:

'Well? What does her father have to do with anything?'

He turns suddenly – fury – and pushes her. My wife knocks into the sink with her waist, falls. She's sitting on the floor.

'Leave me alone!'

Maria crosses the kitchen to where he is, grabs his arm and twists it behind his back. At the same speed she takes him out to the corridor. Taller, stronger, she takes him. He is like a muted, anxious child, afraid of speaking and making it worse, afraid of reacting and making it worse. Maria opens the front door and throws him out into the shadows of the staircase. She bangs the door closed, as though firing a shot.

She waits. Her breathing. Maybe he'll knock at the door. He didn't take his key, he didn't take his jacket, he didn't take his wallet. She waits. She hears the banging of the door to the street. She lowers her eyelids. Her breathing. She walks slowly towards the kitchen and finds my wife on her feet already. They don't say anything. Maria knows that if she were to go to the window she would see her husband heading away in one direction or other. She doesn't want to, she's no longer interested. It's still rage, burning. After a time she goes to the window. Perhaps she'll still see him. She doesn't see him. He has disappeared. The street is deserted. And that's that.

When Marta became pregnant, we were pleased. Marta was twenty years old, she still believed in everything and she was thin. Marta's husband was little more than a boy, he didn't look at other women and he smiled a lot when he heard the news. My wife and I received the news that we were going to be grandparents very naturally. We had a twenty-year-old daughter, and we were going to be grandparents.

At four months, the doctor recommended rest. That was he word he used. To my wife's satisfaction, for the remainder of the time Marta moved to our house. Her husband would arrive at night and have dinner with us, and we would have solemn conversations, and then he would go to bed with Marta. For those months Maria left her bed to sleep in Francisco's room.

Marta spent most of her days in bed. Maria would sit by her and read her romance novels, and they would talk in low voices. Sometimes Marta would come into the kitchen in her dressing-gown and sit by the fire. It was the last months of autumn, then it was the months of winter. Elisa was born at the start of spring.

Marta's belly was round and even. Marta would carefully tie the belt of her dressing-gown over it. Francisco would rest his hand on its shape to feel Elisa's kicks.

'She's moving.'

Maria was not yet quite sure that she was pregnant when she came to tell us. She was. Her eyes were at the bottom of a well, small, and there was a childish tenderness on their surface. It was as though the baby's eyes existed within them. Nobody knew then that Ana's eyes would be exactly the same, as though they were the same eyes.

Some afternoons Simão would go and visit her. Nobody told me, but I was sure of it. He brought her old peanuts that he took out of his pocket. He held out the palms of his dirty hands to her, with peanuts.

Her husband treated her with care. Francisco would go by her house after work. They would talk, and at those times they were the same age. After going to the market, my wife would stop by her house to take her gifts of kale, vegetables, greens.

'Make a soup. Do you want me to make it? It's no trouble.'

Marta had already started to get fat. It could be seen, week after week, as she came in through the front door a little heavier. Elisa ran through the house and kissed her aunt's belly. There was true peace between the sisters, there were healed wounds, there was a good silence and eyes that looked on the past without resentment.

Maria's belly. She wore a blue flannel dress to wait for her husband. She rested her hands on her belly, as though she were carrying it. She smoothed out the dress, and with this gesture emphasised the belly. Her cheeks were flushed, her face affectionately expectant.

When Marta became pregnant for the second time I was already sick, my wife had already lost all possible consolation; Francisco was trying to look after the workshop and ran aimlessly through the streets of Lisbon in the late afternoons;

Simão had disappeared even more from all the places where he'd never been, where he had really never been; Maria fretted and wept for no concrete reason, which she couldn't qualify with any words she knew; Marta was fat, she was of a delicate nature; Marta's husband had his own thoughts, he had women he looked at and touched, whom he called by names that Marta could only imagine being whispered, perhaps affectionate or perhaps feigning affection, which, at the moment when they existed, in that mirror, were still the same as true affection.

When Maria became pregnant for the second time, everyone wanted to be hopeful.

Now it's Saturday. Maria woke up alone, and light. She's in the kitchen, and she's thinking that tomorrow Francisco is going to run in the Olympic Games. Maria confuses tenderness with pity. She feels tenderly towards her brother, but believes she feels some pity. She can't stop remembering when he was little. She always remembers him laughing or smiling. And she feels tenderness, calling it pity inside her thoughts. And she remembers Simão. The image of her brother, blind in one eye, is veiled by a curtain of pity, real pity, the pity of not having seen him for so long, of never hearing any word of him. She throws out some questions, inside herself – where might he be? Is he well? Who's taking care of him? And the cries of the girls in the living room catch her attention. Her attention is a floating boat, rudderless, ruled by the wind and the currents.

In the living room Maria's daughters are playing, and they don't worry because they are children and they can't conceive of anything destroying what they know and expect from every gesture or unknown moment passing: Ana and Íris. My wife is sitting next to them on the sofa. It has been many days, or months, since she has been like this, without any chores, simple and blank. She too is unworried. She is a child in a different way.

The doorbell. Always the same agitation, feverish anxiety, even when they know who it is. And now they don't know who it is. Maria thinks it might be her husband. My wife thinks it might be the gypsy. Always the same agitation – the doorbell. My wife doesn't think about this, but if she did, she could have remembered that it was like when she still used to drink coffee and afterwards had to sit down until the feeling of unease went away. Neither Maria nor my wife try to avoid what they know is inevitable. They are afraid, they are people, but they always confront it, and thus weaken it, destroy it. This is why Maria and my wife come into the corridor at the same time. It's Maria who arrives first as she is closest. A single, firm movement of her arm opens the door.

Marta, Elisa to one side of her, Hermes to the other. Marta – huge – is holding a little suitcase and two plastic bags. All this weight pulls her body down towards the floor and turns her into a gigantic mountain of flesh, in a nearly new fabric dress. And her face – eyes smiling or sad, cheeks reddened by two powder stains, the hairdo that she arranges with water when she leaves the house to get the train. Elisa, a well-behaved little girl, doesn't understand and doesn't ask, she trusts. Hermes wants to play.

Maria and my wife go into the kitchen with Marta, just listening. Her voice. It is outside them, and at the same time it exists within them, too. It is as though they have within their thoughts a kitchen just like the one they're in, with the same gentle lightness, the same serenity, and Marta's voice using the same words to speak of the lack of surprise, vaporous and breathable, that she is speaking of here. My wife and Maria had been expecting to hear those words in that voice for a long time. They couldn't have predicted that she would leave home. They don't remember imagining her talking with such peaceful acceptance, neither sad nor disappointed. Marta tells them her story wearily, using phrases she constructed on her train journey as she watched the landscape. After each word she can see that they know just which word she is going to say next, and she gets wearier. Then she tells them about the decision she has taken. Finally she says:

'I'm never going back.'

And both my wife and Maria can see that, sooner or later, she will go back home. They don't know how long it will take her to go back, but they know she will.

In the living room neither Ana nor Íris ask Elisa or Hermes any questions. They're glad at their arrival and immediately begin playing.

And Saturday passes with a sunny calm, like a day for bicycling without going anywhere, a day for taking a walk, for going round the lake in the park just because it's a route without any problems, just like any other. My wife and my daughters do simple chores, understanding one another. When they pass, their voices are young and they have the resigned wisdom of a lack of urgency. There is plenty of time, and harmony. The hours float by. All the hours float by, and they are identical. The children play and laugh, as though my daughters or my wife could laugh too whenever they felt like it. It is Saturday, and on this day the world has uncomplicated itself.

After putting the children to bed, after a little longer sitting at the kitchen table, after talking about Francisco and agreeing about everything, after remembering many things and laughing more, my wife and my daughters go to bed, and before they fall asleep they think that they could live like this for ever.

Marta hadn't yet been born, my wife was pregnant, we were sitting very close together – sometimes she would sit on my lap – and wondering which of us would die first. It was an anxiety that afflicted us. There were other insoluble conversations which like this one would return every once in a while. A lot of time might go by without us having it, months, years, but when we returned to it we always remembered that it was not the first time we'd talked about it. It was an anxiety that existed underground, and that never completely disappeared. We were too alert to the truth to ignore it. We couldn't pretend it didn't exist. All our children had already been born, we might be lying in bed, naked, we might have just finished making love, and one of us would remember to wonder which of us would die first. And then we also thought about our children. It would be very hard for us to leave them, we weren't sure they could manage themselves on their own, we were afraid they would be incapable, that they'd need us and we wouldn't be there. Marta, Maria, Francisco and even Simão, even Simão. And we thought about what it would be like to die and leave the other, to be left alone. And how long would we be apart? Months? Years? How many years' life would be left to the one who survived the other? I was already very sick, without enough peaceful time to say anything. It was one afternoon.

My wife brought me food that I couldn't eat, I couldn't eat anything. I was at home, in the pyjamas my wife had bought me to wear in hospital. For months I'd spent all my time in pyjamas, thin, my hair frail. And I wanted to sit up in bed, I wanted to hold her hand and press her to my breast. It was one of the last things I said in total consciousness. I was capable of a great deal of hurt. I said to her:

'Now we know who's going to die first.'

There were Sundays. Looking back, it's impossible to avoid the feeling that a lot of them were wasted. Today I feel that just one more Sunday would be enough for me to be able to resolve everything. Then straight after that, I think that it would not. Then straight after that, I think that yes, it would. A single Sunday, from the morning, always bright and unconcerned, a whole day to take advantage of, to waste until the drawing-in of the night – an illusion created by a planet that turns around itself. Today is a Sunday different from every other – Francisco is running the marathon in the Olympic Games. It is this shock of happiness that wakes first Íris, then all the other children, then Maria, Marta, then my wife, who, waking, almost believes she never fell asleep. It is Sunday, Sunday, Sunday, Sunday, Sunday.

Marta combs Hermes's hair in front of the bathroom mirror. Maria gets excited walking up and down the hall runner, followed by Íris, who wants to tell her something, or who just wants to pretend for a few moments that she is big and has important chores to do. Ana and Elisa are talking in the living room. Ana's eyes are shining with the illusion of being a big girl, correct, well-behaved, who does what is expected of her, who understands conversations. My wife is in the kitchen – piano music on the wireless – and she is thinking.

There are not many hours left now until the marathon starts. In Maria's house my wife, like my daughters, like my grandchildren, is alive. The brightness – coming in through the windows, being born beyond the buildings, beyond Lisbon in some pure place without imperfections, without the memory of imperfections – wraps up their lives, just as there is always a glow wrapped around objects that are precious, transforming their simplicity into grandeur.

My wife finds it difficult to persuade Íris and Hermes to leave their playing and come and sit at the table for lunch. When she finally manages it, after picking up Íris under her arms and sitting her down, when she bends down to arrange the chair, Íris pulls her head down with both hands – both arms – and kisses her cheek.

My wife raises her voice. All the voices at the table mingle together, like a web of tangled threads. My wife is trying to talk to Marta, who is trying to talk to Elisa, who is trying to talk to Ana, who is listening to her mother trying to talk to Íris, who is talking to Hermes, who is talking to Íris. They can hear one another, sometimes.

My wife gets up and changes the channel on the wireless on top of the fridge. As though speaking through a funnel, the voice of a commentator is there already, describing the atmosphere inside the Olympic stadium in Stockholm. My daughters and grandchildren suddenly fall quiet. From time to time the commentator says Francisco's name. He says something, and in the middle, says:

'Francisco Lázaro.'

Íris is bubbling in her chair. She puts her hands on the seat,

269

pushing herself up and fidgeting. But no one can resist the enthusiasm. Maria says things in an artificial tone of voice. Marta just smiles. My wife tries to pretend that nothing unusual is happening because that's the form her enthusiasm takes. They can all recognise it, even Hermes giving little cries, even Ana turning her head this way and that, even Elisa who rests her hands in her lap and shrugs in on herself, as though about to implode.

It's a Sunday that is different from all the ones that have already been, and all the ones that will be. My wife begins to take the things off the table, and in order to pretend that she's quite calm, rather distant, she mutters bits of words that not even she is listening to. Her movements and her whole body exist only in that voice coming out of the wireless and the distorted, grey sound of the crowds behind it. And the commentator says that it's very hot in Sweden. Maria comments on every sentence she hears, Marta tells her to be quiet, but very soon she can't contain herself and starts speaking, too. The tablecloth is still on the table, covered in crumbs. Hermes and Íris get down from their chairs and find a spot on the floor, on the tiles. Together they entertain themselves. There's not long before it begins. My wife sits down.

The doorbell rings. Who could it be? They look at one another across the table. No one seems to want to get up. It is Maria's house. Maria gets up. In the kitchen, almost stopping listening to the wireless for a moment, they wait – the expectation. They hear the door open, but they don't hear any voices they can identify.

Maria comes into the kitchen with Simão. Upright, his head lowered, he lifts his face to show himself. For a moment nobody has a heart – an eclipse. Marta places a fist on the table, and with some effort lifts herself up and hugs him. My wife is standing behind her, waiting. It takes all her strength not to cry when he kisses her twice, not to hug him, too, not to say:

'Son.'

Immediately after her, Elisa and Ana give him two kisses, well-mannered, and smile at him. Simão approaches Hermes and Íris and runs his fingers through their hair. And he sits down in a chair. When he doesn't notice, my wife or Marta or Maria look at him.

The marathon is about to begin.

The commentator says my son's name in every phrase, he says Portugal. In the kitchen, my wife, my children and my grandchildren. Together. If they aren't looking at one another they are looking at the wireless or at the air, mixing their thoughts with the commentator's voice.

The marathon has begun.

He's one of the first ones out. He's the only one running with his head uncovered. The commentator's voice is the images of the things he says. They are images that are different in each person's eyes. They come out of the stadium. Francisco is one of the first. Hermes and Íris jump up and down on the tiles, shouting in unison:

'Uncle, Uncle!'

Marta tells them to be quiet. They are quiet. Francisco overtakes a runner. Francisco overtakes another runner. Hermes and my granddaughters are the face of the enthusiasm that also exists, hidden, in the faces of my daughters and my wife. The commentator says again that it is very hot in Sweden.

'I thought it was cold in Sweden,' says Maria.

'Just listen,' says Marta.

After a few kilometres the commentator says that Francisco seems to have something fatty on his skin, perhaps grease, oil. My daughters look at one another, not understanding. The commentator says he's going at a good pace. They smile. He says that if he can keep up this pace for the whole marathon the gold medal will be his. Even my wife smiles. The commentator says Portugal.

Francisco crosses a bridge. In the kitchen, everyone imagines him crossing a bridge. A runner approaches him, is going to overtake him, but he doesn't let him. He takes off running at full speed. For a few minutes Marta and Maria take one another's hand. They squeeze one another's hand. In Sweden it's very hot. In Lisbon, time passes.

Francisco is out on his own in first place. Seven kilometres. The commentator's lit-up voice. My daughters' disbelieving eyes. Ten kilometres. Twelve. Francisco slows. It becomes possible to make out concern on my wife's face. Twenty-one years ago my wife had Francisco in her belly. She didn't know his face and invented everything. Today he's so far away, she can only invent where he is, running in the heat. Will he come back? My wife doesn't want to have this thought and turns her attention back to the voice of the commentator. He says that Francisco is beginning to drop back a few places. He says you can see the tiredness in his face. Hermes and Íris don't understand.

The afternoon slows. Francisco begins to fall behind. Seventeen kilometres. Groups of runners overtake him. The Swedish sun burns. You can see the weakness in Francisco's body. His running is uncoordinated. The sun is tiring him, draining all his energy. Twenty kilometres. The commentator praises the effort of the Portuguese runner. Francisco – the Portuguese runner. The commentator keeps repeating the word 'effort'. He uses various verbs – bear, struggle, cope – and always the word 'effort'. Twenty-one kilometres. Francisco falls.

My daughters' mouths open. My wife and Simão lift their faces as though they have been struck, like martyrs. Ana and Elisa look around to try and understand what they should be feeling. Hermes and Íris, sitting on the floor, play with their fingers and don't understand. They laugh quietly to one another.

Francisco gets up. He runs slowly, disoriented. My wife brings her hands together on her lap, as if she were praying. She is not. Maria makes as if to say something in an anxious voice. Marta tells her to be quiet. The distance passes very slowly now. The runner who is in first place is already very far away. Unreachable. My wife's eyes are closed. Simão is examining the palms of his hands. My daughters' gazes are lost on a non-existent horizon. Twenty-five kilometres – Francisco falls again.

He gets up again. Within the absolute silence of the kitchen the commentator's voice is serious and tormented. Hermes and Íris begin to notice that something is happening that they don't completely understand. On the streets of Lisbon there must be many things happening that no one could have imagined. On the streets that Francisco ran so many times, many things must be happening. The commentator wonders how much longer Francisco can hold out. He's dragging his feet on the ground. Portugal. Thirty kilometres. Francisco falls, exhausted. His body, lying there, is surrounded by people. My daughters, Simão and my wife get up from their chairs and run to the wireless, as if they could get inside it.

I must go and meet my son.

AFTER THEY HAD PUT Francisco on to a stretcher and taken him to the hospital, the commentator said something about death. He said definitely. Marta, trying to keep her voice calm, told Elisa to take her brother and her cousins to the living room. Simão hugged his mother, kept her safe in his arms. Shrunken, she cried and she was a being beneath a tempest, a tempest was passing through her. Her body was small in Simão's arms, it had no will and no shape.

'It's probably nothing,' said Maria, approaching, and deceiving herself.

But the commentator said something about death again. Exhaustion. Maria started a low whimpering, like a wounded animal. Marta, in her huge body, had the prominent eyes, the pursed lips of a little girl. And the commentator spoke in a sorrowful voice. There was no more Sunday. The marathon had finished.

My wife came out from Simão's arms, lost. She wandered, disoriented, one way and another. Our children watched her and there was nothing they could do. The commentator said goodbye to his listeners. His listeners. It was Simão who turned the wireless off.

And nothing. The noise of the refrigerator existing – a vibrating silence. The sad details – the fruit bowl, the kitchen sink, the tiles and the fear, the panic of the window – the height of the window, three storeys, and everyone who had perished beyond it. Simão was crying as though coughing or choking. Marta and Maria cried freely, rivers after a fall of rain. My wife lost all her strength.

She sat down, not reacting. Within her, she had being certain and she had not wanting to believe it. She had definite and impossible. My wife, deciding nothing, remembered our son when he was still small, ten years old, and a dizziness of images tumbled inside her – blood. She remembered our son just born, and at that moment she was dead.

Then the afternoon. No one could understand its calm. Waiting. Each of them abandoned. Time passed, clouded up by the light and distorted by the faces, it went through them, and, clouded up, distorted, installed itself slowly within each of them. Time was a stagnant lake of grey water that slowly grew inside each of them. Simão was the only one who had the courage to approach the window and look at the world, as though it still existed. And it did exist – invisible, meaningless.

There was nothing they could do but wait. Nothing – a void, a vacuum, a single absence, no reply. They had stopped knowing how to wait, but bit by bit they were forced to relearn the unbearable task of waiting. They were forced. There is no need to ask questions of shadows. Hours passed.

At times, Maria or Marta, aware, got up from the chairs where they were getting old and went down the corridor to check that the children were all right. Only Elisa looked at them differently. Ana, Hermes and Íris all smiled, in a normal day. It was still Sunday, for them.

In the kitchen there was only the silence populated by

memories, and all my children's and my wife's fears covering up a certainty, an abyss, that existed, voracious, between them, like a bonfire lighting up their faces. The night was beginning.

Death.

At nine o'clock at night the telephone rang. Nobody knew what to do. The ringing of the telephone tore through them, it was barbed wire dragged across their skin. My wife had her head in her hands, because she couldn't bear it. Marta and Maria went back to being two little girls, sisters. Simão knew it had to be him to answer the telephone. As he walked, he realised that he had legs and arms and hands. He breathed. He held the telephone. Next to him, the chrome-plated frame – the photograph that we all took together in Rossio. He held the telephone. He answered. Time. The faces of my wife and my daughters forgotten in a fault of time. Simão's voice:

'Yes, yes. All right. I'll tell them.' He walked over to my wife, to my daughters, and told them. He stood there, as though looking at his own words and trying to understand them. An infinite, incandescent light. My wife and my daughters watched him, not knowing how to understand him. Francisco's son had just been born.

Francisco's son had just been born.

The words were:

'He's been born, Francisco's little boy.'

Francisco's son had just been born.

ALSO AVAILABLE BY JOSÉ LUÍS PEIXOTO
BLANK GAZE

In a Portuguese village gripped by poverty, José the shepherd meets the Devil in Judas's General Store and slowly his happiness crumbles away. Meanwhile, Siamese twins joined at the tips of their little fingers find their tender communion shattered when one of them falls in love with the local cook. And all despite the advice of Gabriel, wise in his counsel after 120 years. Hardened by hunger and toil, Peixoto's extraordinary characters remain prey to love, jealousy, violence and the overwhelming power of fate in this hauntingly beautiful tale.

*

'Impressive and unusual ... Intensely beautiful writing packed with startling and memorable images ... incredibly rich and resonant'
INDEPENDENT

'You read and breathe as if you were downing a bottle of life in one gulp'
LE FIGARO

'As remarkable for its subtle language as for its characters'
FINANCIAL TIMES BEST BOOKS OF 2007

*